bride squad runaway

CAROLINE GRACE-CASSIDY
AND LISA C. CAREY

BLACK & WHITE PUBLISHING

First published 2019
by Black & White Publishing Ltd
Nautical House, 104 Commercial Street
Edinburgh, EH6 6NF

1 3 5 7 9 10 8 6 4 2   19 20 21 22

ISBN: 978 1 78530 245 9

Typeset by Iolaire Typography, Newtonmore
Printed and bound by CPI Group (UK) Ltd, Croydon, CR0 4YY

For Sarah, with all our love.

Royalties from the sale of this book will be donated to the
Sarah Jennifer Knott Foundation for Cancer of Unknown Primary.

SJKFoundation.org

1

You Know What Would Look Better on Me?

'HOW DOES MY ASS LOOK?' Ava O'Hara steps out from behind the velvet curtain in her bare feet and pulls herself up onto her tippy toes.

'Take a picture from the back for me, will you?' she says, clasping her hands behind her.

'*Aucun problème*! No problem!' Stefan exhales a sharp breath, his eyes taking in all five feet six inches of her. Lifting his flat cap from his knees, he drags it on over his black hair and stands up from the footstool he's perching on. Their eyes lock momentarily, he shifts his gaze, joins his index finger and thumb together.

'Look at you. Come on, *très bien*. You look beautiful.'

Ava smirks a little and deflects from him as she looks away.

'Stefan, seriously? I need your honest opinion. I can't tell you how surreal this is. Seeing myself is bizarre . . . I dunno, it's like an out-of-body experience. Is this really me standing here looking at this as my reflection?' Ava leans in closer, peering into the floor-to-ceiling chrome-framed mirror, her hand slightly shaking.

'*Oui*,' he replies quietly.

She tugs the bobbin loose from her low ponytail, her blonde hair tumbles in beach waves down her back.

'So long, *non*? You always wear it up,' he says.

'I know, I never leave it down for work, just can't concentrate with my hair hanging around my face. Actually, at my hair trial the other day, the hairdresser told me that women my age don't usually have such long hair and fair play to me for not giving a shit! I couldn't believe she could say that, so I applied a wallop of growth serum that night. Literally, I brushed it a hundred times!' Ava fixes her hair to fall over her left shoulder.

'Why does that not surprise me?' Stefan laughs. 'I have never met someone who is as comfortable in their own skin as you.' He unwraps a strip of chewing gum and folds it into his mouth.

'Um, well, I don't know about that, but I'll bank the compliment. Being told what is suitable for us to wear and how long our hair should be . . . Give me a break! I'll be forty in December and I can't wait.' She smooths her hair to the opposite side now, tilting her head.

'You do not look forty –' he starts.

'And I don't feel forty!' she butts in again. 'Because I have no idea what being forty feels like, do I? All I know for sure is that I'm looking forward to finding out. I mean, why is everyone so afraid to age when the alternative is so bloody bleak?' She runs her finger across her throat, her blue eyes wide.

'You're crazy.' He laughs, rolling his eyes back at her.

'True, though, right? I'm not changing my wardrobe or my hair so society can slot me neatly into a survey box. Why are we all so preoccupied with youthful skin and tight necks, when men get away with ageing wonderfully and most of you give less than a shit?' She loses herself in her reflection again, gathering her hair up on top of her head, posing with some exaggeration.

'I do not know, but there is nothing quite so sexy as a woman who owns herself.' He chews slowly, his dark eyes never leaving her mirrored reflection.

'I'll tell you why, Stefan, shall I?'

'Do I have a choice?' he asks, deadpan.

She's on a roll now. 'It's because *we*, us women, are bombarded with fake images all the time. Unattainable, unreal perfection. Instagram pictures that have been trimmed and filtered and God knows what else. It's pure propaganda. Whoever came up with that has a lot to answer for! Now obviously I'm a total hypocrite, so come on ... I need you to photograph my ass!'

Stefan laughs again.

'I'm serious ... *s'il vous plaît*. I need to see myself from all angles!' Ava reprimands herself. 'I'm not part of the solution, I'm part of the bloody epidemic ...'

'Maybe just don't take social media all that seriously. You know it's all fake. Nothing says insecurity like people who pretend to be perfect. Now, the ass capturer. That job will be my absolute pleasure.' He lifts his cap up to scratch his forehead as he adjusts the screen on his phone.

'Thank you!' Ava winks at him playfully and watches as his face suddenly clouds over. 'What?' she says.

'Remind me again why Simon is good enough for you?' he blurts out, shaking his head as though trying to clear his brain.

Ava freezes and stares straight ahead, her heart pounding in her chest.

'Sure, who else would have me?' she manages after a few seconds.

'Don't tempt me,' he responds, turning his phone over and over in between his tense hands.

'I won't – I mean, I was only a spring chicken when I met Simon. Just turned thirty. Not a grey hair or a single crow's foot to be seen. Young and in love. Full of ambition and self-confidence, with no Instagram to drag me down.' Ava smiles ridiculously wide, her face creasing up.

'See? Even that pug face can't make you look unattractive.' Stefan holds her gaze, then grins at her crazy expression.

3

'Bet none of the unfortunate women you date embrace their wrinkles like me? Botox brigade, the lot of them! Or worse, the 'filler-faced femmes-fatales', perish the thought!' Laughing, she pulls her skin tight back across her face with both hands.

'Why do you never believe me when I say I like real women? You've never even seen any of the women I take out, Ava. I hate Botox and fake body parts, inflated lips and ... well, you know.' He bounces his hands up and down in front of his chest area to mime a significant pair of breasts.

Ava gives him a look.

'And, hey, *unfortunate* women – pardon?' He bends his head and looks up at her through his dark lashes.

'Ah, you know I'm only messing with you, but in fairness, you do date a fair few women ... but, unfortunately for *them*, just the once!' She smooths the Alençon lace material across her flat stomach with her hands. 'So much lace,' she mutters and grimaces slightly.

'Maybe I'm waiting for Mrs Right, not Mrs Right Now?' Stefan hunkers down on the footstool again, speedily swiping across the pictures he has just taken of her, studying each one closely, zooming in with his finger and thumb.

Ava turns away from her reflection momentarily and faces him. 'You'll know her when you meet her ... Is that what you're telling me?'

'Something like that, I think,' he says, leaning to his left side to slide his phone back into the pocket of the leather jacket he's sitting on, while never looking up from the cream carpet in the bridal fitting room.

'Can I see my ass, please?' she asks, her hand outstretched.

'Trust me, your ass is good,' he replies.

'Everything okay in there?' An older voice chimes in and breaks the moment, as Ava carefully exhales.

'Yes! All good, thanks a million, Nora,' Ava shouts back.

'I'm just looking for some pins, love, won't be a minute, and I'll be in to you both,' Nora calls.

'This feels pretty surreal for me, too. *Allons-y* ... come on, I can't believe I am taking pictures of you in your wedding dress ... I just ...' Stefan stops chewing and looks up at her again.

She stops posing and holds his gaze once more in the mirror. His expression is swiftly changing.

'Just w-what, Stefan?' she says, and coughs as the words get caught in her mouth.

He stands up faster this time, with a touch more determination. She faces him.

'Just presumed you wouldn't actually marry him, I guess,' he says solemnly.

'But how can you say that? I've been with him for ten years, and we've been engaged since the day I met you ... six months now. I know the actual wedding has come stupidly fast and wasn't exactly planned this way ... it was as big of a shock to me as it was to you ... and this dress is well ... and ... but ...' Ava stammers, apprehensive.

'But you love him?' His voice is barely above a whisper.

Ava coughs again and rests her hand on her neck. 'Sorry, I've a tickle in my throat, I – I ...' She reddens then gulps, as Stefan abruptly holds both his hands up in the air.

'Hey, look. I am sorry, don't mind me. *Oui*, you look beautiful. Simon is a very lucky man, so please, forget what I just said. The dress is perfect, your ass is perfect ... you are ...'

'... perfect?' She narrows her eyes at him, then laughs before he can answer. 'You really do like the dress, though, right?' She grasps the opportunity to change the subject, carefully wiping her clammy hands off each other. 'I trust your opinion the most. You French invented style, isn't that right?' She doesn't wait for his answer. 'I mean, it's, well, it's so … so true to its time, isn't it? Honestly, all that really matters to me is that it's vintage. That there's a story, some history behind it. Who was the girl who stood in this wedding dress all those years ago? What was she thinking? Was she marrying the man of her dreams? Did they live happily ever after like Cinderella and Prince Charming, or did they end up more like *Kramer vs Kramer*? Or worse still, Brad and Angelina!' Ava leans her head on the mirror, deep in thought.

A landline shrills out around The Vintage Bride, as Ava continues to babble.

'I guess I've always loved the idea of long lace sleeves on a wedding dress. The 1970s were cool, weren't they? Like the dresses were gloriously non-fussy, they kept it simple. Like this button-up neck.' She gently touches the lace on the high neck to illustrate her point. 'The bride was always more than just the dress, and they never revealed too much flesh or had to try to be sexy.' She fingers the tiny pearl buttons that go from the bodice right up to her long neck. The heavy lace skirt hits the carpeted floor.

'Is it … beige?' Stefan asks, squinting slightly.

'Ivory!' Ava spins around to face him properly. 'It's my ivory tower.' She waves her hands about, from the tip of her head down to her bare feet. Head to toe in lace. Stefan laughs, his dark eyes playing with her, as he removes his gum packet from the back pocket of his jeans.

'You look perfect in whatever you put on. You were born with that *joie de vivre*, Ava. What I am most liking is that you're smiling.' He unwraps another gum, folds it into his mouth, then places his hands between his legs and eases himself up from the footstool.

'Seriously, how much gum do you actually go through?' Ava shakes her head in disbelief. 'Literally every time I look at you, you're chewing gum.'

She steps back from the mirror, her oval face still only inches away from it as he approaches. He walks around her, then stops, his hand gently touching the lace on the sleeve. Ava reacts instantly to his touch and drops her head to mask the beginning of her rising pink cheeks, as he runs his fingers gently up and down the lace of the sleeve. Her heart thumps in her chest again and her hands turn clammy once more. Stefan continues to move his fingers onto her shoulder, gently touching the lace, brushing her bare skin in between the delicate material. A shiver runs up her spine.

'I – I ...' she stammers. 'I mean ... I should ... I mean ... I – are your hands even clean?' she blurts, at a loss for words, her cheeks red and stinging. Stefan pulls his hands away and shoves them both down deep into his jeans' pockets.

'S-sorry ... Ava, I'm sorry ... I –' He takes a step back. 'I didn't mean ... I shouldn't have ...' He takes another step back and bumps into a rail of dresses behind him.

'It's okay ... I – I know,' she reassures him, as he steadies the rail that is swaying slightly. Stefan looks at her again, then to the rail, then back at Ava, doing a double-take.

'*Attendez* ... hold on! When I came with you the last time on our visit here, you see these *c'est exact*? Still vintage, *non*? *Tu as dit* ... you said ...' He taps his index finger on the left side of his head, trying to recall her words. 'You said that the Dior was your dream dress, *non*?' He pulls his right hand from his pocket and points to the rack of dresses still swaying.

The 'Wow Factor' rail sparkles as the late June afternoon sun flashes through the skylight onto the snow-white materials: a row of vintage designer dresses delicately floating on bright gold hangers. Each one resembles a prima ballerina on the opening night of *Swan Lake* at the Bolshoi Theatre. Dublin's morning sun is like their personal spotlight. Exquisite material. All detailed to pure perfection. With wow price tags to match. Stefan was quite right, Ava *j'adored* the Dior. It was the wedding dress of her dreams.

'The Dior? God! No! No, I prefer this. It's ... it's more me. You know me, I hate fuss. And wasting money. No, not wasting ... *spending* too much money on a dress.'

'On a *dress*? You?' Stefan nearly chokes on his chewing gum. 'She who adores vintage dresses! *Non*? You have piles of old drawings in the back office at the art gallery of wedding dresses from all different times and places that you've sketched. Long ones, short ones, crazy ones, *non*?' He looks more than perplexed.

'Did you look through all those, too?' She twists, looking at him in amazement.

'Of course.' He shrugs. '*Combien de fois* ... sorry, I mean how many times do I have to tell you that I am a great appreciator of art?' He holds up one finger.

'You're pure mad, Stefan.' Ava turns back to the mirror and studies herself once more.

'You aren't lying to me about the dress you really want, though, are you?' he asks, a dark eyebrow raised.

'No, not at all! Absolutely not!' she protests. But when he tilts his head at her, she deflates. 'All right, I can't lie to you. Let's just say I'm not head over heels in love with the dress, but it's fine. It's cute, and thanks for coming with me today.'

'Of course,' he says.

'You really are such a brilliant –' She expends a breath through her nose. 'I mean, what I'm trying to say is, you're more to me than just a work colleague, you know that, right? You're a great friend.'

'*Je sais*. I know ...' He chews slowly.

'I just love how you make me see the world so differently.' Ava hoists up the dress and steps down in her bare feet off the small grey box she is standing on.

'It really helps my art, Stefan. You look at a grey, rainy, miserable Monday morning sky and point out colours to me that I would never usually see. That I never *would* have seen.' She tugs at her hair, winding her fingers through it.

'It's important to really look at things. To really see the whole picture.' He pauses to let her digest his words. 'You weren't really looking before; the almost-purple-grey of the sky, that faintest shade of magenta. The shapes of the low clouds. I remember that day, that sky was so beautiful, and when you looked you were able to capture it all in that painting. The colours in it still fascinate me.'

'Why, thank you, sir!' Ava mock bows. 'I guess I just never had the balls to experiment with that kind of painting before. You made me open my eyes, helped me change the way I take light in. But while you're right about this dress, I have to be realistic and practical, I'm afraid.' She looks a little melancholic.

'I understand.' He purses his lips and lounges against the faux red-brick wall.

'I know you do,' Ava says.

They look at one another.

'Thank you.'

'For what? Standing by and ...' He trails off, scratching his chin. 'Gum?' he offers with a heavy sigh.

'Go on then.' She accepts a piece, unwraps it and chews rapidly.

He wanders away to throw his used gum in the bin near the back of the changing room and she thinks back six months to the moment he'd walked through the door of Art Gallery Space 1, where she worked as the curator, for an interview. They had an instant connection. *Boom*! It was more than peculiar. It totally felt like they had met before. Some place. Somewhere. But they hadn't. They were complete strangers. He'd connected with her like he knew her, too. Effortless eye contact. Both of them standing opposite each other, dressed head to toe in black, in tight black T-shirts and black jeans. The artsy uniform, they'd joked.

When she regained her composure, she had put out her hand to shake his, but Stefan ignored her extended hand and instead kissed her on both cheeks. Ava had felt every hair on the back of her neck stand up. A bolt of electricity – one she really didn't want to acknowledge – shot though her entire body. An explosion of chemistry she couldn't possibly allow. Because on that very day at Art Gallery Space 1 she had been propped up on Vitamin C and painkillers, majorly hungover after a marriage proposal from Simon the night before. Ava O'Hara was now an engaged-to-be-married woman.

Drunken celebrations had rolled on late into the night at a music venue in town where Simon's band, Seventh Hour, were playing. She also remembered smart-arse Mags, her stiff boss and the gallery owner, saying she thought it 'telling' that she'd worn black into work the very day she announced her engagement, as though she were in mourning. Bad karma, she'd exclaimed. But Ava hadn't even thought about what she'd pulled on that day. She was lucky to make it in at all.

After so many long years, she was engaged, even though she wasn't as surprised as she'd made out. If she was being honest, *'about bloody time'* was what went through her mind as Simon proposed from the stage mid-song.

'Marry me, babe,' he'd sung into the microphone clamped between his hands, as he jumped off the stage dramatically and danced towards her. She had feigned shock as he dropped to his knees, more James Brown than Ryan Gosling's Noah in *The Notebook* movie. Ava was sure she'd heard Simon grunt in pain as his knees hit the cement floor. And, as Seventh Hour shifted key, Simon crooned, 'You never close your eyes …' in front of her as the modest crowd cheered.

He didn't have a ring that night, not that Ava had ever demanded one. God, no, nothing like that – she just wanted some official commitment after ten years. Come on. She was a traditional girl, old-fashioned in that ideal. Marriage first, babies later. That's just how she felt. Not in an obsessively maternal way, but the time just felt right in her life. The ticking clock in her head was loud and irritating, like the *Countdown* clock on the game show. Marriage and babies were the next step. Well, it was a natural progression, right? She had a path to follow. That's what women like her did, followed the path.

Mags also liked to go on about how ridiculous it was that her fiancé, Simon, still referred to himself as 'The Tuner' all these years later, even though she'd been one of his band's biggest fans back in the day. Seventh Hour had had a few chart hits and rode the wave for a couple of years, but their glorious musical heydays were well and truly in the past. These days, the band struggled to get any gigs, and the army of fans that once adored them had disappeared to bring up families and stay in at night binge-watching Netflix.

Refusing to give up the ghost, Simon and the band still wrote songs and rehearsed three times a week in Ava and Simon's cramped third-storey apartment, behind the Four Courts near the centre of town. They were committed to the belief it was just a matter of time before they made their valiant rock star return.

Stefan returns and catches Ava's eye in the mirror, and she's forced out of her reverie. She shyly looks away. He's dead right, she thinks. He does know her too well. This is not the dress she wants at all. But Simon is also right. The Dior wedding dress is ridiculously expensive. And, as her fiancé constantly reminds her …

'What's the point in wasting all that money on a dress you'll only wear for one day, babe?'

She watches Stefan as he fills up a miniature plastic cup from the water cooler. Yes, she adores vintage dresses – is a little obsessed even – but she also adores and obsesses over her hero Andy Warhol, but she can't afford one of his works, now, can she? They're far too strapped for cash for this type of wedding indulgence.

Simon always goes on and on about how broke he is. And he is. He rarely has any money, and it's always down to Ava to pay the bills. But he's a musician and she knew that when she met him; it's not like he ever said he would be anything different.

And their wedding had all come together so fast, she's had no time to catch her breath, let alone shop around for a dress. A last-minute cancellation in Kinnitty Castle popped up and Simon took it. Without asking Ava first. She'd been shocked and not sure about the fast-approaching deadline, but he convinced her on the phone that night – well, at three in the morning, when he called her excitedly – that they should just do it. Go for it.

'Seize the day, babe,' he shouted more than enthusiastically. If she'd had the time to browse, she could have found a great vintage dress for a good price. In fact, she probably could have asked Lauren for some help, with her Rolodex of celebrity and fashion industry contacts – but she didn't want it to seem as if she didn't have her life together. Especially to Lauren … Feck that.

As far as Lauren's concerned Ava is living her dream. Okay, so she isn't actually painting for a living any more, but she's doing the next best thing, working in a prestigious art gallery. She's got a job she loves and is now engaged to her boyfriend of ten years. Ava's determined to prove to Lauren that she's made the right decisions in her life. And anyway, it's been so long since she's been truly honest with Lauren McCabe that she's always felt relieved they had more or less lost touch. Until now.

'It is your big day, so once you are sure . . .' Stefan is shrugging heavily, checking his watch. Ava looks at herself again, twisting and turning into the mirror. Hands by her sides. Hands resting on her hips. The dress clinging to her magnificently.

'We have been gone for a long time and Mags could land back on her broomstick at any time. I should get back.' Stefan approaches Ava, kissing her softly on both cheeks. Six months on, this greeting still gives Ava goosebumps.

'I've diverted the gallery phone to my mobile, but yes, wouldn't put it past the witch to swoop in. Go ahead, I won't be long. Plug the coffee machine in, will you?' Ava says, as he tightens the gold-buckled belt on his jeans. She titters to herself as the younger sales assistant gasps from behind the far bridal counter.

That's the thing with Stefan. He's a total fucking ride. Thank God they are just friends and she is very almost married, Ava thinks to herself for the millionth time, because he is just too good to be true. Going hand in hand with his *rideyness*, no doubt, was the fact he was also a commitment-phobe. He'd been on tons of dates in the last six months, but never seemed all that interested in anyone he met. A second date never happened with Stefan, and while Ava didn't like to admit it to herself, this pleased her enormously.

She shoots the assistant a sympathetic half-smile, as Stefan slips his arms into his black leather jacket and pulls down his white T-shirt, which has risen as he's stretched, revealing his taut, tanned stomach.

'I swear you do that abs-flashing move on purpose, Stef.' She bites her bottom lip playfully.

'Take your time. Just be sure, *mon amie*, really look, *oui*?' He winks at her and leaves. The door slams behind him, announcing his exit.

'Jesus wept! Is that your fiancé, hun? Ya wagon!' The slim sales assistant trots over to Ava on towering red heels that sink into the carpet. Ava tries not to laugh – the shoes make her walk as if one of her legs is shorter than the other. How and why anyone would wear sky-scraping heels to work all day was a mystery to her.

'No. Definitely not … I'm afraid Stefan isn't the marrying kind,' she tells her.

'That was a French accent, was it?' she drools as her tongue physically hangs out of her mouth.

'*Oui*, that it was.' Ava is more than amused at her puppy-dog eyes.

'Don't tell me that he's *single*?' The young assistant's jaw drops and she puts her tongue back in her month, as her overfilled lips struggle to meet one another.

'Hmm, define single?' Ava replies, as she tries on an ivory pillar-box hat for size.

'Oh.' The shop assistant looks confused. 'He's gay? What a waste for womankind! He's the spitting image of yer man Olivier Martinez that Kylie Minogue used to go out with, remember him? I mean, I'd give him a …' She reaches out one arm into the crook of her other arm just as an older woman hurries over and smacks her arm down before she can execute her rather vulgar visual manoeuvre.

'Thank you! Thank you, Marina! That is quite enough. I'm pretty sure Miss O'Hara didn't come here to be quizzed like this. Now, back to the desk, please! Can you call Samantha, our Chanel bride in Dalkey, and tell her the dress will arrive in from New York on Tuesday evening? Oh, and make an appointment for her fitting? Tell her absolutely no dark lipstick this time. And if she asks, you can tell her I don't bloody care if it's "Mystical

14

Maroon", she already almost destroyed one of my Yves St Laurent samples the last time.'

'Sorry. Yes, I'll tell her.' Marina meekly hobbles her way back to the counter.

Nora, the boss, raises her eyes to Ava, who just laughs. 'And please, what have I told you about wearing heels in the shop, Marina, you look like Dustin Hoffman in *Midnight Cowboy*.'

'But, oh Chanel ... amazing,' Ava purrs.

'It is quite something, it's 1954 ... short, tea length, with the most exquisite detail I've ever seen.' Nora's eyes roll, so only the whites are visible as she sighs.

Ava holds her hand up. 'Oh, stop, Nora! I can't. I've sketched so many dresses from that period, I'm obsessed. I used to dream I'd get married in the Andy Warhol Museum in Pittsburgh ...' Ava stops suddenly and goes very quiet.

'Now, now, nearly there, love. And please stop trying on hats, we have committed to the delicate veil. You're only confusing yourself, pet.' Nora gently removes the hat from Ava's head and glides away to put it back on the glass hat shelf.

Ava stares closely at her reflection again. 'I look lovely, I know I do. It's a classic vintage wedding dress, so why am I being so critical? Cop on to yourself, O'Hara,' she hisses through gritted teeth.

What would Lauren think about this dress, she wondered? No doubt she'd say it was shit. She had to admit, it had felt so good to talk to her on the phone earlier. Just to hear her voice again. It was well over a year since she'd seen Lauren. The irony was there was a time when they couldn't remember the last time they *hadn't* seen each other! The definition of 'besties'. The problem was Ava met Simon, and Lauren and Simon had never really taken to one another. They just had nothing in common. It had been awkward at the beginning because she liked – no, she *loved* them both. It was a crying shame that when her relationship with Simon progressed and she moved out of the cosy flat she shared with Lauren almost three years ago now, to move in with him, Ava and Lauren just drifted apart.

Stefan had helped her record a video on her phone yesterday in the art gallery. A video message was the only way Ava could think to announce she was getting married in two weeks' time, and to ask Lauren to be her maid of honour. Ava hadn't had the nerve to call her out of the blue and put her on the spot. It just wasn't how she operated. She hated to blindside people. At least this way Lauren could say no if she wanted, politely, by email.

This last year they had drifted so far apart that she really had no idea how Lauren would feel about it. Ava also knew the distance between them was due to the fact she herself had become closer to Cate Connolly recently, another mutual college friend who Ava had also lost touch with. Ava had randomly bumped into Cate at Dublin airport, at the baggage reclaim carousel, they swapped numbers, reconnected on Facebook, started to hang out again. Cate had just moved back to Dublin from London with her two young sons.

Lauren had never quite got over the fact that Cate had given up her career as a speech therapist when she'd got married and had then taken off to live in London and have babies. It also bugged Lauren that Cate was more than a little quirky and really didn't care what people thought of her, she never had. Cate was the no-make-up-in-a-cosy-tracksuit type, while Lauren was the epitome of glamour at all times. Chalk and cheese – that pretty much summed up Lauren and Cate, yet they all used to have so much fun together back in the day. Somehow it all just worked.

Cate was still a stay-at-home mum, but now the proud owner of three small boys. Her latest arrival, Max, had been born just three weeks ago. Lauren was now a social butterfly with a very high-profile, demanding job as the editor of *Irish Gloss* magazine. Simon reckoned Lauren was jealous of Cate, but Ava didn't think so at all. Lauren had no need to be jealous of pretty much anyone, with her glam life floating around Dublin's electric social scene every night of the week, pictured with a flute of champagne in her shellac-nailed hand on the social pages of those overpriced magazines Ava only ever read in the hairdressers. Lauren McCabe – who was, for the longest time, her best friend in the entire world – was now Lauren P. McCabe. Editor. Influencer. Radio and TV contributor. Instagrammer extraordinaire. Big Boss of *Irish Gloss* magazine.

Fair play to her, she'd invested blood, sweat and her entire life into making sure it was Ireland's number one publication. The magazine owed all its success to her. Ava was proud of her, of course she was, but if she was totally honest she felt neglected. Lauren P. McCabe's career and social life consumed her, which left zero time for Ava O'Hara. Right now, she wished Lauren was standing beside her – just like in *Say Yes to the Dress*, friends giggling and going on a proper Prosecco lunch bender afterwards, falling home at tea time. Instead she was alone. About to be married, but ...

'Now, then. Happy, love?' Nora mumbles, interrupting her train of thought once more, her pursed mouth full of the newly found sharp pins with red, green and black round tops she had been searching for.

'Hmm.' Ava shrugs lightly, continuing her blank stare in the mirror.

'Hmm isn't the response I should be hearing from you, pet.' Nora's kind eyes widen as she pulls the pins out and sticks them into a pincushion on the floor beside her. 'Most of my brides are bursting with excitement. I mean, we do exactly what we say on the tin, the shop is called The Vintage Bride. What aren't you sure about, chicken?' Nora gets up slowly from her knees.

'No, it's not that … it's beautiful, Nora. Really. It's just not what I pictured wearing on my wedding day and that's all down to money, I'm afraid,' Ava tells her honestly.

'I understand, dear.' Nora nods.

'I'll pay and take it with me today, if that's okay?' Ava knows her smile is an unconvincing one.

'Pop it off there and I'll just throw an extra hook and eye into the back of it. For added safety.' Nora winks at her. 'And, honey, you would look fantastic in a black sack, but that's not the point. You need to be one hundred per cent happy, you know? Marina mentioned that young man with you wasn't your fiancé?'

'No, he's a … a friend,' Ava tells the older woman cautiously.

'It's been a long time since I've seen a friend look at one of my brides that way,' Nora says, lowering her voice.

'What do you mean?' Ava asks.

'Oh, don't mind me, I'm a hopeless romantic. Let's get you out of your wedding dress, shall we?' Nora continues, bustling around.

Ava, a little dazed, half smiles and nods at Nora, as she stands down off the grey box again, then pads towards the thick velvet curtain. With her wedding in just fourteen days' time, she has an endless to-do list.

'Last chance, would you like to call a friend … your brides-maid, sister, or someone else to come and see it for you before you take it off?' Nora tries again. 'Maybe a fresh pair of eyes can reassure you, pet?'

Ava shakes her head and steps behind the curtain, pulls it across, her thoughts returning to Lauren. Has too much time passed? Was she mad forcing this reunion, especially on the most important day of her life? Not that she thought it was the most important day of her life by any means, but that's what people say, isn't it? Carefully she unbuttons the dress as her mind wanders some more. How had it happened that she and Lauren had drifted so far apart anyway?

So many crazy memories. Travelling around the country with backpacks to every music festival they could scrape the money together for. Howling with laughter about when they'd managed to sneak in backstage at the Rose of Tralee to try on the crystal crown. Sleeping in a one-man tent in random fields, roping in unsuspecting guys to serve as their attentive manservants. They were completely in sync and the laughter never seemed to end – the kind that hurt their bellies and brought running tears to their eyes. And, truth be told, Ava sometimes actually ended the day in damp underwear. Life was so easy then. No complications. She smirks to herself at the distant flashbacks as she slips out of the gown and carefully hands the vintage lace through the curtain.

'I'll get Marina to bag this up, sweetheart,' Nora says, as she gently eases the dress from her.

Ava scrapes her hair back into the neat, low ponytail, pulls on her skinny jeans, and quickly buttons up her tight-fitting charcoal waistcoat. Draping various long necklaces around her neck, she slips her feet into black pumps. Sighing, she thinks of all the stuff she still has to take care of.

'Thank you so much again, Nora!' she calls out after the older woman, not wanting to seem rude.

Her wedding wasn't meant to happen until the following spring. Not that it really mattered – they were always planning to get married at Kinnitty Castle, some day – but they had only been engaged six months. And Ava had really wanted more time to save. Her salary wasn't overly generous, and his salary as a jobbing musician was pretty much non-existent. Sporadic would be one way to describe it. Too many days he had no work at all, so he sat in their overpriced rental apartment, eating ham, cheese and mustard toasties as he mindlessly strummed his guitar. Ava's wonderfully generous dad, Ray, was so adamant about paying for his daughter's big day that she eventually agreed to move the wedding forward. Very forward.

Shaking her daydreams off, Ava breezes out from behind the curtain and tiptoes across the carpet to the till counter. Fifteen seconds later, close to six hundred euro disappear from her bank account in one swift swipe.

'Have a ball, pet. And don't ever say I said this, but remember, it's not about the dress. The most important thing is the partnership, the mutual love and respect.' Nora zips up the gleaming white dress bag and hands her the heavy silver hanger. Ava takes a moment to digest the older woman's words.

'Thanks again, Nora, you've been great,' she says, her smile painted on now.

'See ya, hun, and good luck!' Marina calls out, as Ava waves her goodbye and steps outside onto Dublin's Grafton Street. The smell of the River Liffey is faint on the warm summer air. Buskers sing and crowds mingle past as Ava takes a moment, then she strides back towards the gallery, the muslin bag with her vintage wedding dress hanging heavy over her shoulder.

2

Drinking Dinner.

'OH, HERE SHE IS. A MODERN-DAY PRINCESS GRACE.' Stefan comes from behind the counter to offer help, an espresso cupped in the palm of his hand.

Ava is breathless as she steps into the grey brick gallery on the corner of Dawson Street. 'It's so hot out there. Global warming is a really scary fact,' she tells him. 'That's proper Mediterranean factor fifty heat. No sign of Mags on her broomstick, I see. Have we been busy?'

Stefan shakes his head, puts his cup down on the solid timber floor.

'*Non*,' he says, taking the heavy dress bag from her sticky hands. 'May I?'

'Oh, thank you.' She sighs with relief.

'Just a few email enquiries about the exhibition, I logged them in the book. But I still couldn't get Laurence Kilroy on the phone. I am starting to become nervous ...' he tells her as he carefully lays the dress bag across the glass display table, where towers of flyers and art brochures sit neatly at each end.

'Thanks, I'll call him again after I grab a coffee. What is he playing at? I can't stand flaky artists.' Ava walks around the triangular gallery, with its pure white brick walls, straightening the displayed artwork. 'Kilroy was due to drop in over the weekend when I was in here and was a no-show then, too,' she continues.

Happy with the gallery now, Ava goes towards the Nespresso machine.

'He better not let us down,' she says, 'we've put too much work into this. Lots of media coverage confirmed, and we don't have a hope in hell of getting another artist talented enough to fill that slot now.'

Mags had asked Ava to send out dozens of invites, and there had been lots of RSVPs coming in. She'd even gone so far as to do cute flyers for him, *and* he was printed in the brochure.

'I swear to God,' she says, thinking about it all, 'if that was me and I had that opportunity, I'd be ...' She trails off, knowing she's said too much.

'You know your charcoal of the lamp post on the Ha'penny Bridge at night with the young woman in the background ... that bright yellow pastel moon? So, a man, he spotted it and he enquired about the price. You really should think about selling your work again,' Stefan adds, trying to raise her spirits.

'Stefan! Seriously, stop showing my work to people when I'm not here! It's not for sale. He couldn't have spotted it in the back, you brought it out to show him, didn't you? I'm not a commercial artist. My stuff is just in storage here until I can find a landlord that will allow us to put holes in the bloody walls! It will all come with me when I move. In fact, now I think of it, I must bring in my portfolio next week and take all my work home. Need to start getting my life in order!' Ava extends her hands out wide.

'*Tu es folle* ... you're crazy, Ava. You're so talented,' he says good-humouredly.

'Not interested.' Ava puts her hands firmly on her hips and stares him down.

'If you were more supported, I think perhaps you would be?'

Stefan pipes up boldly, as he stands close to her at the coffee machine.

'Not this again ...' She takes a capsule of coffee from the ceramic bowl and slides it into the slot, pressing a button to whir the machine into action. Stefan leans back against the sink and crosses one leg over the other.

'Does Simon ever remind you what a talented artist you are? *Non* ... But you tell him all the time that he is a great musician!' His eyebrows are raised.

'I'm not that type of artist any more. I don't want to be, it's too hard,' Ava almost snaps at him. 'I just want to work in a gallery, earn a proper wage, be around art, and draw, paint, sketch when it takes my fancy. But for my eyes only. That's quite enough for me right now.'

'Once upon a time you had a successful exhibition ... You sold paintings, *oui*?' Stefan's voice raises a notch, as he lifts his broad shoulders high, questioning her.

'When I was twenty-nine ... a lifetime ago.' She moves to the mini fridge and removes a carton of milk. Opening the top, she sniffs it, then puts it back on the counter top.

'The commercial artist thing just didn't happen for me. And this conversation is over.' Ava twists her long ponytail around her slim fingers.

'*Un instant, s'il vous plaît, un moment ...*' He puts down his coffee, holds up his index finger and disappears into the storage room next to the kitchenette. He returns seconds later holding a large painting in a sharp white glossed frame.

'This,' he holds it up, shaking it gently, 'is exquisite.'

'So? What do you want me to say, Stefan?' Ava pours a drop of milk into her coffee and stirs it roughly, throwing the teaspoon into the sink, and takes the steaming cup in her hand as she moves towards him. She stares intently at the framed painting she did of a young mother feeding her baby under a tree in Dublin's St Stephen's Green that Stefan is holding. The mother's eyes are a pale blue, just like her own. The only bright colour in the picture. She had chosen a carriage-green paint for the trees, so dark it's almost black, and the grass such a burnt orange it's almost brown. Stefan watches her closely as she analyses her work.

'That baby must be in school by now,' she mutters to herself.

'I know a bit about art, I did study it in Paris for four years under Marie-Madeleine Rabec-Mailiard, you know.' Stefan holds up four fingers to emphasise his point.

'Thank you, Stefan, I can count.' She tuts.

'And I did my internship in the Louvre, remember?' He squeezes his dark eyes at her and she blushes despite herself. He puts his cup in the sink.

'I know, and thank you. Really, what would I do without you?'

'Not have a constant headache?' he offers, smiling, folding a strip of gum into his mouth.

'Maybe.' She lifts the cup to her mouth and blows the hot liquid gently.

Stefan goes out to the main gallery and places the framed picture on the floor by Ava's desk.

'Put that painting back in storage, Stefan! Seriously. Now!' she calls after him.

'*Oui*,' he calls back.

'You know, I really do thank my lucky stars you came to work here,' Ava shouts through to him.

'I know, especially since I was only supposed to stay in Dublin for a few months and I'm still here. But, I don't know for how much longer,' he adds nonchalantly, returning from the gallery floor, running his hands through his hair. Ava is forced to look away from his gaze.

24

'Don't ... don't be stupid ... you're not going anywhere!' She shakes her head.

'I'll see ...' He moves closer to her. She can smell his cologne, always La Nuit de l'Homme by Yves Saint Laurent. Little does he know that she sometimes sneaks into Brown Thomas department store on her way home from the gallery and sprays her wrists with it. She loves the musky smell so much, not that she'd be caught dead ever admitting it.

The gallery door tinkles loudly outside and Ava puts her half-finished coffee cup into the sink, then delicately pushes him out of her way with both hands on his shoulders. Out in the gallery a young woman, pushing a pink buggy, walks around slowly and studies the walls. Ava politely interrupts her to hand her a brochure and flyer for Laurence Kilroy's upcoming exhibition.

'His work is very thought-provoking, lovely experimentation with visual textures, it's frighteningly fresh. Any questions, I'm happy to help. Otherwise feel free to browse around.'

Ava feels slightly uneasy, still a little shaken from Stefan's suggestion that he might be leaving Dublin. He comes out to stand beside her, and they remain quiet, side by side, as the young woman wanders around, checking out the walls. Ava looks at her watch.

'Eh, it's almost wine o'clock on a Friday evening ... fancy a glass of vino, Stefan?' she whispers to him. 'Let's close up early? It doesn't look like Mags is going to swoop back in tonight after all. She'll never know. I'd murder a freezing cold Pinot Grigio.' Ava adjusts her necklaces, looking away from his direct stare, conscious of her shoulder rubbing against his arm.

'*Bonne idée, cherie! Oui!*' Stefan enthuses.

The young woman waves the elegant cream and black Laurence Kilroy flyer at Ava. 'Thank you.' She smiles. 'I'll try to come back for this, it looks interesting. I'm really looking for something for my sister's birthday, she's a real art lover and I think I've seen something special that she could relate to. I'll be back, I tend to have more time in the evenings.' Ava smiles at her baby in the buggy, kicking her chubby legs around in the air, and holds the door open for her.

'Oh, that's great. We'll be delighted to welcome you back! We'll also be hosting a little wine and cheese reception after the Kilroy exhibition, which you're more than welcome to stay for. It should be a good night.' Ava smiles as she closes the door behind her.

Stefan almost runs to the door to flip the neon sign to 'Closed'.

'Yes! Wine time, baby! Been a funny old day for me, really, hasn't it?' Ava takes her clutch from under her desk and applies some rose-tinted Vaseline to her lips.

'*Oui*. It has for me, too. A glass of wine should help,' Stefan responds.

'First drink on me, so. Better make it a bottle,' Ava tells him.

He raises his hand and they high-five.

Ava looks around wistfully. Black paintings surround her. Some have the odd splash of colour, mainly splashes of bumblebee yellow or pomegranate purple, though the mood of the gallery is dark this week. Funnily enough, she curated these walls herself in Mags's absence, and she's not sure why they are so gloomy.

★ ★ ★

'Not exactly what you might call a marriage *blanc* – a *white wedding* wall, is it?' Stefan's fingertips were covered in black paint. He was looking at her sombre choices.

'No, I guess not.' She'd stepped forward to straighten a picture with a level.

'Rather melancholy, *non*?' He'd pulled a baby wipe from a packet and cleaned his hands.

'Are you saying my wall has been curated with pensive sadness, Stefan?' she'd teased him.

'*Non,* just not exactly Veronese ... no pomp or celebration, considering your upcoming wedding?' He'd dropped the used wipe into the bin by Ava's desk and folded a piece of gum into his mouth.

'I saw his works at the National Gallery four years ago. It was, in fact, Henry James who professed him the happiest of painters, the person who produced the happiest pictures in the world. This is how I feel right now. Happiness is a not so much a trait but a current state of mind.'

'That's revealing.' Stefan had raised his eyebrows.

'We might prefer that Veronese displayed a hint of Michelangelo's *Terribilità,* or Leonardo's intellectual restlessness or Titian's all-encompassing human sympathy but ...'

'I have to run,' Stefan had interrupted her. 'I have a date. I need to get cleaned up. Oh, and I tackled that outer wall.'

More interested in his upcoming date than the outer wall, Ava had spun around to face him. 'Where are you taking this date?'

'She loves the theatre, so I got tickets to a show she mentioned in passing. I'm a good listener, if nothing else.'

Seeing Ava's approval of his plan, he'd curled his lips. She'd nodded and stared after him as he'd sauntered out of the gallery.

Outside, the rain had been sleeting down across the road. He'd pulled on his cap, shoved his hands deep into his jeans pockets and looked back in, just as she'd quickly looked back to the cheerless wall in front of her.

★ ★ ★

But now, Ava liked her curation. It was honest. Real. It was her mood. Weirdly.

'I'm going to miss this place when Simon and I get married,' she says to Stefan now, back in the moment.

'I just cannot believe you are moving to the County of Clare. When will I get to see you?' Stefan turns his attention away from her as he lifts one foot onto the counter to tie the laces on his grey runners.

'You just say County Clare and I know, it's bananas. I've always been such a Dubliner. It still hasn't really sunk in I'm leaving. It's only to the village of Liscasey, it's less than a three-hour drive from here, but it was all I – all that *we* – could afford. Only way we could own our own home was to buy in County Clare. Edenvale. That's the original name on our house. We literally drove down and just bought it on the spot. It's the cutest cottage but needs a ton of work, as you know, that's why I'm doing so much weekend overtime, to save for the renovations.

'Simon's been up and down, overseeing the project in between travelling to gigs. He's been away so much lately. We'll figure out a way to get together every now and then, Stefan, don't worry. I'll be up and down. I still have to sort a job down there, and it's seriously stressing me out. But all this crazy money we are emptying into our landlord's pockets is pure madness. I can't be a part of the problem here, with the housing and rental crisis any more, and as Simon's work is so sporadic he suggested –'

'You leave the job you love and move all the way to County Clare?' Stefan interrupts, pulling his lace way tighter than he needs to.

'No … *our* idea, Stefan. Simon's been trying … he *does* try.' Ava pulls her pink cashmere cardigan from the back of her chair and drapes it across her shoulders.

'Uh-huh.' Stefan raises his right eyebrow sharply.

'I want my own home, Stefan. At least a house is an investment, it's not dead rent money. Maybe it's a uniquely Irish thing, needing to own a house. Yes, it's little far, but I do have a car, you know, I can come up to Dublin whenever I like. I have to, I mean, to see my friends, and you …'

Stefan looks Ava in the eye.

'And me?'

'You know what I mean!' Ava nudges him.

'I only want what's best for you, Ava, and I'm not sure …' Stefan responds before she cuts him off.

'You really don't like Simon, do you?'

Stefan straightens himself awkwardly and thinks for a moment, chews slowly, then shrugs. 'It's just, how you say – The Tuner is more of a dreamer than a doer.' His observation isn't lost on Ava.

'It's just who he is. I can't criticise him for being true to himself.'

'I can,' Stefan jumps in.

'But he has always been nice to you, right?' she enquires.

'That is true … *man*.' Stefan's handsome face breaks into a cringey grimace.

'Stop! It's only a word he uses … a lot. But it's just how he talks. All the musos do.' Ava slaps Stefan playfully on his arm. 'Right so, tapas, or are we drinking dinner tonight?' She takes the muslin dress bag up from the glass table and moves to the storeroom, where she hangs her dress carefully and closes the door behind her.

'Alcohol for our entrées, *oui*?' Stefan nods as Ava's phone rings. 'But then we must eat, you crazy Irish,' he says. Ava answers without looking at the caller ID.

'Ava O'Hara, how can I help you?' she sing-songs into her phone.

'Using our full names today, are we? Well, hello Ava O'Hara! It's Lauren P. McCabe again!' Lauren's excited voice sounds on the other end of the phone.

'Oh, Lauren! Hi! Sorry! I forwarded the gallery calls to my phone when I was out collecting my wedding dress. So please tell me it's a yes, and you can get the time off work?' Ava sits back on her egg chair and waves at Stefan to sit. He obliges and crosses his long legs, listening intently to Ava's phone call.

'Collecting your frock! How exciting! Yes, good news. I got work cover confirmed. This chief will be there with bells on, sunshine! Now listen, you can't make me wear some meringue horror, okay? Oh, and I need to leave by seven thirty sharp on Saturday morning. I've got to put the magazine summer bumper edition to bed and it has been bloody chaos around here. I won't be able to go mad, I'm afraid.

'Now, on to the important stuff ... please tell me there'll be some hot single guys there. I need a ride, Ava. It's been a while, like at least six weeks. Oh, and get this, last month I went on a Tinder date with this guy Rylan who works for RTÉ Sports, and do you know what the dry shite said to me? He said he had never seen a girl get so drunk on a dinner date in his life. And you know what, Ava? I felt proud! What the eff is wrong with me? He was an insufferable misogynist prat, so boozing my face off was the only way for me to get through the torturous date. Better that than crawl out the bathroom window in the skirt I was wearing! I'd have been done for indecent exposure.

'But anyway, back to your big day, I'm so happy for you and The Tuner. A wedding! It's what you've always wanted.'

'Ah, well, here now, I don't know about that!' Ava responds before she checks herself. 'But ... thanks, we are verrrrry happy together, I'm a verrrrry lucky girl.' Ava manages to interrupt Lauren's million-miles-an-hour talk as she slowly turns her back on Stefan and swings the chair around to face the gloomy gallery wall.

'But I'm thrilled you'll be by my side. It really means a lot to me, Lauren. Cate's just had another new baby. I'm not sure if you knew?'

'What? How many is that now? Five?' Lauren shrieks.

'Three. Max, another gorgeous little guy. I've only seen pictures. She's very tied up unfortunately and, oh, Lauren, you can wear whatever you like. You know me, never was going to be the Bridezilla type. And you, of all people, have so many amazing designer dresses. I just want you to be comfortable ...'
Ava clutches her phone tight to her ear.

'Ah here, no one ever got laid at a wedding by being comfort-able, Ava!' Lauren cuts her off, laughing. 'And you know me! I have something, black, halter, with a sexy slit up the side. It's not too slutty, but I've almost caused a few strokes with guys wearing it to various events before. Can I be comfortable in that?'

'Totally.' Ava laughs along with her.

'Deadly! So, I'm thinking high strappy Jimmy Choos, and a sharp blow-dry. I've a blunt bob and poker straight bangs right now, don't know if you saw my new headshot in the cover fold of the magazine? Anyway, you know me, always changing my hairstyles and colour. Hair is supposed to be barely black, it's actually more raven black. Cleopatra, eat your heart out! Starting to get a wine belly, mind you, so I better abstain for the next couple of weeks ... and by abstaining I mean vodka and sparkling water, obviously. So I guess I'll see you in two weeks? Kinnitty ... wow ... all those chats we had about that place, all the times we stayed down in Offaly in your dad's when he moved. And your gorgeous mum, God rest her ...' Lauren's voice slows.

A moment passes and Ava clears her throat to speak, but Lauren intercepts.

'Right, got to go, I have to blog about California Glow, a fake tan that actually made me look like an Oompa Loompa when I tried it last night. I'm still luminous! Toxic too, probably! Just need to hashtag *amazing* hashtag *musthave* the shite out of it, sure that's what they pay me the big bucks for. Isn't that right, Julia? Are you recording? Don't start recording yet! Oh God, sorry, Ava, my assistant Julia is shooting a video for the Instagram story post for me and waving me down like a lunatic to get on with it before the shitty tan streaks again. I've got a wind blower on me at full blast at the moment, and it's still pouring off my leg. My assistant Julia is a millennial, ever so dramatic and opinionated. She also doesn't really like to do actual work, isn't that right, Julia? Got to fly, talk soon! Be really great to see you, love.'

Lauren rings off.

'Who was that?' Stefan asks.

'My long-lost bestie.' She spins back around and hugs the pink cardigan around her, a huge smile on her face. 'She had to go, rub herself in cream or something.'

'Ohhh, *intéressant*!' Stefan flicks his dark hair up, rubs his eyes and uncrosses his legs.

'No, I refuse to let *that* happen!' Ava shakes her head and opens her clutch bag to drop her phone in.

'Is she married?'

'No.'

'Hot?'

'Very.'

'Hot and single.' Stefan licks his lips playfully.

'That's grotesque, Stefan, and Lauren would eat you for breakfast. Let's go.' Ava stands up and flicks off the bright overhead fluorescent light behind her. Stefan pulls his cap out from inside his jacket pocket and follows her out the door, laughing as he adjusts it on his head.

★ ★ ★

Minutes later, they're sitting cosily on two high-backed stools at the candlelit bar in Rosilita's Wine Bistro, off Grafton Street.

'Our regular seats.' Stefan settles himself on the high stool, draping his leather jacket over the back. Ava can't help but take in the strain of the muscles in his arms as he reaches round.

'God, we really are quite the regulars here, aren't we? Probably not a good thing, but hey, it's the only time we really get to chat on our own, so ... to friendship!' Ava raises her frosted glass of Pinot Grigio.

'*Mon amie*,' he says to her, as he twirls the wine in the glass, then takes a sip.

'Today's stressed me out big time, Stefan. I mean, not just getting the dress but the realisation that I still need to find a job in Liscasey ... Well, anywhere in Clare. Did I tell you about the full-time position teaching art to kids in a place in Ennis I saw?'

Stefan shakes his head.

'The pay is actually pretty good, saw an ad in the window of that Murphy and Rose's recruitment place across from the gallery. They advertise all sorts of rural jobs too. It's an after-school gig, so I don't need a teaching degree, it's more fun-based. Make and do kind of thing. But whatever you do, don't breathe a word to Mags about it. She can't know I'm leaving just yet, in case she sacks me two weeks before my wedding. What is it with her, anyway? I mean, I'm working there three years and I barely know anything about her. She is borderline rude to me. God knows, I'm relying on those two weeks' wages to pay for the vintage Rolls-Royce I have my heart set on. Most bridal traditions I could take or leave, but the vintage dress and vintage car are the two things I really care about.' Ava's aware she's ranting, but Stefan remains attentive.

'Never mind cars. I wish you did not have to leave. I'll really miss you,' he says earnestly.

'Ah stop, I wish you could come with me! The Clare girls would love a dashing French man knocking around the place!' She tilts her head to smile at him, her eyes focused on his.

'Oh . . . oh, me too.' Stefan eyes widen, and she raises her glass to his and they clink again, then gulp in unison.

'I'm sure Mags will have another Ava employed for you before you can say "Abstract Expressionism". Maybe you'll be promoted?' Ava laughs a little too energetically.

'I don't think so . . . and work responsibility is not what I came to Ireland for, you know. I just wanted to see this beautiful country and experience the culture, which I did, and then I saw the job opportunity and thought I'd like to live in Dublin a little while longer. I don't want your position, if Mags were to offer it. Without you there . . . *non.*' Stefan rubs his hands over his light overgrowth of stubble.

'What?' Ava puts her glass down, her face falling. 'You were serious earlier when you said you might leave Ireland?'

'*Oui*, perhaps.' He shrugs.

'You can't!'

'*Pourquoi?*'

'I'd never see you . . . like, ever again?' Ava pulls a sad face.

'You could visit? We'll always stay in touch, no matter where in the world we are.' He whispers close to her ear, 'I mean, we'll always see the same stars, Ava O'Hara.'

He is trying not to laugh, but she bursts out laughing.

'Nice line, Stefan. So romantic – not!' Ava does finger quotations on the word *not*. 'Look at you, forever the French charmer! You can take the boy out of Paris, but . . .' She trails off, slightly flushed.

'*J'aime ton sourire*! I just love your smile.' Stefan beams at her, as he takes another long gulp, holding his wine out in front of him, twirling the glass by the stem.

'But where would you go? I always thought Dublin was special to you.' Ava avoids his gaze and picks at a thread from the top button on her waistcoat.

'I don't know … London, maybe? Barcelona, perhaps?'

'London's amazing, so cosmopolitan. So hip. Just your scene!' she says, trying to sound supportive.

'*Oui*, I have many friends there.'

'It sort of feels like we're breaking up, doesn't it, Stefan? I don't like it, so let's just change the subject. And I'm feeling a bit emotional, probably just nervous about the wedding. Dad has spent a small fortune, and that alone makes me uncomfortable. He wanted to pay, insisted on it, as I'm his only daughter. His only family, actually. It's been so last-minute getting that cancellation and all, and Kinnitty Castle is the furthest thing from cheap! I just never thought it would actually happen, really I don't think …' Ava opens her silver clutch bag and applies some more rose-tinted Vaseline, then snaps it shut as she smacks her lips together.

'I know my room was two hundred and thirty euro. For one night!' Stefan says. 'It will be worth it if you can match me with the *magnifique* Lauren, though!' he teases her.

'Quit it! It's not happening. Although when she sees you I may have to tie her hands together with the celebrant's sash. Sure, I don't even know if Lauren will stay overnight, to be honest. She has to run back to work, as always. To her glamorous lifestyle. When I was ranting about the fakeness of Instagram earlier, she, in particular, came to my mind. Lauren is the Instagram queen.' Ava twirls the thin stem of her wine glass now too, glancing at the sparkle on her left hand.

'Such a beautiful ring,' Stefan mutters, following her change of thought.

'Isn't it? Dad saved so hard to buy this for my mum, bless him.

35

He bought it in Dublin at the Happy Ring House on Westmoreland Street. They got dressed up in their best Sunday clobber and met under Clerys clock. You know that iconic Dublin meeting place, right? I should bring you there before I . . . Anyway, Mum always told me from the time I was a little girl that one day it would be mine. I just . . .' She stops and drains her wine, settling the empty glass steadily back on its doily.

'Just what?' Stefan does the same, his long fingers resting around the stem.

'Oh, I don't know. I just never thought it would end up as *my* engagement ring too, you know? And that she wouldn't be here. That I'd have to grow up without her. It's not that I don't adore it . . .' Ava stops and rubs the four-claw diamond solitaire ring gently. Stefan looks less than convinced.

'Did you want to pick your own ring?'

'No, it's not that . . .'

'You told me you had been saving for a ring, both of you?' He raises his eyebrows.

'We were . . . actually we had a bit put away. I saw this ring from 1908, the year my granny was born, in that little antique jewellers, Harlequin, on South Anne Street. This gorgeous little rose flower diamond. It wasn't pricey or anything; it was so pretty and dainty, so we opened a little account and put a few euros in every month. Anyway, look, he was right, it wasn't a necessity and we used that few bob for his new guitar case, so . . . he needs it for travelling to his gigs. It makes sense, right?' Ava holds her hand up to the light and admires her mother's ring.

'Romance and practicality have never been something that I'd put together,' Stefan adds, with more than a tinge of sarcasm.

'I do love this, of course . . .' Ava stops babbling abruptly.

'But?' Stefan crosses his legs on the high stool and leans a little closer.

'But I guess it sat in my jewellery box by my bed for years. I was too scared to wear it, so I just admired it. For the delicate piece of art that it is. I was always so scared I would lose it or something. It feels wrong on my finger somehow ... It just means so much more to me than a ring. Oh, listen to me moaning ... This is a glass of wine on an empty stomach talking. I'm such a lightweight when it comes to drinking these days. Look, don't mind me. I'm being stupid.'

Ava pulls the bobbin from her ponytail for the second time that day and lets it fall loose. She slides her hair across her face and out of her eyes. 'Why waste money we can't afford? Anyway, enough about all that!'

Stefan says nothing and studies her for a moment. Then he opens his mouth to say something, but closes it again and smiles.

'So ... tell me, the video we made, this bridesmaid of yours, this single Lauren ...' Stefan swiftly moves the conversation in another direction.

'Maid of honour!' Ava interrupts. 'I think we both know our bridesmaid days arc well and truly behind us!'

'Maid of honour,' Stefan corrects himself. '*Comment* ... how come you never talk about her? I mean, for someone who made your eyes light up like that on the phone? I've never even heard you mention her name before. Where did you meet this Lauren?' Stefan asks as he holds up a fifty-euro note to get the attention of the bartender.

'Well ... we've kind of drifted a bit now, sadly. It's a long story.'

'I have all night.'

'Well, we met in Trinity College. I was studying fine art, Lauren was studying English and politics. It was one night in the Buttery, the crazy campus bar. At a karaoke final, believe it or not. Oh, the singing shame!' Her face lights up and Ava removes her cardigan and drapes it on the back of the stool, fixes her various necklaces.

'Are you ready for this? First round it was musicals, I belted out "A Woman's Touch" from *Calamity Jane*, and Lauren sang "Just You Wait" from *My Fair Lady*. Round two was the final, just me and Lauren. I screeched "Viva Forever", and Lauren belted out "Spice Up Your Life", as if she was Geri Halliwell. Obviously, we thought it was absolutely hilarious that we both chose a Spice Girls song and it turned out that we both loved Baby, Sporty, Scary, Ginger and Posh as much as the other – as did the entire pub. Got free drinks sent over to us all night to thank us for the entertainment. I'll never forget it, my hair was shaved at one side, I was wearing this fabulous 1960s mod outfit, this skin-tight black-and-white shift dress; it was obnoxiously short.'

'Ohh, you have a picture?' Stefan can't help himself, gently waving his fifty note at the bartender, flirting to get her attention.

'Quit it, Stefan! Anyway, we just got talking and never shut up. We'd so much in common, and I don't mean to sound cheesy but I'd never really had a proper' – Ava does finger quotations for the second time today – '"best friend" before Lauren. Then Cate Connolly came on the scene, she was studying speech therapy in Trinity. Cate was knocked out in the first round of the musicals, mind you. She sang a song from *Calamity Jane* too, "Just Blew in from the Windy City". I swear I'll never forget the stomping dance she did while singing it. It was priceless. Anyway, Lauren and me were both single and loved the same things. Namely going out, getting drunk, cheesy pop, following bands around, and eating sweet and sour chicken with fried rice. We moved into a tiny flat in Grosvenor Square in Rathmines three weeks later and lived there together for the next three years.'

'Wow . . . but what happened?' he asks.

'Then . . . I met Simon.' Ava tightens her grip around her glass.

'It was, of course, at a Seventh Hour gig in Whelan's bar. Funnily enough, Lauren and I were out celebrating. It was the day I sold my very first painting. Remember the one with the red balloon that blew away and got stuck in a tree ... the one you like?'

Stefan nods. 'I do! The contrast of the balloon so bright red against the dull tree.'

'I've always loved that one myself,' Ava replies, but as Stefan goes to speak she puts her hand across his mouth.

'*When* I was an artist, Stefan! Don't start! Anyway, I bought Simon a shot at the bar because I thought he was hot, and I was a bit star-struck as I adored Seventh Hour. We were flirty and giddy, and that was that really. He started to stay over in the flat in Rathmines a lot as he was in between places and the band was taking off and getting a lot of hype, and it was all so exciting for me, but ...'

'But not so much for Lauren?' Stefan instantly recognises the problem.

'No, no, probably not ...' Ava digests what he's just said. 'Do you know, I've never really thought about that properly before, like seen it from her side.'

'Who won the Spice Girls karaoke competition in the end?' Stefan wonders.

'Lauren. As she always does. Lauren just wins at life.' Ava's little laugh has a clear tinge of frustration.

'Why is she not committed?' Stefan's waving finally gets the attention of the pretty bartender. 'Same again please, *mademoiselle*,' he flirts charmingly with her.

The bartender blushes, drying her hands on the off-white tea towel slung over her shoulder. 'You again,' she says, flirting right back. 'That seat should have your name engraved on it.'

Ava looks at them, from one to the other briefly, leans in closer to Stefan then continues chatting.

'Lauren? God, no! Lauren will never get married, she loves herself too much … In a good way, I mean. And she just wouldn't be the marrying or maternal type at all. It's like Lauren never wanted to meet someone. Oh, don't get me wrong, she was always up for snogging random guys, but ridiculously picky when it came to having a boyfriend. It was just her excuse to never have to settle down, I think. All work and all play, that's Lauren's life.' Ava drinks from the already drained glass, a single droplet sliding down her throat. 'I was thinking about this earlier. I started hanging out with Cate a bit more, but for some reason as we got older she and Lauren started to rub each other up the wrong way. Cate didn't get the world Lauren ended up in, and vice versa. I was always the peacekeeper, piggy in the middle, it became exhausting so …' Ava shrugs.

Stefan hands her a fresh drink and takes his change from the bartender.

'Enjoy.' The bartender only has eyes for Stefan.

'*Merci*.' He smiles at her.

'*De rien*.' She grins back, ignoring a phone ringing behind the bar.

'*Tu parles français?*' He raises his eyebrows again.

'*Oui … un peu*.' She uses her index finger with a shimmering gold nail to push her trendy black-framed glasses up her nose.

Ava makes a guttural sound and they both look at her. She coughs to mask it and smiles sweetly at them both.

'May I ask for your number, perhaps?' He rummages behind him in his leather jacket pocket and then slides the white doily and a silver pen across the bar to her. The bartender giggles, blushes again, tucks her hair behind her ears and scribbles her number on the doily.

'*Merci beaucoup*…Suzanne!' Stefan says, as he reads and folds it into his back pocket. Ava shakes her head, rolling her eyes.

'*Tu peux me téléphoner,*' she says as she sashays away.

'Puhlease!' Ava turns her head and sniggers.

'What?' He looks at her.

'As if...we all know "*un peu*",' Ava grimaces, imitating Suzanne.

'You don't believe she speaks French, *non*?' he asks, raising his eyebrows.

'*Non!*' Ava widens her eyes and makes a face at Stefan. 'I believe she fancies you, knows you're French and decided to learn a few lines. Fair play to her, I mean. A for effort.' Ava checks herself. 'You'd make a very attractive couple, and hey, another date, Stefan, how do you have the energy?' She lightens her tone.

'I suppose I'm trying to find what you have, Ava. True love, *non*? What do you think?' His eyes serious now, daring her to pick up the bait. Ava returns his look but says nothing and starts fiddling with her necklaces. They sit in silence for a few moments.

'I do believe in true love, Ava.' He wipes the counter with the palm of his hand.

'What's that supposed to mean?' she asks him, her eyes lost in the dark pupils of his.

'I'd never settle for anything less.' His words hang heavy in the air, as Ava picks at her nail polish.

'I think whoever you fall in love with will be the luckiest girl in the world ... I hope you do find that true love, Stefan. Listen, I better get back to Simon. And I've got to grab my dress from the gallery on the way home.' Ava drops her hand and dips her eyes to the marble bar counter.

'What time do you finish, Suzanne?' Stefan lifts his head to call after the bartender.

'*Dix heures!*' she calls from the bottom of the bar, uncorking a bottle of wine.

'You are relentless!' Ava shakes her head at him. She pulls on her cardigan and stands up to leave.

'Not relentless enough, I'm afraid, but *une question* for you before you leave me again: why have this Lauren woman as your maid of honour, if you never really see her? I could have been your pretty-in-pink-maid-of-man!' He pouts dramatically.

'Gay you are not, every woman knows that!' Ava says, but then looks him straight in the eye. 'Because the truth is, I really, really miss her.'

There, she's finally admitted it out loud.

3

All Sorts of Jittery.

S OMEWHAT UNSTEADILY, AVA HAULS her dress up the three flights of stairs to the city centre apartment she shares with Simon. City centre traffic whizzes by outside the Four Courts on the near empty quays. She hiccups as she rummages in her clutch for her keys. The door suddenly swings open.

'Ohhh, the wanderer returns?' Simon tuts, hair standing on end as he rubs his long goatee beard. Dressed in navy shorts with white sports socks pulled up to his calves, chunky headphones sit around his neck and a bottle of Corona dangles from his right hand.

'Oh, hi, love! Sorry I'm so late, was dress shopping – collecting even – exciting!' Ava struggles under the weight of the dress on her shoulder. 'And then I went for *one* with Stefan. But you know how the French love their wine! I didn't stay for food.' Ava rolls her slightly glazed eyes.

'Thought so. I couldn't text you, I've no credit again, and I'm starving, but I'm guessing you didn't bring any food back with you?' He ushers her in ahead of him, then closes the door behind them with a quiet click.

'No, sorry, I decided to save the few euro and eat at home. I did a big shop yesterday in Aldi, though.' Ava stops. 'Eh, can you give me a hand here, Simon? This is heavy!' She nods towards the dress.

'Oh, sorry.' He grabs the hanger and hooks it on to the door frame, as Ava slips off her pumps and turns to face him.

'The lads dropped by to jam earlier and ate what was in the fridge . . . again.' Simon laughs, nonchalantly, taking a swig from his bottle.

'That's not on, Simon, it's not fair. We barely have the cash to feed ourselves, let alone all your band mates. This is ridiculous,' Ava says, her hackles up.

'No, I know, man . . . You're right, you're totally right. I'll tell them that next time.' He pads back into the living room, as Ava is suddenly distracted. There's a stunning bouquet of colourful flowers sitting on the floor.

'Wow! What are they? They're fabulous.' Her eyes light up. 'Did you . . . ?'

'Oh, I dunno, they arrived earlier.' Simon shrugs.

'Did you leave the apartment at all today, Simon?' she asks him, distracted.

'Nope, got sucked into watching an old VH1 Pink Floyd documentary and played some Fortnite, then the boys landed over.' He takes another swig from his bottle as Ava, ignoring him, walks over to pick the enormous bouquet up. She opens the tiny brown envelope and removes the card:

Here's to you – the almost Mrs Tuner. I need to start buying strange men more shots in Whelan's! Can't wait to see you in two weeks. I'm so thrilled to be your maid of honour. I miss you, Ava. Love, Lauren xx #TheTunersWedding.

'Oh, I miss you too, Lauren . . .' Ava breathes the words out as she inhales the bouquet and takes it into the kitchen. Rummaging under the sink, she finds an old vase. She runs the cold tap, fills it and carefully arranges the delicate flowers.

'It's been such a long time since anyone's sent me flowers,' she says to herself, settling the vase on the kitchen table, standing back to admire them.

'Can you rustle up anything in there, love? I'm starvin'!' Simon yells, as Ava pulls opens the fridge door and peers inside.

'There is some packet ham and a few cherry tomatoes left. I could make you one of my special toasties?' she calls back.

'Any onion?' he shouts.

Ava rummages in the vegetable basket at the side of the fridge.

'Found one!' She sticks her head around the kitchen door.

'Mustard?' He doesn't look up as he shouts again, head buried in his phone. Ava sighs, steps back into the kitchen, opens the press and takes out the mustard.

'Yes!' she calls back, shaking the almost empty mustard bottle.

'And tea, please?'

Ava stomps barefoot to the kitchen door again and peers around into the living room. He is still texting, thumbs a blur, and doesn't look up.

'What did your last slave die of?' she says, as he jumps out of his skin and shoves his phone into his back pocket.

'I thought you'd no credit?' she says.

'Eh, I don't. I was emailing our builders back, they ... they're a bit behind this week. I may have to head down there in the morning. These lads can't be trusted.'

'What do you mean, can't be trusted? We're paying them really well, aren't we? Exactly how far behind are they? Let me see –' And she moves towards him, hand outstretched for his phone.

'Ah, no. Don't worry,' Simon dismisses her. 'It's grand. I'm on top of it.'

Shaking her head, Ava goes back into the kitchen and clicks on the kettle. 'How did the songwriting go today?' she asks, as she grabs two mugs out of the cupboard.

'Eh, we've some ... hit songs written, babe, just need to get them down, ya know ...'

'Studios cost a fortune, Simon,' she calls back to him, rolling her eyes as she pours hot water into two mugs and starts preparing two ham, cheese and onion toasties. Simon comes in, pulls out a chair, turns it the wrong way around and sits opposite her, listening to what's playing on his headphones.

'Have you heard anything I've said?' Ava asks loudly.

'Sorry, man,' Simon replies, reluctantly removing his headphones.

He watches as she opens his toastie and squirts a load of mustard onto the filling.

'This is nearly empty. You need to get some more,' he says, shaking the bottle viciously and squirting the last of the liquid out.

Ava doesn't respond, as she takes a sip of her tea. He tears at the toastie, groaning as he inhales it.

'Imagine, two weeks tomorrow we will be husband and wife,' she muses, drumming her fingers around the cup.

'Eh, meant to say ... about the honeymoon. There's a chance the band will have a few gigs in the diary that week, so we may need to ... well, put it off for a few weeks. That's cool, right?'

'No way! That's so not cool with me, Simon! Is this about the builders not being finished on time, because you paid them in full, right? They signed that contract! I've been working my ass off for this house and I'm dying to see it all renovated. Leave that contract out for me to look at, will you? Just in case.'

'Okay.' Simon doesn't look up. 'Ten years, man, that's a long time to be with the same person, all the same,' he mumbles, still not meeting her eyes and blowing into his hot tea to cool it down.

'God, it is ...' Ava is lost in thought. 'And, you know, my anxiety is reaching weird levels. Like, I keep thinking what if I can't get pregnant because I've left it too late? I've been on the pill for over ten years.' She narrows her eyes at him. 'What's the last decade been all about then?'

He shrugs again, takes another bite and chews noisily. 'I haven't spent too much time thinking about it, I guess,' he says eventually, looking up at her, and they eat in silence for a while.

'Well, we want kids, don't we? I mean ... isn't that the main point of us getting married?' Ava starts again. 'We've talked about it often enough over the years. I'm just worried about our financial situation.'

'Are you starting on about money again? It's always the same. Every time you have a few drinks it's money, money, money. I'm a musician, Ava. You've always known that. I will not conform to pay for what is my privilege. My destiny is in my own hands, I'll never work for the man, man.' He licks his baby finger, gathers crumbs, then licks the remaining crumbs off the plate with his tongue.

'Jesus! What age are you, Simon? Licking your plate? Really? And no, I'm not saying that. I'm just saying we aren't in a great place financially. You know how much I support your career. I always have, you can't throw that one at me. Sure, aren't I giving up my job at the art gallery so I can try to make more money when we move and have the cottage?' she asks, then trails off as Simon belches, his hand covering his mouth.

'The pay in that place is a joke anyway. You work too hard for that shit money. I told you the night I met you that selling art is obnoxious. Art should be free, man! You're wasting your time with all that trying-to-sell-art crap. It's only for rich prats!' He gestures wildly, warming up to one of his favourite subjects.

'Steady on, Simon.' Ava juts out her chin. 'But it's okay to pay for music? In that case, shouldn't music be free?' she asks him.

'Music is free, man. You've gotta listen to what your soul is telling you ...' He taps his chest.

47

Ava sticks her fingers in her ears briefly. 'I've heard this a million times, Simon, and, actually, Stefan thinks I should paint *more*. He thinks I have real talent . . .' she says to him, then realises that she is more than a little tipsy. She takes her half-eaten toastie plate to the sink, annoyed by Simon's soapbox posturing.

'Is that who really sent you the flowers? That German dude, Steven?' he asks casually.

'He's French. His name is Stefan. And no, I told you, they're from Lauren,' Ava reaffirms.

'Oh, so you went ahead and invited her to the wedding then?' He laughs, more easily now.

'I asked her to be my maid of honour, actually.'

Simon bursts out laughing.

'You did not? Woah, man. That girl's a total man-eater. I must WhatsApp the lads in the band to warn them. And you haven't heard from that one at all in, what, must be well over a year? You don't need to hear from her, mind you, she's never off Instagram, talking shite about every product under the sun. She'd sell her soul for a euro, that one. Never warmed to her, the hashtag bitch.' He stands up rather abruptly and leaves the table.

'She was very good to you, lest you forget!' she shouts after him. 'I mean, she let you stay in our flat rent-free for months on end and never said a word. Lauren was a really good friend to you, Simon, even though deep down I don't think she liked you that much either. And bring your plate over, I'm not your cleaner!'

She scrapes the remains of her half-eaten toastie into the bin, then turns to the sink, scrubbing the plate angrily with a wet cloth. Leaving it to drip-dry, she upends a washed pint glass and fills it with water.

Simon walks back into the kitchen. 'Listen, it's late. You've had a few, and I'm not getting into a fight here about Lauren and the builders. Make love not war, right?' He stands and moves towards her with his plate and cup and puts his hands around her waist. 'The great news is that we've finally got all the songs together for the new album. We've booked MindWill Recording Studio beside the house in Clare for a few weeks next month, so you won't see me for a bit, all going well.' Simon crosses both his fingers.

'How did you guys afford that?' Ava turns to him in amazement.

'That was the other thing I wanted to talk to you about actually . . .' He hesitates.

'What?' Ava pauses.

'Maybe the band recording a few tracks in the new house? You see, we don't have –'

'Not a chance, Simon! Don't even go there.' Ava shuts the conversation down.

'Uh, eh . . . but . . .'

'It's a no.' Ava shakes her head, firmly.

'I don't need your permission to make music now, do I?' Simon adjusts his position.

'Only if I'm the one who pays for it.'

'Forget it . . . did I say how damn sexy you look this evening? I love that waistcoat on you, man, very rock 'n' roll, my soon-to-be ball and chain. You were always my favourite groupie.' He kisses her neck gently as Ava dries her hands and turns into him.

'I don't think you did tell me I look sexy, actually. In fact, I can't remember the last time . . .'

The effects of the wine swim warmly through her head and she opens her lips to find his.

'Think I'm terribly on edge, for some reason,' she whispers, putting her arms around his neck. 'I'm over-analysing everything. I'm seeing problems that probably don't exist.'

'I think we both have massive wedding jitters, man,' he whispers into her ear. 'You know what's good for jitters?' He moves his pelvis tight against her, as she steps back, the flowers catching her eye again.

'I'll be in in a bit, Simon, there's something I want to do.' She turns to admire the bouquet on the table.

'Cool, man.' Simon adjusts himself, slides his headphones back over his ears and heads off. Ava opens out a drawer under the sink. She removes an oversized plastic storage box containing a yellow and red paint-splattered portfolio book of heavyweight wood pulp paper, a box of coloured pencils and pastels, paints and paintbrushes of all different shapes and sizes. She lays her art supplies on the table and opens the portfolio and starts flipping through various drawings to find a blank page. She stares at the colourful flowers before snapping pictures of them on her phone from all sorts of angles. Propping her phone up against a thick, well-used cookbook, she sketches an outline then starts to paint, her hand moving with speed and accuracy across the page as her worries melt away.

4

Dying to Know. Afraid to Find Out.

'WAIT, YOU STAYED THE NIGHT AT HER PLACE?' Ava swiftly turns her head to look at Stefan, who is stacking the Art Gallery Space 1 summer brochures by the long window.

'Uh-huh.' He continues to stack, dressed today in a grey hoody and black jeans. 'Apologies, I didn't get home to change.' He chews gum slowly as he responds and continues stacking.

'Oh ... but you *never* stay over after a date.' Ava shifts her weight from foot to foot. She twists the small diamond earring in her left lobe around and around as she watches him.

'Dates ... plural!' He grins at her mischievously.

'Oh, really? I only left you Friday night. Did you go out with that girl Suzanne afterwards?' she asks.

'*Oui*. I stayed for another when you left, and when she finished her shift we went to Davey Byrne's. Then on *samedi*, Saturday, we went to a Farmers' Market in Phoenix Park and then she cooked for me – organic Beef Bourgogne!' Stefan smacks his lips.

'You stayed in her place *all* weekend?' Ava tries to control the tone in her voice as it rises. 'This girl ... it is Suzanne, isn't it? She must be really something to hold your attention like that.' She twists the diamond earring more vigorously and the back pops off. Glad of the distraction, she searches the timber floor for it, finds it and concentrates on attaching it back to the bar.

'Suzanne? *Oui* ... She is kind of special.' Stefan straightens his pile of brochures neatly against the window and moves back towards Ava.

'Special, how?' Ava walks to meet him, her runners squeaking on the timber floor.

'Just ... special.' He stands up straight now, as Ava faces him. There is a mischievous glint in his eye.

'You don't say.' Ava smiles weakly at him.

'I do, or no, *je suis désolé*, that is what *you* will say in two weeks' time to The Tuner. I do. I do forever.' He shoves his hands deep into his pockets.

'I guess.' Ava shrugs.

'And you'll live happily ever after!' Stefan adds.

'I guess ... I mean, yes!' She tries to hide her rising frustration.

'Good. So, what did *you* do over the weekend? You weren't working, right?' he asks her, as they stand inches apart in the middle of the gallery floor.

'Nothing much, Simon's band were rehearsing in our apartment. It was terribly noisy and totally unrelaxing, so I just did some watercolour work in my room and I read, and oh, actually, on Friday night ... you'll appreciate this!' Ava skips back to her desk and pulls her portfolio art book from underneath, flips it open and shows Stefan the sketch she did of Lauren's flowers.

'Is this your portfolio? All your work?' He takes the heavy book carefully in both his hands.

'Yeah, I brought it in to collect all the loose drawing in the back room, best to start getting it all together for the big move. And if nothing else it will stop you from pestering our customers with my drawings!' she exclaims, as he brings it to the window. He holds it up to the light.

'This is just *merveilleux* ...Wonderful, Ava, the outline strokes so light, the dishevelled strokes so real ...Is that the new natural hair bristle brush? It copes so well with the heavy texture of the paint.'

'Yes, doesn't it? It really manages to maintain their shape,' Ava muses.

'It's exposed, and these blooms ... so uncomplicated.' Stefan examines the painting intently.

'Right,' Ava enthuses. 'That's it exactly! I was just going to bed and they just kind of said that to me. I looked beyond, like you always tell me to do. Lauren sent them to me ...I photographed them first, as we both know the life of a flower is so temporary, but I just couldn't stop sketching. Weird, it was pulling something out of me. I didn't finish the actual painting part until five in the morning, got totally lost in it.'

'No one uses brush colour like you ...' Stefan continues studying the picture closely.

'Why, thank you!' Ava does a small curtsey. 'I am kind of pleased with it, actually. Might get this framed for my new house. I can't envision the place done up, so have to wait until I actually see it. Then I'll know where to hang it!' Ava smiles as Stefan flips the page back; straight away her smile vanishes, as realisation spreads across her face.

'Oh no! Shit! Please ... No! Don't, please, Stefan!' Ava panics as she jumps to grab her portfolio; he jokingly holds the heavy book over his head. She jumps again to try and reclaim it from him, snatching at thin air.

'Too late.' He grins and turns the page. 'These are good. Really, really good!' He flips to another page.

'Please give it back, I'm serious, Stefan!' she shouts, as he flips through the pages. Suddenly his grin vanishes; he pauses and becomes silent.

'*C'est moi?*' His words rush out.

Ava purses her lips tightly, flushing red from her neck to her face.

'Can I have it back, please?' She takes the book, as he hands it to her.

'Ava?' He takes her arm, as she pulls away.

'Just leave it, Stefan, okay?' She stomps towards her desk and shoves the portfolio back underneath it.

'I – I – can we talk about this?' He follows her, but then the door tinkles and Ava spins around to see Suzanne standing in the doorway with two small brown paper sandwich bags dangling from each hand.

'*Bonjour.* Lunch? I was just passing.' She smiles at Stefan, fresh-faced under her glasses, wearing workout gear with two plaits hanging on either side of her pretty face.

'Suzanne, *salut* . . . so nice of you!' He looks to Ava, who looks away immediately and pulls out her phone.

'It's lunchtime, of course! The morning has flown. Mags will be in soon, so you go, take a long lunch,' Ava suggests.

'*Non* . . . no, I will stay, I have to –'

'Not at all, go. He's all yours, Suzanne,' Ava cuts him off, a bright smile lighting her face, and she ushers him away with a flicker of her hand. 'Sure, I've enough stuff to arrange here with Laurence Kilroy's exhibition fast approaching. Been chasing him for various confirmations all week. I need to get on that now.' Ava tries to act normal, her heart racing and her mouth dry as she leans against the pillar near the door of the gallery.

Suzanne smiles at Ava, handing a brown paper bag to Stefan. 'Homemade bread,' she tells him, crinkling up her cute freckles. 'Great place you guys work in. Stefan was telling me all about it over the weekend.'

Suzanne bites her bottom lip, then opens her brown paper bag and pulls out an apple. Rubbing it clean with the end of her tight Lycra top, she bites into it.

'We like it,' Ava says, sitting and holding up her phone, as though she's about to make a call.

'Stefan's going to take me to the National Art Gallery this Sunday. I've never been, imagine that? Am totes excited!' She crunches into her apple.

'We will talk when I get back from lunch, *oui*? I'll help you track down Laurence Kilroy?' Stefan shakes his fist in the air, joking, but he is flushed in the face.

'Sure will!' Ava paints a bright smile on her face.

'Can I bring you back anything?' he asks her, folding a piece of gum into his mouth as she shakes her head. He slips his jacket on. Ava looks immediately to Suzanne, who is intently focused on Stefan.

'Have a nice lunch and enjoy the NAG on Sunday. It's a special place, you'll love it.' Ava smiles weakly, as Stefan and Suzanne leave, then she drops her head into her hands.

'Oh my God, what was I thinking? *Morto*! You moron, Ava!' She scrunches her hair tightly between her fingers, then stands and flings her phone onto the timber floor, where it bounces with a bang. 'Oh shit! Oh no! Oh shit!' Ava scrambles around on the ground. 'Great. This is just bloody great!' She picks up her cracked iPhone and carefully punches in a number, hits loudspeaker and it goes straight to voicemail.

'Hello. Mags Crowley here.' A clipped voice rings out. 'You know what to do.'

'Hello, Mags, I . . .'

The door tinkles an arrival as an elegant older woman, sharply dressed in a tweed cape and tan knee-high boots, marches in.

'Hate the walls.' She throws her hands out and drops her bag on Ava's desk.

'Hello to you too, Mags. I was just leaving you a voice message.' Ava hangs up and greets her boss.

'Where is our originality, Ava? Where is our soul? Because I'm certainly not feeling it here. There is no inspiration on these walls, which is most unlike you.' Mags throws off her tweed cape and click-clacks around the gallery.

'I'm not sure, Mags.' Ava swallows and stands up. 'To be brutally honest, I'm not sure about anything any more.'

'You are better than this. *Way* better than this!' Mags looks at her, her sharp features creasing in disapproval.

'I have to talk to you, I-I need to hand in my notice, Mags … I'm moving to Liscasey in Clare after the wedding. I …' Ava stutters, finding it impossible to articulate such life-changing news.

'Moving to Liscasey? Why?' Mags looks aghast.

'Because we bought the house there. I told you that,' Ava replies.

'Yes, as a holiday home, I thought? A summer runaround?' Mags isn't impressed.

'No, forever. I can't afford summer runarounds, Mags. We have to live there, we can't afford Dublin any more, it's outgrown us financially.' Ava pinches the bridge of her nose and can't meet her boss's eyes, as Mags leans on the edge of Ava's desk.

'I have to look for another job down there. I haven't yet. It's been all so fast – the wedding, and the move.'

'Ava, dear, when you came to me first you were a bright commercial artist, you wanted to display and exhibit. I respected your work. Then you just stopped being an artist and asked me for a desk job. I presumed you were going through what we call a dry period? I assumed you'd paint again.' Mags shrugs and shakes her head.

'I need security, Mags.' Ava runs her hands through her hair.

'Security? With The Tuner?'

'You know what I mean. Simon is an artist ...'

'And you are *not*?' Mags is indignant.

'No, not any more. Why can't you and Stefan respect that? You two are always giving me a hard time,' Ava says, frustrated.

'It breaks my heart to see you settle like this. That's all.' Mags sits on the edge now.

'I am not settling, Mags, we've been together for ten years. I love him, I want to take the next step. Why can't anybody understand that?' Ava protests.

'Don't do anything rash about your job here. Just take some time off for now, Ava.' Mags gets off the edge of the desk and pulls Ava's jacket from the back of her egg chair. 'Go.'

'What, right now?' Ava looks at her messy desk.

'Yes, right now, this very second. Your wedding is in what, eleven days? Relax, get a facial, meditate, get your glam on ... find your smile.' She hands Ava her jacket and drags her up from her chair by the elbow.

'But ... but Stefan?' Ava says, as Mags tucks her clutch bag under her arm, her hand in the small of Ava's back.

'Stefan will still be here when you get back,' Mags tells her in a softer tone than she has ever heard, as she frog-marches Ava out the door and it tinkles behind her.

5

Something Old. New.
Borrowed . . . WTF?

'Not long to go till he puts a ring on it!'

The big day upon her, Ava looks at her father uncertainly.

'What? Isn't what they say nowadays? Look!' Ray O'Hara points to a sign for Kinnitty Castle, on the rural outskirts of County Offaly, as he wriggles his sizeable arse in the back seat of a vintage Rolls-Royce. Ava, a vision in her high-neck, lace, vintage wedding dress, sits beside him, holding his hand tightly.

'Oh. Oh. Oh. Oh. Oh. Oh. Oh. Oh. Oh. Ohhhhhh!' Her dad sings the chorus to 'Single Ladies' like he's just stood on a chunk of Lego in his bare feet.

'You're so hip and down with the kids, Dad,' Ava tells him, but she can't stop laughing at his seriously off-key Beyoncé impersonation.

'You know me, love!' he says, a little out of breath.

'Oh, Dad, my nerves are shattered!'

'You look beautiful, Ava. Perfect. Try and relax, you'll be grand,' he reassures her, as she tries to steady her nerves by inhaling deeply and slowly, smoothing her full lace ivory skirt down with her hands. She knows that her delicate veil complements her oval-shaped face perfectly.

She had insisted on getting ready from her parents' house in Offaly, so she did her own hair and make-up. Her parents had moved there from Dublin just before her mother got sick. Checking her face in her compact mirror, she nods approvingly at her natural-looking glow with a bold red lip.

'Bet The Tuner is getting the jitters now, too. No doubt he's calming his nerves with a few drinks. Doing what he does best, talking non-stop about himself,' her dad pipes up, breaking the silence. 'I hope you brought an extra set of keys for that new honeymoon house of yours, love. You know what he's like with remembering important stuff,' he adds, a little sarcastically. 'Brain like a sieve!'

'Ah, Dad, stop! And please don't call him by his bloody band name. Today of all days! It's Simon! S-I-M-O-N! And yes, of course I've got that stuff covered.' Ava pokes her dad's arm.

'Remind me, how did he even get that stupid *Tuner* name in the first place, Ava? I've never even asked him. And he's not exactly the world greatest conversationalist.' Ray blows his nose loudly.

'Dad!' Ava gives him the eye. 'Okay, I've told you this before, but in case any guests ask, you really should know. In his previous life, prior to the band thing starting, he got into music by tuning guitars in a music store upstairs in Rathfarnham Shopping Centre. Then the band formed and it just stuck. It drives me mental how everyone calls him The Tuner – I'm the only person who calls him by his actual name. He's almost forty himself, and I agree he really needs to ... Oh, Dad, look!'

The grand turret of the castle had come into view.

Ava falls quiet, squeezing her dad's strong hand tighter.

'We should be very grateful, Ava. We're lucky. We have each other.' Ray crumples up his tissue.

'I am, Dad. What isn't there to be incredibly grateful for, having a man like you by my side for forty years, to have you here beside

59

me today?' she says to him. 'I'm a very lucky girl. And now I've a new, long life ahead of me with Simon.' She swallows the lump that is lodged in her throat. The same lump that has been lodged in her throat all week.

'Your hands are still shaking. Are you sure you're okay, love?' her dad asks his sing-song tone.

Ava sighs. 'I love how your Galway accent is as strong as the day you left for Dublin all those years ago, Dad. Yeah, just a few butterflies, it's normal, I guess . . . isn't it?' she gulps, looking him straight in the eye now, questioningly.

'The day I married your mother in Salthill, it was bucketing down rain. I woke at five in the morning and I looked out the window at the heavens pouring and I said to myself, "Ray O'Hara, you are the luckiest man in the world." Then I stepped outside and I did a little rain dance.'

'You did not?' Ava looks lovingly at him.

'I bloody did!'

'Wow, no nerves?'

'Not one,' he admits.

'You danced for Mum in the rain on the morning of your wedding! Why have you never told me that before? It's the most romantic thing I've ever heard. I'm sure Simon would do that for me, too.' She looks at her dad for reassurance; he doesn't let her down.

'I know he would.' He pats her cheek a little harder than he might have meant. Ava looks quizzically at him.

'Oh, look, Dad. I know – maybe you think I could do better, but don't all dads think that about their daughters?'

'Listen, sweetheart, I'm happy if you're happy.'

A moment of uncomfortable silence pervades the Rolls, then Ava leans forward between the front seats of the car to talk to the uniformed driver.

'Any chance you could you stick some talk radio drivel on there? I need a distraction for this last bit of the drive.' Ava sinks back on the soft leather seat and shuts her eyes, feeling the delicate flutter of her semi-permanent false eyelashes high on her cheekbones. The driver nods silently at her in his rear-view mirror and fiddles with the round dial on the antique radio. The deep voice of Joe Duffy fills the car.

'And you are very welcome back to Talk to Joe ... Now folks, we're still chatting on the topic of "Biggest Regrets", so call in and share your stories. We've got Tracy on Line One. Go ahead, caller.'

'Am I on? Am I on? Ahhh ... how are ya, Joe? I'm talkin' to the famous Joe! This is a mad buzz!' she squeals, her heavy Dublin accent flooding the airwaves.

'Hello, Tracy ... your biggest regret, please?' Joe says again, patiently.

'My biggest regret, Joe, is permanently marked across me back. Got totally hammered on me hen's weekend in Liverpool three years ago. You know how it is with them mind freeze shots, sure they're only brutal! Went to a twenty-four-hour tattoo parlour beside Anfield with me sister and me friends when we were all locked and up for a few laughs. So anyways, I always called me fella Jason, 'Sweet Pea', now he's more of a bleedin' bitter lemon ... an' anyways we're still together by the mercy of God ... So, I wanted to dedicate my tattoo to him, but didn't the tattoo fella spell it wrong and we didn't cop it until the next morning when we were sober, well almost sober. So now I'm left with Sweet P E E. Do ya get me, Joe? P-E-E as in p-i-s –'

Joe butts in to cut off her impending swear word with a laugh. 'That's one hell of a permanent big regret, Tracy.'

'Biggest regrets, interesting topic,' Ray muses, smiling at Ava.

'You all know my feelings about tattoos in general, listeners.

I'm allergic. I mean, who wants to be a wrinkly old granny with a tattoo?' Joe asks Tracy the caller.

'Who wants to be a wrinkly old granny, period?' Tracy spits back.

'Well, that's, eh, one for the books, all right! Right so, over to another caller on Line Two. Chloe, are you there?' Joe waits through the dead air. 'Eh, come in, Chloe. Wow, folks, this is what we call literally radio silence!' Joe clears his throat away from the microphone. 'Let's take a quick commercial break and see if we can get the young lady to chat with us then. Come back to us in three, you're talking to Joe.'

A jingle plays out as Ava, looking out the window, catches sight of the splendour of Kinnitty Castle getting closer.

As the Rolls turns and purrs up the winding avenue, Ava gasps as she sees the breath taking views of the nineteenth-century castle seated on its six hundred and fifty acres of lush green parkland. Her heart beats faster.

'Isn't it something else?' her dad says wistfully. 'Wouldn't your mum have been proud as anything today. God, she loved this place.' He brings his white linen handkerchief to his eyes with a gentle dab.

'I know, Dad, I really do.' Ava runs her thumb along the solitaire stone of the ring around her wedding finger. 'There's no one I wish were here more than Mum.'

'She's with us, love. I can feel it.'

Ava pats his leg. She has loved Kinnitty Castle ever since she was twelve years old and her mother was gravely ill. The family had moved to Offaly only a few months before and came here for a memorable day. Mother, father and daughter. Her mother so brave, still so elegant with her salmon-pink silk headwrap, always smiling, and always doing her best to create memories for young Ava. It was this weekend that changed Ava's life forever. Their last weekend as a family of three.

It was also a turning point, when Ava became attached to old things. It became a way of life for her, made her somehow feel closer to her mother. Growing up, she stood out from the crowd with her unique vintage style, in her clothes and even in how she furnished her bedroom. She wore her hair in fancy headscarves she had kept from her mother's bedside drawer, because her Chanel No. 5 still lingered on them. Some people called her 'weirdo', but she didn't care. Maybe she was. Most evenings, she was content to listen to music and paint in her bedroom – her happy place. It was only when she got to Trinity College that she really found her tribe.

Ava's eyes widen now, as she takes in the medieval castle, drenched in ornate original features, the place where she always knew she would, one day, be married.

'The Tuner's in the bar already, no doubt. Sorry, I mean "Simon",' her father adds sarcastically, as he folds his hankie back into his top pocket.

'Dad! You've just blown your nose in that!' Ava protests.

'Ah, who's to know, love. I won't take it out again. It'll spoil the look of the suit if I don't have a white hanky in my front pocket. It's all the wedding fashion!'

'So gross, Dad!' But she can't help but smile at her dad with his daft ways. She loves how he never cares what others think.

'Yes,' she admits, 'the band all stayed at the castle last night too, and no doubt they're all hungover today, chasing the cure.'

'They have the fear of God in them, in every sense!' Her dad laughs.

'Lauren is meeting us in the lobby with the photographer. Can't say I'm looking forward to all these photos, but at least she's an expert at posing!' Ava sighs and lowers the window to get some extra air, but the draught gives her a sudden shiver, so she pulls it up again quickly, despite the warmth of the early June afternoon.

DJ Joe's deep voice can be heard on the radio again.

'It's a tough one this topic, I know. Biggest Regrets ... They can be tough to talk about, but you have taken the first step and called in. Go ahead, Chloe ...'

'Yeah, I'm here, Joe,' a posh female voice says softly. 'Honestly, I'm not sure if I should even be calling in like this, but I felt I just had to, because it involves someone marrying someone today, and this guy is just a cheating pri— Uhm, rat.' She pauses.

'Go ahead, Chloe, we're listening,' Joe pushes.

Chloe pauses again. This time Joe remains silent.

'Oh,' she says at last, 'have I got a good biggest regret story for you, Joe.'

Another pause, as Ava feels her dad holding his breath alongside her. The driver has even shifted in his seat to listen closely.

'Okay, so, here goes ... I'm a bit nervous, so bear with me. So I met this guy in a Dublin nightclub about three months ago. He was in a band performing there that night. And a good few drinks later, we got chatting and somehow ended up back at my place. And well, yeah, you know yourself, we got a bit carried away. Anyway, I started dating him after that night, on and off ... you know. But here's the thing, I was so happy to have met a guy who seemed so normal and down to earth. I am – was – mad about him, Joe, he was so attentive, so different to every other guy I'd met before then. He just seemed so genuine. That was until he finished things two weeks ago. He literally disappeared off the face of the earth. The di – sorry, *prat* – ghosted me completely. No explanation. Nothing. So I was pretty upset and confused, couldn't figure out what had happened. And yeah, you could say I was kind of angry.' Chloe pauses again, her voice cracking with nerves.

'Oh my God, imagine that!' Ava looks at her dad, bewildered. After a dramatic pause, the radio conversation continues.

'So, anyway, I decided to do some investigating to track him down on social media, as us girls do, and I found out the ass – piece of work, is actually engaged and getting married – today! To some poor girl he's been going out with for years! And I bet you she has no idea she's marrying a lying, cheating, dirty scumbag ...'

'C-can we higher this up?' Ava asks slowly.

'Wow, that's terrible, Chloe. I'm so sorry. Did you get a hold of him in the end, to tell him he was busted?' Joe asks. 'And did I hear you correctly – this guy is getting married today?'

'You did, but I took it one step further, Joe. I found the hashtag him and his poor unfortunate wife-to-be have for their wedding and, well, I posted drunk photos I took of him and me in bed together with that hashtag. Just put them up there an hour ago – put it on Instastories too, so I can see who and how many have seen it. It's blowing up. My face is blurred as my boobs are showing a bit, but you can see his face perfectly. I'm hoping to let that poor girl know her groom-to-be is a serial shagger. I mean, I'd want to know if it was me, and there's no denying it's him ...'

'That is quite the story, Chloe,' Joe chimes in, the excitement clear in his voice. 'I hope that girl has good support ... Obviously, I have to say your alleged accusations are very serious and, well, we wish her and you well. Thanks, Chloe, and if anyone out there has more big regrets stories, call 1800 Talk to Joe now ... Coming up ...'

'Girls, listen, don't let this cheating liar be your biggest regret!' Chloe butts in. 'If you come across a guy calling himself The Tuner from the band Seventh –'

'Sorry to end the conversation so quickly there, but we can't name names and of course all these claims are alleged by the caller, and this radio station doesn't condone the naming of third parties,' Joe jumps in frantically.

Ava and her dad turn towards each other sharply.

'Oh. My. God. Dad!' Ava shrieks. 'Driver, STOP! Now!'

The car screeches to a halt as Ava swings the door open and runs to open the boot, where she rummages to grab her ringing phone from her suitcase.

'Ava, it's me, Lauren, something awful has happened. Your wedding Instagram page has sex photos of The Tuner and some random girl. She has a whole story about how she's been dating him for a few months. She found out he's getting married today and has gone public to warn you. She's going apeshit! I only just saw it, as I had to post thanking my make-up artist. Anyway, a lot of people are commenting, and it's spreading like wildfire. Like, people are adding their own hashtags in sympathy ... it's up as an Instastory too. I need to shut this shit down, fast. I'm on it. I reported the hashtag.' Lauren's voice is panicked, she is panting breathlessly.

'Oh, we'll shut this down fast all right, Lauren. Get down to the castle entrance right now, I'm coming up the driveway,' Ava says, getting back into the car, her voice shaking. 'You need to help me get the hell out of here now!'

'Keep your phone in your hand,' Lauren yells again down the line as she ends the call.

'Oh, Dad, I'm so sorry.' Ava gulps for a breath.

'I'm bloody not! I'll take care of everything, just let Lauren get you out of here.'

6

Prince Charmless.

Lauren is pacing up and down nervously at the castle entrance as Ava and her dad pull up in the majestic vintage Rolls-Royce, the gravel crunching loudly under the wheels to announce their entrance. She teeters as fast as she can towards the car in her heels and tight dress, pulling a designer case behind her. She yanks the car door open and hears Ray O'Hara's low comforting tone as he tries to reassure his daughter.

'That's my girl ... that's my Ava. You can handle this, you are strong like your mother.' They both stare up at Lauren.

'Ava ... fuck – sorry, Mr O'Hara – I honestly don't know what to say.' She squeezes into the back of the Rolls and holds Ava in a tight hug. Ava's breathing fast and furious. Of all the people who could have been waiting for her today, Ava realises her best friend is the perfect one.

'I think I'm going to puke, Lauren.' Ava looks up at her.

'No, you are not. Not on my watch.' Lauren holds her up straight by her lace-clad shoulders.

'Thank you for coming ... for being ...' Ava stops as Ray O'Hara interrupts the moment.

'Right, girls. Let me handle everything here. Lauren, please help me get my daughter away as fast you can. I don't want that asshole to set eyes on her. He isn't even entitled to that.' He exits the car, moving faster than he has for years.

'Come on, Avz, it's going to be okay, I promise.' Lauren backs out of the Rolls and extends her hand to Ava, who takes it, shaking.

'My immaculate French manicure that will never be seen,' Ava says as she stands by the car with her dad and hugs him tightly.

'Have you got everything, love?' he asks.

'My case! I need my stuff! I only have my phone, everything else is in the case, my wallet, everything. Can you grab it out of the back of the car, Lauren?' Ava shrieks.

Lauren knocks on the window. The driver is open-mouthed, speechless as he watches this all unfold.

'Boot!' Lauren shouts. 'Can you get her case from the boot? Come on, come on!'

Obediently, the driver gets out and pulls out Ava's honeymoon case and her bag from the boot.

'Give me two minutes!' Lauren says as she opens her own case and reefs out a huge rattling bunch of keys, then quickly disappears again. Ava stands over her case and drapes her bag over her shoulder.

'Don't you worry, darling. It'll be my bloody pleasure to tell that Simon the wedding is most definitely off. I swear to God, when I get my hands on him ...' Ray spits his words into Ava's ear as he holds her close.

'Oh, come on, Lauren!' Ava mutters in frustration. Then, 'Dad, please, your blood pressure. It's not worth it. Dr Atkinson warned you about losing the rag. Please, just don't. Oh my God, I just wish the ground could swallow me up. Everyone is staring at us. I think I might pass out.'

Groups of wedding guests are gawking at the unexplained

commotion from the castle steps. The last-minute church crowd, finishing their oversized glasses of gin and tonic, perched on outside benches, start to mutter questioningly to one another. A gossipy hum is now travelling between them all, all eyes on Ava, who keeps her head down on her dad's chest.

'Oh, come on, Lauren!' she hisses to the gravel just as her vintage car tyres crunch away slowly from the castle and a black Range Rover comes to a screeching halt beside them. Lauren jumps out of the car with the engine still running and bundles Ava into the front seat. She pops the boot open, throwing Ava's case in as she runs back to the driver's side.

'Sorry, the alarm keeps acting up, so safer to keep the engine running. It's a pain in the arse,' she shouts as she hops into her seat and frantically pulls her seat belt on.

The last-minute crowd, all dressed to the nines, stare blankly as Lauren navigates her way across the noisy gravel of the car park, expertly avoiding all the slow friendly waves and bemused expressions. The colour of Ava's face now matches her wedding dress as her eyes lock with Stefan's. He stands, in a sharp black suit and ivory tie, a flute of champagne in one hand and his other arm draped around Suzanne's bare shoulders.

'Ava?' she sees him mouth, his face alarmed as his arm falls away from Suzanne's shoulders. Ava twists her head away.

'Lauren, move it! I can't cope. I've never been so mortified in my life,' she gasps, burying her head in her lace lap now, hiding from view. 'Stefan brought Suzanne? I didn't even offer him a plus one! I just assumed he'd be on his own! He only paid for a single room!' she screams, her head face down now into her dress skirt.

'Who? Who are they? I'm going as fast as I can. I don't want to run over a wandering wedding guest. This shit is bad enough!' Lauren says, her head darting at the wheel.

'Where was she going to sit, on his knee? Share his bloody dinner?' Ava sounds off.

'What? What are you talking about?' Lauren asks, confused, as she continues to navigate her way out as carefully as she can, her head bobbing as she checks all three mirrors. 'God, why are they all so nosey?' she asks irritably. 'Move it! Who are most of these people anyway? And why are most of them dressed like they are going to a Queen concert at Slane? Gobshites, the hack of them! Stay down, Avz!' Lauren takes a second to look out her driver's window at most of The Tuner's friends, smoking rollies and wearing fedora hats.

'Is this actually happening to me right now?' Ava heaves the words into her dress.

'Shit! There's some fella chasing the car!' Lauren stares intently in her rear-view mirror. 'And he's catching up!'

Ava spins her head to look out the back of the car. Stefan is chasing after them, waving his hands frantically, his ivory tie blowing in the wind.

'Don't stop, Lauren! Put your foot down! He's the last person I need to see me like this,' Ava screams, as Lauren speeds up, but Stefan continues to give chase.

'Who is that guy?' Lauren is confused. 'He's like the feckin' Terminator!'

'How long is this bloody driveway?' Ava ignores the question.

'One more minute until the coast is clear!'

Lauren signals and exits the castle grounds onto the windy country road. The two pant in their seats, catching their breath.

'Where are we going?' Ava whispers, pulling herself upright on the seat now the narrow road is free of wedding gawkers.

'I don't know exactly, let's just say we're going on a mystery road trip. Far away from this shit-show! I can't believe this is happening.' Lauren repeats herself again, louder, as she puts pedal to the floor.

'I am *that* woman, Lauren. The living cliché of the wretched woman dumped at the altar. The urban legend you hear about and you imagine how horrendous it would be if it happened to you. The sheer mortification . . . I'll never live it down.' Ava heaves.

'You left *him* at the altar!' Lauren doesn't take her eyes off the road. 'You took your power back!'

'But only because I found out he was a lying, cheating scumbag.' Ava's voice breaks again.

'Still, you left him. You walked away. You did the right thing.' Lauren nods in approval. 'He's the loser asshole standing at the top, waiting . . . *You* left him at the altar!' Lauren's rant is interrupted by a loud guttural noise coming from Ava.

'S-s-s-sorry!' Ava sobs hysterically, huge tears rolling down her face, her nose running like a tap, make-up sliding away.

'Oh, Ava . . . oh, love . . . oh, shush . . . it's going to be okay, I promise. He's so not worth it. He never deserved you.' Lauren finds a packet of tissues in the compartment beside her, as Ava bawls. Lauren leans across her and opens the glove compartment, removing two miniature bottles of vodka. She presses them into Ava's hand.

'You needed that ugly cry. Now, get these into you, you're in shock. You might as well start now. Listen to me very carefully, Ava. Simon's a total and utter dick. He is, and always has been, a self-centred, washed-up, wannabe rock star muppet. He's delusional, and . . .' Lauren's floodgates have truly opened.

'I just can't,' Ava responds. 'This is not the time, Lauren, let's not . . .'

'No, *this* is the perfect time, Ava! He's such a screaming prick! Even your dad didn't like him, and Ray likes everyone. He even felt sorry for Ivan Drago in the *Rocky* movie, remember? And

71

he had a soft spot for the Wicked Witch of the West way before *Wicked* the musical was ever written!' Lauren smiles at Ava, hoping to chase away some of the despair filling the car.

'H-he did, didn't he?' Ava splutters and inhales deeply, smiling weakly back at Lauren. She shuts her eyes. 'But seriously, what am I going to do? I need to talk to Dad, Lauren!' Ava rummages in her bag for her phone, her voice rising in panic again.

'No, no phone calls for you, young lady. For all we know the Terminator could still be chasing us,' Lauren tells her, constantly checking her rear-view mirror.

Ava holds her phone in her tense, white-knuckled hands.

'I'm afraid to turn it back on,' she whimpers.

'Good! Don't! Seriously, you're the last person that needs to be making phone calls right now. Your dad's got the wedding situation handled. Oh, to be a fly on the wall when he confronts The Tuner . . . give me, give me your phone. Now!' Lauren grabs the phone out of Ava's hand and stashes it between her legs before Ava can stop her.

'I mean, *the mortification*. I've been dumped right in it on my wedding day, live on the radio too,' Ava whimpers.

'What are you talking about?' Lauren is confused. 'Radio?'

'Simon's bit on the side was on the "Talk to Joe" radio show! I'm the laughing stock of the entire country. Stefan's face said it all. Never mind my family and friends. Jesus, how could he do this to me? After ten years. What am I going to do? How could he do this? How many times has he done this?' Ava's brain is struggling to register the situation.

'Stop thinking and drink the vodka!' Lauren orders from the driver's seat.

'I hate vodka.' Her hands shake as she struggles to open the tiny red cap. Lauren reaches for it and deftly twists the bottle open with one hand.

'Sip!' she orders again. 'You know what, Ava? I'm not sorry. I'll say it again: Simon Dwyer never deserved you.' Lauren whacks her hands off the steering wheel as she tries for the second time to overtake the car in front.

'Oh, come on, missus, some of us have a crisis going on!' she shouts, then indicates and overtakes at speed.

'Okay, we need a plan, a good one ... where do we go from here? Maybe we should call around and make a reservation somewhere for the night? What do you think? Maybe head back to Powerscourt Hotel? I get a deal there through the magazine ...' Lauren slams the brakes at a red light as the car behind slowly trails up behind her.

'I want to go on my honeymoon. To Clare,' Ava whispers.

'I know you want to, sweetie, I know. I know you do.' Lauren pats Ava's arm gently.

'Will you come with me?'

'Wait, what are you talking about?' Lauren says, shifting gears up into first as the light goes green, fanning herself with her other hand.

'I want to go to our new house in Clare. Edenvale, it's called. It's where Simon and I were going to live. I mean *my* house. I paid for it out of Mum's inheritance money, so I'm guessing *I* own it now, since we're not husband and wife. He was looking after the renovations, it was going to be a surprise reveal for me after we were married.' Ava sips the vodka, wincing.

'You were moving to Clare? When were you planning to tell me about this? God, I'm sweating!' Lauren rolls down her window and welcomes in the cool breeze.

'We bought a little house in Clare. It was supposed to be our escape from the crazy Dublin rent situation, we never could have afforded to buy anything there. A wooden shed, maybe, but ...' Ava explains.

'Wait, did you just say you used the inheritance money you got from your mother to buy you and The Tuner a house?' Lauren butts in, wiping some perspiration from her top lip.

'Yeah, I did.' Ava nods.

'And what exactly did The Tuner contribute to this little house on the prairie?' Lauren purses her shiny lips together.

'Well, nothing to the actual purchase price because, well ... he doesn't have any money ... we have a joint account, that's where I put any of my leftover wages from all my overtime. My weekly wages pay the rent on our apartment, and Simon was putting all his gig money into that renovation account.'

'*All* his gig money? You mean maybe a few euros from the three random weddings he plays a year with the band? Or am I missing something here?' Lauren sounds incensed.

'I don't care about all that now, Lauren! So, you will come with me? To Edenvale?' Ava asks again hopefully, deliberately diverting from the subject of Simon.

'What? Me? Oh God no, not a chance, Ava. I can't! I've got to work. I've to put the magazine July bumper issue to bed. Work is manic. I've to do all the California Glow posts ... there's literally no one else who can do what I do. And it's not like I can rely on Julia.' Lauren indicates and shifts lanes, indignantly.

'P-please, Lauren.'

'I just can't, Ava.' Lauren shakes her raven hair roughly. 'I wish I could.'

'Whatever,' Ava mumbles, her tone suddenly frosty. 'Just drive me there then and you can go back home. To your fabulous life.'

'I can't leave you alone, Avz, that's crazy talk. Let's just find a hotel for the night, get a bit of dinner, maybe have a couple of drinks. We'll have a good chat about everything, a good cry will help, you'll see ... it's what you need now, love, honestly,' Lauren offers, gently fanning herself again.

'Dinner! I don't need a nice fucking dinner, Lauren! Let me out! Stop this car!' Ava slams her hands off the dashboard as Lauren jumps out of her skin.

'And welcome … rage.' Lauren pats Ava's knee supportively.

'Let me out! I mean it. Stop. Now!' Ava roars like a woman possessed, the veins in her slim neck bulging like Udon noodles.

'Calm down, stop this,' Lauren tries to reason with her.

'I will literally jump out of this car. I will pull a Ladybird, I don't care if it's moving!' Ava rests her hand on the handle of the Range Rover passenger door, the mini bottle of vodka spilling on her dress, slowly creating a wet pattern.

'Okay! Okay! You win! I'll try figure out how the hell I'm going to pull off going to Clare with you! Relax. We can't just go right now, I've a lot of work stuff to sort out. It's serious, it's my life.' Lauren wipes her sweating brow.

'Work problems? I just got the rug pulled out from under my entire fucking life! And you think you've got "stuff" to worry about? Really? Puhlease!' Ava rolls her eyes, raising her voice. Lauren pulls over and pushes on her hazard lights as she bites her lip nervously. She rummages under the editions of *Irish Gloss* and finds her phone.

'Who the hell has rang me twenty-three times?' she asks, looking at her screen. 'Oh God, that's Cate Connolly. Her number ends in 007, doesn't it? I must have removed her from my contacts. Eh, by accident.' She quickly taps out a message on her iPhone, then exhales deeply in the uncomfortable silence that follows.

'I've got it. We'll head to my uncle Lar's mobile home in Roscrea. He's never there, always off gallivanting. And if I know Lar, the key will be left somewhere obvious, to confuse any potential burglars in the area,' Lauren announces, trying to engage Ava in lighter conversation again. 'It's only half an hour away. We'll get our bearings, and I'll take you to your house in Clare in the morning. Deal?'

'Erm, yeah, okay ...' Ava mutters as Lauren continues tapping on her phone.

'That's Cate answered, will stop her harassing me for now. But first things first, I need to stop at a garage. We're almost out of petrol, but *most* importantly, I need to get booze for later. Oh, and salt 'n' vinegar Taytos. And Curly Wurlys. Oh, and toilet roll ...There's no shops around Lar's caravan field ...' As Lauren recites her random thoughts aloud, Ava rolls down her window, removes her veil and lets it fly away in the breeze. An awkward silence follows, as Ava and Lauren watch the delicate white netting wrap around a nearby stop sign.

'A screaming metaphor?' Lauren raises an eyebrow at Ava.

'Wish I stopped it ten years ago,' she replies.

'Lovely dress, by the way,' Lauren tells her awkwardly.

'It's not. It's shit,' Ava replies, deadpan.

'It is. But why did you of all people pick such a shit dress?' Lauren replies, in agreement.

'It was cheap,' Ava admits.

Lauren says nothing, turns the key and the engine roars to life. She breathes a sigh of relief and indicates. After a few minutes on the road she swerves abruptly and pulls into a garage.

'Jesus Christ, Lauren, some of us want to live. Well, *maybe* want to,' Ava squeals as her head bounces off the passenger window.

'Relax, I would have missed it, and I've no idea how far up the next garage is. I seriously need petrol and when did you become so ...'

Lauren parks the Range Rover, pulling up the handbrake.

'So, what?' Ava rubs her head, the other hand in her mouth as she nibbles on her bare thumbnail, the manicure now non-existent.

'So ... nothing, never mind.' Lauren leaves the missing word hanging as she tugs at the neckline of her skin-tight dress.

'I don't think being aware of dangerous driving makes me anything, Lauren,' Ava says. 'This is supposed to be my wedding day. Is this even real? Or just a bad dream? This doesn't really happen to people, it's only in movies, like ... horror movies.' Ava's voice is chipmunk-like, it's so high-pitched, then she suddenly heaves and retches.

'Oh no! Don't puke! Okay, out of the car! Come on, let's go!' Lauren jumps out and totters around to the passenger door as fast as her heels will allow. She pulls it open and leads a retching Ava by the laced sleeve towards the garage shop, as her phone starts ringing loudly.

'Oh, sweet Jesus, this is all we need!' Lauren sighs, showing the incoming caller ID to Ava.

'I just need to get some air, got the watery feeling in my mouth ... you talk to her.' Ava waves the phone away from her, swallowing loudly.

Taking a deep breath, Lauren puts her phone to her ear as she gathers up the lace skirt of the dress and helps Ava sit down on a low stone wall.

'Cate, hiiii, how are youuu? You got my text then?' she gushes insincerely, rolling her eyes. 'She is. I know. Viral? Well, sure, isn't everything classified as viral these days ... I wasn't listening to the radio, no ... I was getting ready to walk down the aisle with her, just two besties and ...' Lauren paces back and forward, her sleek blow-dry blowing in the summer's breeze.

' ... No, don't worry, I'm taking care of her. I know you would if you could ... yes, I know you had a new baby ... I have a card ... somewhere ... Yes, I know you now have *three* children, Cate, you mention them ... often ... and I can do the maths ... Listen, I'm taking her to my uncle Lar's mobile home in Roscrea for the night, so I better go. I'll get her to call you from there later, okay? I will . . . I know . . . she is . . . we should . . . I know . . . where does the time go . . . you're right . . . Okay, bye-bye.' Lauren hangs up.

'She's so good to keep calling,' Ava mumbles, her head between her legs.

'Isn't she just.' Lauren grits her teeth. 'Now, you sit there and chill out. I will get petrol and supplies.'

'Chill out? Are you off your rocker?' Ava's words hang heavy in the air. 'I need to check my phone! I can't just bury my head in the sand like this!' She gets up as the hem of the dress gets caught in a jagged stone and rips.

'Oh, Ava!' Lauren's hand flies to her mouth as she tries to pull the torn material together.

'Just leave it! It's worthless now anyway.' Ava roughly pulls it out of Lauren's hands. 'I need to turn on my phone.'

'Wait. Why would you want to turn on your phone?' Lauren says. 'Like you need to read all those pity party messages right now? Fuck that. It's only going to make you feel worse, believe me. And Simon has no right to contact you. When we do turn it on you are blocking that asshole forever! You don't need it right now, Ava, honestly. Anyway, look! You can't use your phone in a garage.' Lauren points to the sign with a huge red 'X' through mobile phones.

'I have to face the music sooner or later,' Ava tells her.

'Later. Later is always better.'

'Oh, never mind, Okay, okay, let's just hurry up, can we?'

Ava recoils as a car pulls in and the driver stares at them both. Lauren replaces the pump and they walk into the garage shop in their bridal finery. Two employees at the cash register swivel and stare as Lauren smiles sweetly at them. Ava marches straight for the wine section and grabs as many bottles as she can physically hold. Clinking bottles ring out.

'I figured this was the one day I wouldn't need my purse!' Ava tells Lauren as she grabs popcorn and extra-large bags of cheese and onion crisps.

'Twenty Silk Cut Blue, the wine and the crisps, fifty unleaded, and a receipt please.' Lauren grabs a handful of Curly Wurlys and shoves all the stuff at the assistant, then stands at the service hatch and takes out her credit card.

'Complements of *Irish Gloss*,' she tells Ava. The assistant gawks at them, open-mouthed.

'We are making a movie,' Lauren lies. 'It's kind of like *Bridesmaids* but without the woeful street diarrhoea scene. Never sat right with me, that scene.' Lauren makes a face of disgust.

'I didn't know you started smoking again too, Lauren,' Ava says.

'Neither did I. And a lighter, please. Check it works, will you? There's a lot we didn't know about today, Ava,' Lauren replies.

'Pardon me, but are these twist caps?' Ava asks the assistant, as she checks the lighter and nods.

'Great!' Ava lifts a scanned bottle from the counter and tears off the black foil then twists the cap as she lifts the bottle to her mouth and gulps.

'Ah, here now, you can't drink wine on the premises, love!' The assistant hurriedly tears off the credit card receipt and pushes it through the hatch to Lauren. 'We've CCTV too, by the way.'

'Thank you, we'd better get back to the set. She's very method. Oliver Reid was her granddad. It's in the genes,' Lauren says as she follows Ava back to the Range Rover. Lauren puts the rest of the supplies in the boot, then she hops back in beside Ava, who holds onto two bottles of red on her lap. Lauren starts the engine.

'Is it me or is it absolutely roasting?' Lauren rolls down the window.

'I'm cold,' Ava says as she shivers and lifts the bottle to her mouth.

'Shock. Okay, let's get you to Lar's mobile home, you'll be okay, I promise. Lauren's here.' Lauren looks to Ava, who raises the bottle in a mock toast, her face void of any emotion.

7

If You Hurt My Best Friend.

'LORD ABOVE! WHEN WAS THE LAST TIME Lar flushed his toilet, never mind bleached it?' Lauren holds her nose between finger and thumb as she walks out, her dress hoisted up.

'Seriously, beyond gross in there, like a portaloo at a music festival on the last day. But the relief of getting those Spanx off is pure bliss. However, now I'm knickerless.' Lauren waves her skin-coloured knickers in the air. Ava sits by the window, staring blankly out at the vast field of mismatched mobile homes.

'I wasn't thinking we'd end up, well, here. . . and I want to get out of this dress!' Ava holds up the vodka-stained, ripped skirt.

'Cleanliness isn't Lar's thing, I suppose. Now, where's that red wine?' Lauren flops onto the brown velour couch.

'This caravan living area has always freaked me out. It's just a couch and a table . . .' Lauren looks around. 'Though I had my first-ever kiss around the back of it, and many thoroughly enjoyable summer fumbles from that day on. I learned a lot about my body down here, Avz. Me and Marvin Kelly, I thought we'd be together forever until I found him snogging the farmer's son!' Lauren laughs, but Ava doesn't react.

'Oh, and this gross yellowing net curtain – and faded wallpaper that's actually peeling in the corners. That freaks me out too.'

Ava continues to stare out the window, an unlit cigarette in her right hand and an open bottle of red wine hanging like an extension of her left.

'I shouldn't have bought those cigarettes. Remember how hard it was for us to give up?' Lauren eyes Ava with concern.

'I'll give up again tomorrow, Lauren. I haven't smoked in over fifteen years. I need something right now and this is it.' Ava flicks the lighter and lights up, she takes a long hard drag and exhales. She coughs hard and stubs it out into an already overflowing ashtray on the table. 'I'm ... I'm so ... unsure about how I feel, Lauren, it's really weird.' Ava pulls a piece of loose tobacco from her tongue. 'I mean, all I'm feeling now is utter embarrassment that I ran away from my wedding. That's not right though, is it? I mean ... how am I feeling about my ruined relationship? About the fact that Simon has been shagging other women behind my back? I mean, we don't use protection, as I've been on the pill for so long. And now I find out he's been putting my health at risk too?' Ava turns to face Lauren.

'Oh, I know, the whole thing is horrific.' Lauren moves out and finds a glass above the kitchen table on a shelf, blows into it to clear the dust and pours herself a large glass of wine.

'Everybody knows, everybody feels sorry for me. Is there anything worse than knowing people feel sorry for you?'

'I couldn't care less what people think of me any more, that's the one big plus of turning forty.' Lauren sits and pats the space next to her, as Ava moves from the window and flops down beside her.

'Stefan never liked him.'

'Who is this Stefan?' Lauren asks, swigging at her wine. 'Huh?'

'A guy I work with, my friend at the gallery. We hang out together. He's French.'

'*Excusez-moi?*' Lauren raises a perfect HD eyebrow.

'He's just a friend, Lauren,' Ava replies.

'Ohhh la la ...' Lauren offers.

Ava stares at her blankly.

'He was the guy who was chasing your car as we left the grounds of the castle,' Ava tells her, a little more volume in her voice now.

'Ohhh La La LA LA LA! That was him?' Lauren sits up.

'He's a really nice guy.'

'Do you have the hots for him or something?' Both Lauren's HD eyebrows are now raised.

'Well, you can't help but fancy Stefan a bit, he's just ...' Ava gets up and walks to the window again.

'I didn't get a good look at him – I was trying not to kill people – but please go on ...' Lauren urges her.

'Artistic. Proper true to himself. He's like a piece of art himself actually.'

'Is he now?' Lauren starts.

'No ... don't go there, I don't need any more complications in my life right now. We wouldn't pass the Bechdel test!' Ava shakes her head vigorously.

'The what test?' Lauren asks.

'The Bechdel test. If this were a film or a book we'd be failures, Lauren, for only talking about men. Sort of means that we must talk to each other about something other than a man.'

'Oh, okay ... um ... speaking of art, I bought you a little present. Hang on a sec.' Lauren rummages for her car keys and goes out the door. Ava hears the car alarm screech from the Range Rover and Lauren swearing loudly. It stops and Lauren comes back in and shuts the door.

'Starting to lash rain out there,' Lauren says.

'What is wrong with your car? Why was the alarm going off?'

'Oh, it's nothing major. Like I said earlier, it just goes off at random times. I have to get it fixed. If I don't have to turn off the engine, it's fine. Anyway ... here!' Lauren hands Ava a white bag with black rope handles.

'What's this?' Ava takes it.

'You have to open it to see!' Lauren says, laughing.

Ava opens the gift bag and removes a huge sketch pad and boxes of pastels and paintbrushes.

'I know how much you love to sketch. I bought it in Paris actually, on my last trip. Not for your wedding present or anything, just for you, but then I just never saw you. Well, I never really see you ... and ...' Lauren trails off.

'This is amazing.' Ava flips open the cover page and removes a pastel from the box. A huge smile appears on her face for the first time that day, as Lauren steps closer to her.

'I've missed you, Avz ... I've ...'

The door bursts open and Ava and Lauren grab onto one another.

'Only me!' Cate Connolly breezes in, drops her small blue suitcase on the floor and kicks the door shut behind her.

'Cate!' Ava can't believe her eyes. 'What the ... ? How did you ...?'

'Lauren texted me, so I got a bus down to the town, then grabbed a taxi here. Talk about a wild goose chase! But never mind me. How is my poor friend?' Cate rushes towards Ava and wraps her in a bear hug that lifts her off the ground.

'I can barely breathe, Cate,' Ava croaks, stepping back to take in her larger-than-life friend. Tall and athletic, with a face free of any make-up and her wild red hair in a messy knot piled on top of her head, she's casually dressed in jeans and a T-shirt with a light beige trench coat draped over her arm.

'Jesus Christ, Cate, I nearly shat myself! Don't do that to me!'

'As dramatic as ever, I see. Hello to you too, Lauren, for a change this isn't about you.' She brings Ava's head close to her ample chest.

'What's that supposed to mean exactly?' Lauren asks, her lip curled.

'Oh, never mind, now is not the time, Lauren. Now, Ava, I've heard exactly what happened, I saw the hashtags, and then I called your dad, who told me Lauren had whisked you away. I figured she'd take you here to Lar's, all things considered. I remember how much she talked about losing her virginity here to that farmer's son. Remember him, Lauren? What was his name, Marvin or something? So, anyway, when I chatted to Lauren later and she told me she was in fact on her way to Lar's with you, I was already on my way ... didn't tell her that, so here I am. What. A. Dickhead. I can't imagine how you are feeling, but don't feel you have to re-tell me the events right now. We can talk properly later. But I haven't just come all this way to offer my sympathy, I think have a solution. I've come prepared, equipped if you will. Cate has brought some magic! First, let me make us all a nice hot sweet cup of tea ...'

'Tea!' Lauren shoots back sarcastically. 'Are you high, Cate?'

'I'm trying to calm our friend down, Lauren. I could do without the smart-arse comments. Maybe a little appreciation, just maybe *try* to be nice?' Cate says, ignoring Lauren's snide remark.

'What do you think I've been doing all day? Tweeting updates?' Lauren says, fanning herself with an old beer mat.

'No, though it wouldn't necessarily surprise me, you are never off Twitter and Instagram. I don't know where you find the time, Lauren. There, there ...'

Ava breaks her head free from Cate's claustrophobic embrace and looks at her squabbling friends.

'Well, how would you know that unless you are on there too?

I see you online all the time, but yet you never post a thing. Too busy snooping on what I'm up to, by the sounds of it!' Lauren's face is redder than ever now.

'I've more important things in my life that don't include snooping on you, Miss McCabe,' Cate says, propping one hand on her hip. 'Get a grip!'

'Hello! Hi! Me here! I'm just after running away from my wedding in case you both hadn't noticed!' Ava yells, tugging at the neck of her dress and ripping it slightly more down the neck.

Lauren and Cate stop in their hostile tracks, mouths open.

'Sorry, Ava,' Cate says carefully, swallowing hard.

'Yeah, sorry, Avz,' Lauren chimes in, knowing she needs to defuse the rising tension.

'Look, Cate,' Ava interjects, giving Lauren a sharp look. 'It's great to see you and thank you for coming all this way. I know you've got a lot going on right now with the new baby, and ...'

'I'm – I'm sorry, Cate. It's been ... it's been a really long and stressful day so far, as you can imagine. You just scared the shit out of me, springing us like that.' Lauren mutters her apology unconvincingly.

'It's fine. It's totally fiiiiine!' Cate fake smiles at Lauren. 'Anyway, yes, Simon is a total dick, but I have a plan. I know how we're going to remove him from Ava's life. Permanently! But we need to move fast on this.'

'Murder him? Castrate him?' Lauren offers, with a serious glint in her eye.

'Smash his stupid guitar over his stupid cheating head, and bury him alive with his stupid vinyl collection?' Ava chimes in.

'If only we could. Anyway, you want to hear my plan? You just need to trust me and follow my directions carefully,' Cate says with authority. 'And you need to take it seriously.'

'Okaaaaay ...' Lauren looks dubious.

'You're actually kind of starting to scare me a bit, Cate.' Ava looks nervous, as Cate moves into the tiny kitchen space and starts rattling cutlery drawers and rifling through cupboards.

'Okay, first, I need candles. *We* need candles. I have a very special one I stopped off to buy on the way here. It's in my case, but it'll be way more powerful if we have a few more,' Cate calls to the other two in the living room area, continuing to search through various cupboards, opening and shutting them at speed.

'Yessss! Found what I need!' she shouts gleefully and hurries back into the living area with three, tall, glass-covered candles, each with a picture of Pope John Paul II on them.

'Now I have everything!' Cate claps her hands.

'Wait, you've a naked Simon tied up in the boot of your car, and we're going to roast him alive on top of a bonfire of holy candles?' Lauren can't contain her sarcasm.

'Look, Lauren, if you're not going to take this seriously, well ...' Cate says, not bothering to hide her annoyance.

'I'm sorry, Cate. Really. I'll stop being immature ... go on ...' Lauren looks at Ava, who seems to be paying close attention.

'Okay. So, first things first. Get that dress off you, Ava. It's toxic. I just need you two to put some clothes on that make you both feel powerful. As women. Think Beyoncé fierce, it can be anything at all.'

'Guess I'm shit out of luck there, hun. All I have is this!' Ava looks down at her sad, stained, ripped wedding dress.

'That's where you're wrong, young lady! I have your suitcase in the boot of my car, remember? With mine!' Lauren responds, delighted with her problem-solving skills, as she grabs her keys and skips out.

'What's that?' Cate twists her head to the door as the car alarm sounds again.

'Her alarm keeps going off,' Ava informs her, as Lauren returns.

87

'Okay, won't open yet, give it a few minutes.' Lauren throws her keys onto the couch. 'Would there be anything of poor departed Mavis's left in the wardrobe, I wonder?' she suggests.

'Yeah, perfect, you two go to search around the bedroom, see what you can rustle up, and change. Bet you'll find all sorts of random stuff in there,' Cate says.

'I don't want to be wearing any of Mavis's old clothes, Cate. She's dead, and that's just weird,' Ava says, appalled.

'Look, we all have to commit to this little ceremony for it to work. I'll get set up here; you two go figure it out. You're the creative one, Ava, go be creative!' Cate ushers them down the back of the mobile home to the bedroom. Lauren pops her head back around the door two minutes later.

'Hang on, Cate, did I hear you say *ceremony*? Don't you think we've had enough of the ceremonies for one day?' she asks her.

'Don't worry, this is a very different type of thing. Now go, get yourselves sorted. As I said, just throw on something that makes you feel empowered as a woman. It's all about how you feel on the inside. Put some thought into it . . . use your imaginations! I'll take care of the rest.' Cate shoos her away, then kneels down to open her blue suitcase.

★ ★ ★

'This is the bedroom,' says Ava, gently pushing the flimsy plastic door open.

'I'm seriously creeped out already,' Lauren says, removing her phone. 'And I'm claustrophobic, but this is a good photo opp. Sure, I'll take a pic of my tanned decollate and then hashtag California Glow, hashtag despite the lashing rain.'

'Can you put your phone away? It feels like you haven't put it down all day!' Ava gasps, rolling her eyes.

'It's work – I don't have a choice. And why is it so hot in here?' Perspiration has started to form on Lauren's top lip. It shines as she takes a selfie.

'I'm freezing! How in the name of God are you always so hot?' Ava, standing by the compact bed, squeezes past Lauren and slides the door open.

'Holy shit, look at all this!' Lauren says, pulling an embroidered red dress from a plastic hanger.

'*All* this? You can't swing a cat in here, it's so tiny!' Ava quips.

'Wonder, do these clothes belong to Lar or were they poor Mavis's? You never really know these days, do ya?'

A few minutes later they re-enter the living room, Ava wearing the flamboyant red dress, with a thick black unibrow drawn across her forehead. Lauren is still wearing the same sexy black dress from earlier, but now has a dusty black top hat with a large feather perched on her head.

'Cate! Woah!' Ava's hand finds her open mouth and covers it. Cate is sitting on the couch wearing a black lacy bra and matching knickers. On her feet are a pair of dangerously high stilettos. Ava can't help herself, despite it all she bursts out laughing. 'What the actual?' Ava shakes her head.

'Look at us!' Lauren says as she dissolves into peals of laughter too.

'That's what I like to hear. Come on, sit down and relax so I can explain. This is going to be classic!' Cate smiles gleefully, as Lauren and Ava follow her directions. They sit down on the couch. 'Okay, first let's explain who we are, so we're all on the same page before we begin,' Cate announces. 'Lauren, you start! And you are?'

'I'm representing my hero, the eternal female badass: Stevie Nicks,' Lauren offers, defiantly.

'Ex'Laurent! Remember we used to say that?' Cate stamps

her high heels as they clip-clop off the linoleum floor. 'Ava?'

'I'm the Mexican art queen. Frida. Frida Kahlo. I mean, if the one eyebrow didn't give that away,' Ava tells them, still unsure of what the hell is going on.

'Brilliant, ten out of ten for participation, girls!' Cate claps her hands.

'Turns out my good old Auntie Mavis had a bit of a wild side. I mean, look at these epic outfits we found in a caravan wardrobe.' Lauren laughs. 'Now, Cate, who are you? You look smokin' hot, by the way.'

Cate smiles at Lauren's unexpected compliment. 'I am representing Josephine Skriver when she was a Victoria's Secret supermodel,' Cate adds, laughing, sucking in her post-baby belly spilling over her teeny black lace underwear. 'I didn't realise my lady garden was quite so in need of a landscape, but anyway ...' She coughs loudly to clear her throat. 'So, my girls, we're all here present and our heads are in the right place, so let's begin! Welcome to our "Cleansing" ceremony. The purpose here is to rid our dear friend Ava O'Hara of all the former bad energy from her ex, Simon Dwyer. Our mission is to clean her chakras and restore all her sexual energy so she can attract and welcome as many hot men into her company as she can handle. Not necessarily now, but in the future ... when she's ready ...'

'Umm, Cate, there's a Bechdel test she'd like to adhere to ...' Lauren starts.

'Forget it! I love the sound of this!' Ava shouts, hitting her friend on her arm.

'Cool ... So, in that case, can you include me in your hot-men-sex-spell-casting? I could do with some help there.' Lauren laughs.

'I thought you went on a hot date every week with all those celebs?' Cate turns to Lauren, her eyebrows raised.

'Nah, just ask Ava about my tragic love life,' Lauren says carefully, but means it.

'You certainly tell a different story on social media,' Cate adds, looking genuinely confused.

'That's my job. Not my reality,' Lauren replies.

'Stop interrupting. I'm getting into this witchy shit!' Ava hushes her.

Cate stands up and opens her little suitcase again. She carefully unwraps purple crêpe paper from a mysterious object and holds it up in the air with both hands, examining it carefully.

'What is that?' Ava squints.

'Is that a p-p-penis candle?' Lauren stutters.

'Correct, Lauren. It is indeed.' Cate towers over the girls in her heels as she lights the large penis-shaped candle in her hands and rests it down in the middle of the coffee table.

'Ohhh, I'm liking where this is going, Cate!' Lauren's eyes light up. Cate removes three large envelopes from her suitcase.

'For you!' She hands one to Ava. 'And for you.' She thrusts another towards Lauren. 'So, Ava, this penis candle represents Simon Dwyer. Now, please remove the contents of your envelope and place it on our altar. By that, I mean over there ...' She points to a little plastic side table.

Ava quickly rips her envelope open and removes a bright red garnet crystal and gently places it on Cate's makeshift altar – in front of the burning penis candle.

'This crystal represents sexual prowess and romance,' Cate announces. 'Lauren, you're next.'

Lauren removes a stick of sage from her envelope and places it on their makeshift altar.

'And this smudge sage will help us cleanse Ava of all Simon's shitty energy so we can restore her aura. Clear her of any STDs too, with a bit of luck. Please light the sage, Lauren, and place it on that saucer.' Lauren obliges, and plumes of sage smoke quickly fill the mobile home.

'Christ, it smells like weed!' Lauren sniffs the air hard, then splutters, coughing loudly.

'And for my gift for our altar, I solemnly present you with ...' Cate reaches into her suitcase again and produces a large bottle of Jose Cuervo tequila. 'Ceremonial shots!' She holds the bottle out, laid straight across her two hands.

'Oh, Cate, you never cease to amaze me! You legend!' Lauren claps her hands together, clambering to grab the bottle from Cate's hands. Lauren twists the lid off and throws it onto the couch. 'We won't be needing that any more – lids are for unfinished products!' She holds the glass bottle to her mouth and takes a large gulp, physically shivering as the alcohol hits the back of her throat. She hands the bottle across to Ava.

'Oh, oh ... I don't know, I might stick to the wine ... I hate tequila. Remember the time that gorgeous promotions girl dressed as a cowgirl came around Streets Bar selling shots from her holster? I knocked one back and immediately puked it up on the counter right in front of that guy I fancied at the time! Jimmy, was it?' Ava holds her hand up.

'It's medicinal ...' Lauren smiles, gently pushing the bottle towards Ava's mouth.

'Oh, okay.' Ava takes a long gulp, then jumps up and hops up and down on the spot.

'Your turn, Mummy.' Lauren takes the bottle back and hands it to Cate.

'I don't really drink any more, to be honest. Plus, I'm breastfeeding, so ...' Cate replies.

'So why did you bring the tequila if you're not going to drink any of it?' Lauren makes a face, then knocks back another large gulp.

'For Ava ... thought she might need it?' Cate shakes her head at Lauren, whose eyes water as she smiles though the burning sensation. Then Cate extracts the burning sage from the saucer and waves it over Ava, spinning her around. Lauren takes another swig, observing the ritual.

'Now we will all turn our palms upwards. Oh, and close your eyes!' Cate tells Lauren and Ava. They steal a quick glance at one another, then follow her orders, giggling. 'As mistress of ceremonies, I ask the gods to cleanse our Ava of Simon Dwyer, and protect her libido. May it live long and prosper. And may only good, honest and ideally hot men come her way from this point onwards. Lauren, too, by the way, gods ...' Cate chants, eyes closed. 'I now pronounce Ava officially cleansed!'

After a minute of silence, she puts the burning sage into a glass of water. The smoke is filling the room and leaving a ghastly smell.

'Where in the name of God did you learn all this crazy chakra-cleansing stuff, Cate?' asks Ava, fascinated.

'When I was in London for those three years. One of my ex-yoga friends taught me a bit about it. Amy Doberman was her name. Mad as a box of cats! But enough about her, don't want to talk about *that* witch and *that* situation ...' Cate replies, trying to change the subject. 'So, how do you feel now, Ava?'

'Wait, we want to know about this Amy Doberman first. You can't just throw a witch reference out there and expect us to not to jump all over it!' Ava is sitting forward now, enthralled.

'You'll think I'm off my rocker if I tell you *that* story,' Cate tells them.

'Probably,' Lauren says under her breath.

'Oh no, we won't! Come on, Cate, spill. . . I need more of this distraction.' Ava leans further forward towards her friend, nudging her. Cate sighs loudly.

'Okay, okay. So ... after we moved to London with our eldest son, JP, who was only a baby, I guess you could say I went through a bit of a phase. Got an unexpected dose of post-natal depression for a bit. Happens, ya know? Felt like crap all the time, zero energy, basically didn't feel like going outside the door ...'

'Cate, you never told me. You should have gotten in touch?' Ava offers, sympathetically.

'Eh, yeah, I know,' Cate says awkwardly. 'But I wasn't thinking straight. It's hard to explain what it's like, or talk to anyone about it, to be honest. It's kind of like a big dark cloud that just comes over you. No warning. It really knocked me for six. And JP was just a baby, like I said, and so needy, and we were up to our eyes in the thick of all the new baby craziness, wrecked all the time ...' Cate continues. 'So, my mam was a bit worried about me and encouraged me to join a yoga class, thought it might help me relax and clear my head a bit. I think she thought it would be great if I could meet some other first-time mums in the same "what-the-fuck?" boat as me. So I signed up for a Mommy and Me yoga class at a local studio. It was great cos I could take baby JP with me.'

'Wait, they've got new babies doing yoga in London?' Lauren nearly chokes on her words.

'No, you just lay them on the mats with you while you're doing the downward dog shite. JP would just totally zone out, it was great!'

'Keep going,' Ava says. 'I want to know *everything*. Did it help?'

'Yes and no. So, I got to know the yoga teacher – this girl, Amy. She seemed totally cool at the start; we just really hit it off. And we started hanging out a bit outside of the yoga classes. She was mad into all this meditation and chakra-cleansing stuff, taught me a good bit about it ... It's actually pretty fascinating.'

'I thought you said she was a witch?' Lauren pipes in.

'Wait, I'm getting to it …' Cate takes a breath. 'Anyway, one night we invited her and her partner Becky over for dinner and, long story short, after they left I noticed a couple of things missing from the house.' Cates eyes widen dramatically.

'Whaaat? What kind of things were missing?' Ava asks.

'So this is where it gets interesting. It was totally random. First thing I noticed was these crystal salt and pepper thingies we got as a wedding present. But I got really pissed off when my B*Witched greatest hits album went AWOL. I listen to it every morning when I'm making breakfast for the kids and JP loves "C'est La Vie", it's "our song" and, well, it always just seems to put me in a good mood. Reminds me of you pair, to be honest. Nostalgic, ya know?' Cate adds.

'Your B*Witched greatest hits album? Are you actually serious?' Lauren bursts out laughing.

'Eh, hello, Posh Spice? I know, don't ask, yes, I'll admit I was a little obsessed with them back in the day. Like us three and the musicals, and you two and the Spice Girls. We all have our guilty pleasures, come on!' Cate smiles broadly with a wink.

'Annnnnnd … what else was missing?' Ava asks, eyes widening.

'Well, I got this gorgeous silver pendant necklace after JP was born, my push present, I called it! Wore it all the time. I'd left it in the kitchen when I was preparing dinner the night Amy was over, on the counter like I always did. The next morning when I went to look for the necklace it wasn't where I left it. Turned the entire house upside down looking for it. I was frantic!'

'Nightmare! That's so upsetting.' Ava looks horrified.

'Yeah, I assumed JP had buried it somewhere in the house, so I had to get over it. Figured I'd find it somewhere eventually. And I did find it, a week later. I was sitting cross-legged in my Mommy and Me yoga class and there it was – swinging around Amy's neck!'

'You're joking! What did you do? Rip it off her, I hope, just like she blatantly ripped you off!' Lauren gasps, incredulous, suddenly more interested in the conversation.

'Well, I nearly had a fit, the furthest possible thing from Zen. But, somehow, I managed to keep my cool and waited for the class to end. And then I approached her.'

'Christ, I need popcorn for this shit! Annnnnnd? What did you say to her? "Hey, klepto?"' Lauren grabs the bottle again, now completely engrossed in the story.

'She said I must be mistaken, that it was hers. Said how offended she was that I'd ever accuse her of stealing. She said it was just a coincidence we had the same necklace. But she had this crazy intense look in her eyes, this robotic Stepford wife-type smile plastered on her face. It was in that very moment I realised she was nuts, and obviously had a problem with stealing things. And that was the last time I ever saw her. No more Mommy and Me yoga for JP and me! I got better after that, probably because I didn't have to sit with those cliquey, self-satisfied yogis ever again!'

'Wait, you let her get away with it?' Lauren asks, appalled.

'Not much I could do, Lauren. Had to take the high road. She took it. She argued it was hers and I couldn't prove it wasn't, so I just had to let it go. I was so upset, but after that drama I came across this Facebook page of hers where she goes by the name of "Goddess Amy", who practises magick . . . like magic with a "K", all powerful energy direction stuff. It's very in vogue apparently, but I sure as shit wasn't going to mess with her. She could have put a hex on me!'

'Wow, I would have . . . actually, I don't know what I would've done,' Ava adds. 'But I totally get the scared part.'

'That's some serious Hansel and Gretel-level shit, Cate,' Lauren adds, shaking her head.

'Yup, so that's how I learned about chakra-cleansing. At least one good thing came out of the kleptomaniac Amy Doberman... I cleansed Ava of Simon Dwyer!' Cate breaks into a beaming smile.

'Sounds like we both dodged bullets.' Ava nods her head.

'And here's to that, Cate!' Lauren raises the bottle and the three girls cheer in unison.

'And to kleptomaniacs! Screw them all! Simon thinks he stole my heart, well, I just reclaimed it, bitches!' Ava chimes in, nodding towards the tequila bottle, as Lauren passes it to her.

'Bottoms up, ladies!' Lauren toasts.

'Shots, shots, shots!' Ava starts chanting like a woman possessed.

The other two join in unison as the tequila bottle gets passed between them.

8

I. Am. Never. Drinking. Again.

'WHAT TIME IS IT?' AVA CROAKS through a mouth as dry as burnt toast. 'For me, it's at least blow my face off o'clock. I'm sober and the nightmare begins all over again. Oh my God, the fear is off the scales. That asshole ... that absolute shit of an excuse for a man! I want to break his bloody neck!' Ava sits up, hands firmly pressed down on her throbbing head in her creased red dress and smudged unibrow. 'I swear I haven't drunk tequila since I threw up on that poor Jimmy fella in Streets Bar. Or was his name Timmy?' Ava tries to open her eyes but they are glued shut, one eyelash hanging down. 'I need my phone! I have to see what's going on with the mess that is my life now. Please, Lauren, give me my phone? I better face the music now. Maybe look at the shitstorm that Chloe bitch caused online.'

'I'm. Never. Drinking. Again.' Lauren's voice is barely audible as she rises from the couch beside Ava, her dark blunt bangs standing up in the air. 'Did we all manage to sleep on top of each other on this tiny couch?' she asks, as she spots the empty tequila bottle on the table. 'I guess so,' she answers herself, shrugging.

'Not exactly how I'd imagined waking up today.' Ava is standing slowly, holding onto the wooden arm of the old couch.

'You had a lucky escape.' Lauren tuts, as a low moan from the couch interrupts her.

'What were ye thinking? Why did I bring that tequila? I didn't think you two would drink the entire bottle!' Cate, face planted down on the couch, drools into the old embroidered, buttoned cushion. 'I haven't slept so well in years! I feel great! But what is the gross smell from this cushion?' Cate stretches happily, her wild red hair tangled like a bird's nest.

'I don't know, but all I do know is that I forgot my mortification for a few hours and that was a big win in my book. Tequila-tastic, actually.' Ava perches on the edge beside Cate now.

'Try that stupid car again, will you, Lauren? We need to get our bags out, and I really do need to check in with my life, my dad especially. My poor, gorgeous dad. And I want to hear what Simon's had to say for himself.' Ava drops her head into her hands at the thought.

'I presumed you blocked him?' Cate asks.

'Not yet. I haven't had the balls to turn my phone on since this shitstorm broke and Lauren confiscated it. But I'm going to call him now from one of your phones if I have to. He's not getting away that lightly. I want to know how bad he feels today. I hope he feels like the biggest piece of shit. He better be packing up and getting the hell out of our apartment, too. I need to change the locks on the Edenvale house. Simon-proof everywhere,' Ava adds, sighing.

'I'd say that's exactly how he feels.' Cate rubs her hand on Ava's shoulder as she does some lunges, her arms aloft like a true yoga goddess.

'Seriously, how can you?' Ava moans.

'I feel great! I can't remember the last time I had six solid hours of sleep!' Cate adds, perkily, as Lauren makes a face behind her back. 'Although, my boobs are murdering me, like I can't even tip off them! Ouch! And I'm sure baby Max is wondering where they've disappeared to.'

'What if he begs your forgiveness? We didn't exactly get a chance to discuss that scenario!' Lauren says, purposely ignoring Cate, as she moves like a newborn baby deer to get their bags.

'Nothing he could ever say, or attempt to sing, would ever drag me back to him. Ever. It's so over. I can't tell you. I have a lot of faults, sure, but one of them isn't a lack of self-respect. If there is one thing my dad taught me after Mum passed away, it was to always have complete self-respect. Non-negotiable,' Ava tells them.

Lauren nods at her in agreement, and gets her keys and heads to the car as Cate rises slowly and starts to rummage in her open suitcase on the floor.

'Oh, I know you're in here somewhere ... I always come prepared. Come to Mamma.' She finds a box of painkillers and throws the red box at Lauren, who walks back in the door at that exact moment, pulling Ava's case overnight bag behind her in one hand and hers in the other. They fall at her feet. She drops the cases and grabs them.

'Genius, Cate! Thank you,' Lauren says, planting butterfly kisses all over the red box.

'Okay, who's attempting to make the tea, please. Someone? Anyone?' Ava croaks.

Lauren hands Ava's case to her, raising her hand. 'I will. I'm never fully dressed without my morning cuppa, in fairness,' she says, staggering into the tiny kitchenette.

'Lauren, fizz those bad boys up while you're in there, will you? We need them. Stat,' Ava calls after her.

'I think the last time we all had a session like that together – well, when you joined in, Cate – was, hmmm, I actually can't remember ...' Ava opens her neatly packed honeymoon case, deep in thought. 'Do I need to abandon my cheating fiancé at the altar every time I want to see you girls?' she half jokes, as Lauren passes her phone to her.

'After all the kerfuffle of choosing this' – she holds up a padded white silk clothes hanger with delicate black lingerie hanging from it – 'it never so much as left the hanger. Best laid plans and all that.' She drops it back into her overnight bag. 'And this was the suit I bought for today.' She holds up a sleek white suit jacket and throws it over the side of the couch. 'This is torture!' She blesses herself as she holds out her phone.

'Do you want me to look?' Cate offers.

'No, thanks ... this is my shitstorm and in I go. Just pray for me.' Ava sits back down onto the couch and turns on her phone, types in her password slowly, then swipes it into life.

'I'd say the fact that we can't remember our last major session was because that was probably our mission at the time ... to not remember,' Cate says wryly, trying to make conversation to give Ava some space as her phone repeatedly bings with messages.

'Jesus,' Ava says.

'It's not that I don't want to party, but I seriously can't cope with the hangovers. I need to face it, I can't drink any more. Waking up hungover with three kids is ...'

'You're not with your kids now, though?' Lauren says to her.

'No, but I am breastfeeding and have to pump and dump, and my hangovers don't just last a morning, they last a week, and I can't cope!' Cate snaps.

'Calm down,' Lauren tells her, and wins a smile back from Cate.

'Are you calling your dad?' Cate turns to face Ava, who is engrossed in the phone.

'Hmmmm. So many messages here ... when will we ever learn that we aren't eighteen any more? Like seriously. When are we going to cop on to ourselves? Why do we always turn to booze?' Ava mumbles, her thumbs ablur on the phone as she scrolls through all the messages.

'Ideally, well ... never ... never ever,' Lauren mutters, as she shimmies past Ava holding a mug of pain relief in one hand and puts the other cup beside Ava on the table.

'I'm not reading the content, just seeing who they are from. Every cousin I barely know, it's horrific the embarrassment, and I'm not sure if I can even stomach pain relief right now. You know me, I can't even brush my teeth with a hangover without gagging.' Ava hesitates before reaching out and picking up her mug, sipping it slowly, phone still grasped in her hand.

'Has Simon texted?' Cate asks hurriedly.

Ava ignores her.

'Em ... well ... at least it was only us here. I usually get a text the morning after a work event with six words no woman ever wants to hear – "I heard about you last night" – nearly always from my assistant, Julia, the millennial I was telling you about, Avz. Attitude for days. I honestly doubt her parents ever corrected her throughout her entire life ...' Lauren rolls her eyes at Cate.

'Come on, call your dad. Who gives a shit what people are saying? Sure, you don't even know half of them.' Cate nods again at the phone clutched in Ava's hand, her knuckles white.

'The struggle is real,' Lauren sighs, as Ava dials.

They wait expectantly, silence filling the air. It rings then they hear Ray's voice.

'Dad? It's me ... I am, I'm fine. How are you? What's the latest?' Ava enquires nervously.

'Go on, ask him what Simon had to say for himself? What did Simple Simon say?' Cate pleads, whispering in her other ear.

'He said shit happens and legged it!' Ava cries, eyes flashing in amazement. She can hardly believe what she is hearing. Hand over the phone speaker, her eyes suddenly light up. 'Oh, he did, did he? Okay, great, thanks, Dad ... he is ... he is great,' Ava responds. 'That's okay, you go ... I love you, too. Yes, the girls are looking after me. Cate's here now, too. Call me if you need me, okay, Dad? Bye.' She rings off.

'What? Lauren, listen to your voicemails quick! I'll do the same,' Cate says aghast.

'Me too actually,' Lauren says and dials in first. She puts the phone on loudspeaker and the automated voice fills the room:

'*You have six new voice messages. This message was left 23 June at 1.16 p.m.* "Lauren . . . it's me . . . like, I can't serio do all this stuff on my own . . . my therapist said I should avoid all stress and my dermatologist said the same . . . eh, call me back!"'

'Who the hell is that?' Cate asks Lauren.

'Julia, my useless assistant.' Lauren rolls her eyes.

'*This message was left 23 June at 1.21 p.m.* "Seriously! I have to go, Lauren. I've a deep pool yoga therapy appointment at twelve and I can't come back after it. I have to go to bed . . . you need to get back to the office!"'

'She's a real keeper, right?' Lauren rolls her eyes again.

'I've no messages at all,' Cate says, dropping her phone onto her lap.

Ava hits loudspeaker on hers.

'Okay, brace yourselves.' She puts her head between her knees.

'*This message was left 23 June at 9.16 p.m.* "It's Dad, love, just letting you know everything is fine, it's all over now, and ya know what? I've me feet up at home watching *Coronation Street* with a steaming cup of milky coffee and I'm eating a massive chunk of the fabulous chocolate biscuit wedding cake! Absolutely delicious, by the way. I'm celebrating here. Simon was a louser. A selfish yolk. Ya know what he said to me? "Shit happens, man." *Shit happens all right,* I said back to him, and he saw my face and turned and ran like the coward he is. Thank God he didn't get his hands on your mother's inheritance. He's not entitled to any of that cottage now you aren't husband and wife. Ring me when you feel like a chat, go on, ya have him on the ropes ... Hold on, I'm coming now, Gina."' The doorbell rings and the message cuts off.

Laurens messages are still playing out. '*This message was left 24 June at 8.51 a.m.* "Hi, Lauren, it's the Well Woman clinic here, we just wanted to see ... "'

Lauren jumps up to cut the voice message off. 'Ah, just a ... a thing ... for the magazine ...' She puts her phone away, and an entirely different voice fills the room next.

'*This message was left at 3.16 p.m.* "Hey, *c'est moi* ... I don't know what happened, but Mags tells me that you are gone ... call me? Please?'

'Who's that?' Lauren asks.

'No one ... um, someone from the gallery.' Ava hits off her messages. 'Last thing ... okay, here I go, into Instagram. Pray for me,' Ava says as Lauren grabs her phone out of her hand.

'Not a chance, sweetheart! Why would you torture yourself like that?' Lauren stuffs Ava's phone down her top. 'Although, speaking of social media, reminds me I seriously do have to post a story for that California Glow crap ...' Lauren looks up and catches Cate's narrowed eyes.

'I can't believe Simon didn't try to contact you immediately?' Cate is dumbstruck.

'I can,' Ava said.

'Why?' Cate asks.

'Oh, well, Simon doesn't do confrontation. He'll "wait until I have calmed down, *man*".'

'He doesn't do *anything*,' Lauren mutters under her breath.

'It's mind-blowing that he didn't try to contact you at all ...' Cate talks over Lauren, totally dumbfounded. 'After ten years together, and everything he did to you?'

'Who could calm down after finding out on national radio that their fiancé has been having an affair? On their wedding day, no less,' Lauren says, hands out wide.

'Me, probably,' Ava says sadly, shrugging her shoulders. She ties her blonde hair up with a bobbin.

'I don't know what to say, Ava.' Cate moves over to sit beside her.

'Other than you're still rocking that unibrow?' Lauren adds.

'There is nothing to say ... I ...' Ava rubs at her unibrow, only smudging it more.

'He never deserved you, I know it's not what you want to hear now, love, but he was always a langer, everyone could see that.'

'So why didn't you tell me, Lauren?' Ava throws her hands up in the air. 'Why? I thought friends were supposed to be totally honest with each other!'

'How could I? Think about it! It would only have come between us, not that it didn't happen anyway, but imagine if I'd have met you and said, "Yo! Hey, Ava, Simon's a bona fide prick!" How would you have taken that?' Lauren hits back.

'Well, I would have ...' Ava tries to respond.

'I disagree,' Lauren says, shaking her head, and Ava has no choice but to nod slowly.

'I had to shut my mouth when you told me you were moving out of our flat and giving up your art work to go full-time at the gallery. Wasting all your artistic talent to support Simon's career. I shut my mouth because I didn't want to lose you. But I lost you anyway. That's the bit that fucking bugs me the most!' Lauren sighs.

'And you, Cate? Did you think he was a prick, too?' Ava turns to Cate, who is cradling her cup of tea tightly.

'Oh ... oh, I don't know,' Cate frowns.

'Oh, get off the fence, Cate!' Lauren yells.

'Don't tell me how I feel, Lauren. I think he's a prick now

obviously, but no one knows what goes on in anyone's relationship, not even your nearest and dearest,' Cate snaps, clearly riled. 'Not that you would know – you have never been in a real relationship in your entire life, you haven't a clue.'

'So because I've never been in a "real relationship", I can't have an opinion? Is that what you're saying?' Lauren narrows her eyes at Cate.

'No, you can, but you can't tell Ava that Simon's always been a prick. She accepted his proposal of marriage, for God's sake. She clearly didn't think he was a prick or she wouldn't have agreed to marry him, would she?' Cate spits.

'I do now,' Ava mutters, dejected in the midst of their venom.

'But he was cheating on her! He was screwing other women, Cate!' Lauren stands up, flattening her fringe with her palms.

'Well, one that we know of. But thanks for the loud reminder, Lauren.' Ava leans back, her eyes teary.

'We don't know for sure if it was other women or just that one woman on the radio, Lauren. Let's not overdramatise this, when we don't have all the facts yet,' Cate offers.

'What does it matter if it was one woman or five hundred?' Lauren asks.

'It doesn't. All I'm saying is we are just here to support Ava, not tell her what to do.' Cate lowers her tone, trying to calm this spat between her and Lauren.

'She's my best mate, I will freely share exactly what I think she should do!' Lauren adds defiantly.

'This is a great help, guys – you guys at each other's throats. Thanks.' Ava pushes herself up off the couch and moves to the window.

'Okay, listen, Lauren, this isn't the time. You're both horribly hungover right now, of course we shouldn't be ranting on.' Cate shoots a sympathetic look towards Ava.

'How are you always so together, Cate?' Lauren fires at her. Cate ignores her passive-aggressive compliment.

'Right, so, we've got to get a game plan together. Let's get ready to head back home, we can all come over to mine tonight and I can make a nice dinner ... And, Ava, I can make up the boys' den and you can stay with us as long as you want to. We have a really comfy blow-up bed,' Cate suggests.

'Do you want to let Cate in on your plan?' Lauren asks Ava, a slight smirk spreading across her face.

'What plan?' Cate asks, sipping her tea as Lauren rubs her hands together.

'So, Cate, we are going to head to Edenvale today. You know, the new house in Clare I told you about? It was supposed to be a surprise reveal from Simon for our honeymoon. He was managing all the renovations. And well, I got an even bigger surprise in the car on my way to the wedding yesterday ...' Ava's eyes fill with sadness again.

'Guess I was the only one who hadn't heard anything about it, then,' Lauren mutters under her breath, irritated.

Ava ignores her comment. 'Please say you'll come with us, Cate! For me?' Ava looks hopefully at her. 'It will be just like old times. The Three Musketeers!'

'More like the Witches of Eastwick.' Lauren can't help herself. Panic floods Cate's face as she grabs her breasts.

'Ava, you know I'd love to, but ... but I only left quick instructions on the fridge for last night as I ran out the door to get to you after I saw the wedding commotion on Instagram. I left the three boys with a neighbour. And JP has a birthday party to go to. And Jake has an awful cold. And Max ... I'm still breastfeeding, as you can see. I need to pump ... my boobs are murdering me right now.' Cate winces.

'Don't you freeze your breast milk, though? You told me you

did. For emergencies? This is an emergency!' Ava interjects, looking at Cate intensely.

'Yeah, I do, um, I mean, I have some in the freezer ... um, okay, so if I was to not go home today at all ... Okay ... let me see what I can do, I need to figure it out.' Cate paces about, trying to reassure Ava.

'Calpol, check. Nappies, check. Breast milk, check. Birthday present for Jaime Carter next door, check.' Cate recites her mental notes loudly, pacing while talking frantically to herself. Lauren, watching her, grabs for her phone and starts furiously texting a mile a minute.

'Child seats are all in my car, and sure there is enough pasta in the press and pasta sauce sachets in the fridge, and ...' Cate uses her fingers now as she counts. 'I have the portable pump in my bag.'

'Bloody Julia. She's always asking how she can step up and take on more responsibility in editorial. I give her this one opportunity to do it and she freaks out. I mean, I'll be back tomorrow, for God's sake. All I need her to do is keep things moving along at the magazine. Deep pool therapy, me arse!' Lauren sighs, her eyes never leaving her text conversation. 'I have to do everything!' She wipes her top lip, perspiring again. 'The only time that damn Julia ever really paid attention recently was when I showed her how to make scrambled eggs in a microwave. It was a mind-blowing revelation to a millennial, apparently.'

'That's why they pay you the big bucks, McCabe. You're the only one that can do everything.' Ava tries to ease her frustration.

'I can't do everything actually. Well, not the things I really want to do, Avz, but that's a story for another day,' Lauren replies, suddenly quieter but still engaged in text combat on her phone.

'Okay, Ava, let me check in at home. I'm sure it'll be all good. Well, as good as it can be when I'm not there.' Cate is anxious.

'I'll give a lengthy checklist, and snack schedules, and bedtime story recommendations, and what clothes to dress them in tomorrow so they don't look like hobos, and ...'

'And can your wife wipe her own backside?' Lauren looks up from her phone.

'Oh, piss off, Lauren, I'm really not in the mood!' Cate snaps.

'Cate, breathe!' Ava jumps in. 'Lily is a fantastic mother. She'll be just fine! Relax.' She takes the sketch pad Lauren bought her up from the table. Cate sits down on the couch, inhaling deeply.

'I know, it's just ... As you know, Ava, I do it all and, well, Lily works so hard in the restaurant. They kept their Michelin star and it's crazy busy right now ...' Cate nods her head towards Lauren and makes a face at Ava, who swipes her hand at her in a gesture to just ignore her. Cate's phone beeps.

'Oh, she's an angel, she said that I can go.' Cate throws her head back.

'What, like a permission slip?' Lauren laughs. 'A kitchen pass?'

'Exactly like a permission slip, Lauren, that's exactly how we roll: mutual respect for one another and the insane workload that's involved in bringing up three boys. We're a team and we have rules and schedules.'

'Oh, keep your yummy mummy wig on, Cate!' Lauren says as her phone beeps.

'It's Julia. She's has assured me she will try her best to keep everything rolling at the office, so I'm in too. I'll be on my phone a lot, but once you're cool with that it's all good,' she chimes in.

'Right, I better get dressed and out of this gear.' Cate opens her case. 'I mean, who will write those intriguingly powerful articles on the importance of facial filler if you aren't there?' She smiles up innocently at Lauren.

'Like you said yourself a few minutes ago, piss off, Cate! I'm not in the mood.' Lauren rubs her hands together. 'It's so good to see you drawing, Ava, nothing like heartbreak to get the creative juices flowing.' Lauren walks over to the window where Ava is.

'Oh, it's so therapeutic sitting here looking out at the open fields,' Ava says, relieved as she closes her sketch pad. 'I did give up doing the things I love for Simon, and that's beyond pathetic,' she says. 'No self-respect at all, actually.'

'New chapter, love,' Lauren tells her. 'Right, we need to get cracking. There's a bit of a shower in the bathroom, but you'll have to really squeeze yourself in, it's bloody tiny! Is there any coffee around? I actually feel strong enough to stomach one now. Let's get this show on the road.' Ava stands up, looking slightly better as the pills take hold.

'Jesus help me,' Cate squeaks.

'What now, pelvic floor let you down?' Lauren says, spinning around.

'Please God, someone help me.' Cate voice cracks as the words leave her mouth in a frenzied whisper.

'Oh, fucking hell,' Ava hisses.

'What is it? What's wrong?' Lauren asks again, as she looks at Cate's whiter-than-white face. A huge black rat with a tail as long as a serving spoon is perched on her lap.

'Okay, okay, calm, it's a rat . . . balls . . . okay, don't move, Cate . . . I did a feature on rats once in the magazine. Erm, okay, think, Lauren, think! Oh yes, they carry Weil's disease.' Lauren tiptoes from the window to the couch. The rat stands on its back legs and stares Cate down. She is frozen to the spot.

'N-n-not helpful,' Cate pants, rooted to the couch. The rat rubs its claws together, still staring into Cate's face.

'I'm going to attempt to throw this cushion at it.' Ava slowly bends and removes the round cushion with buttons from the end of the couch. The rat doesn't stir.

'I – I – I think I've just slightly peed myself,' Cate puffs. Breathing in and out rapidly.

'Just pretend you're back in her Lamaze classes. Breathe! In and out, slowly,' Lauren suggests. 'Oh . . . there . . . is . . . another . . . one . . . throw the fucking cushion, Ava!' Lauren jumps onto the table, startling the rat just as Ava throws the cushion and whacks Cate in the face with it. Cate screams. The rat jumps onto Cate's shoulder.

'I-I'm going to p-p-p-pass out.' Cate turns her head impossibly slowly to make eye contact with the rat. Lauren jumps off the table and runs for the door.

'Oh shit . . . oh shit . . . oh shit,' Ava puffs. 'Ohhh . . . okay . . . don't move, Cate.'

Lauren runs back in and grabs her and Ava's bags; she picks up Cate's beige trench coat and Ava's blazer and hauls them out the door at speed.

'O-oh . . . help me, Ava . . . please, just do something . . . anything!' Tears stream down Cate's face.

'I – I – I'm terrified of rats too, Cate . . .' Ava squeaks just as the rat jumps back onto Cate's lap and stands upright on its two back legs. Cate makes a sound like Ava has never heard in her life. Like the noise a rusted steel door might make that hasn't been opened in a hundred years. Lauren runs back in to the mobile home.

'What are ye doing? Get out of here, this mobile kip is clearly rat infested. Oh, Jesus, we drank out of the glasses and cups, and slept on that manky couch.' Lauren stands at the door. 'All those brown things on the floor. I thought were scorch marks. They're rat droppings!'

'I think I'm going to be sick.' Ava retches repeatedly, then vomits all over the floor. The rat, startled by the noise, jumps off Cate's lap and runs through the vomit, skidding as it scurries into the kitchen.

'Go!' Lauren yells. Ava, hyperventilating, makes for the door, while Cate, bawling hysterically, runs out the caravan door.

'Agggghhh!' Cate screeches, itching herself all over, jumping up and down on the spot.

'Oh, Jesus, like I need that shit. Haven't I had enough rats to last a lifetime already?' Ava wipes her mouth with the back of her hand and falls to the gravel on her knees.

★ ★ ★

'Edenvale, here we come!' Lauren clicks her seatbelt, as Ava clambers into the passenger seat of the Range Rover.

'Cate, you okay back there?' Lauren looks back at Cate, who is still sobbing and shaking.

'It was only a rat, Cate, it wasn't a bomb! Calm yourself down.'

'Rats are my biggest fear, Lauren.' Cate sobs harder. 'Just like commitment is for you!' she mutters.

'Well, look at it this way. You have' – Lauren ignores Cate's dig and turns the ignition on – 'I won't say overcome, but faced, your biggest fear ...' The engine roars to a start and Lauren breathes a sigh of relief.

'I've w-w-wet myself and my boobs are leaking.' Cate's hands run up and down her body.

'At least you know all your womanly faculties are in good working order.' Lauren screeches away on the grass from the mobile home, then steers down the long narrow field, where branches of untended brambles scrape her Range Rover.

'We're still dressed like this!' Ava suddenly realises. 'Christ, we have to change!'

'We will, just let me get out onto a main road and find some- where. Relax, we can change in a hotel bathroom or whatever. We're lucky to get out of there alive,' Lauren shouts back at her.

'Put your coat on, Cate.' Ava throws the beige trench coat over into the back and Cate clambers into it, covering her underwear.

'Y-y-y-you are right, Lauren. I d-d-d-did face my f-f-f-ears,' Cate says, trying to catch her breath and sniffing loudly, as she picks up an *Irish Gloss* magazine from the huge pile resting beside her in the back seat of the car. 'A-a-although this is all I – I – I have to read for the journey, so I have to face another m-m-major fear . . .' Cate hiccups loudly. 'Being forced to read *Irish Gloss*.'

'Oh, she's back! Touché . . . Well, it is Ireland's best-selling magazine, Cate, for the third year running. We can't all be wrong.' Lauren shrugs and adjusts her seat, then tips Ava beside her.

'Don't let me forget, Avz, I have to post another Instastory soon for that California Glow crowd, it's a three-posts-a-day contract . . . It's lucrative for me to talk shite. It will have to be something clever to get the likes this time. But hey, a contract is a contract unfortunately.' Lauren looks around for inspiration, as she fans herself with her hand.

'I can't post the next Instagram story still dressed like this. I've no idea how many people are seeing my post. Guess a quick tweet and hashtag will have to do.' Lauren rubs her hands down her body. 'Christ, I'm sweating bullets here,' she adds, wiping her hands on her dress.

'Must be torture having to make up stories all the time. I couldn't do t-t-t-that,' Cate says, hiccupping again as she speedily flicks though the glossy pages. 'I mean . . .' She tries to cover now, as she sees Lauren's face redden deeply in the rear-view mirror.

'No, you don't do social media because you're way better than me, Cate.' Lauren's eyes cloud over. 'You're just way better than everyone!'

'The scenery is lovely. I'd love to just capture that right there.' Ava points out the passenger window as fields full of grazing cows zoom by. The rain starts to spit and Lauren flicks on the wipers.

'It's funny how totally rural your uncle Lar's mobile really is,' Ava adds, trying hard to banish the tension that's filled the car like a bad smell.

'That's not what I meant, and you know it, Lauren. I – I just don't like looking at people pretending to be having fun all the time, that's all. None of it is real life, it's all filtered and Photoshopped and, honestly, it's all pretty pathetic.' Cate snorts in the back seat, rolling her eyes.

'You don't like any of it because you are knee-deep in nappies and it's all a million miles away from what you can relate to right now! Is it because it's such a different world?' Lauren digs.

'No, I *choose* to be knee-deep in nappies. I don't want to live a fake life. It's just all nonsense and ...' Cate dumps the magazine back on the pile.

'And what?' Lauren's voice is slightly raised.

'I don't know exactly, that's just how I feel,' Cate mutters, uncomfortably.

'No, I think you do know what you mean, Cate. Spit it out!' Lauren challenges her, adjusting the rear-view mirror to see all of Cate's face in the back seat.

'Guys, are you actually serious? Are you listening to a word I've said? This really isn't helping, and my head is thumping. Come on, let it go!' Ava leans her head on the window, exasperated.

'And actually a lot of us are being real, living real lives, bringing up kids, and yes, knee-deep in shitty nappies, post-natal depression, and, hey, torn vaginas. Must be hard for all the beautiful people to stomach sometimes, that's all.' Cate squeezes a rolled-up edition of *Irish Gloss* between her hands.

'But you aren't on social media, Cate, so how do you *have* to look at it?' Lauren points to her in the mirror as one might to the accused in the dock.

'Seriously?' Ava mutters, closing her eyes tight.

'S-s-sometimes I go on social media, yeah ... like mainly when I'm on the toilet! I look at your page when I'm consti-pated, Lauren, if you must know,' Cate blurts out. 'You help me shit! And you know what else? I look at these photos people are posting and I swear to God, I want to comment with "Stop editing your pics. What if you go missing? How can we find you if you look like Kate Moss on Facebook but a potato in real life?"' She smiles and starts laughing out loud at her own joke. Lauren doesn't laugh.

'I fucking knew it! It's people like you who drive me *mad*! Telling me I'm never off social media, judging me, when they couldn't possibly know that unless they were on there too. The green button bastards, I call you lot. You always see these social stalkers online, but they never post a thing ... No, no, they just snoop around on other people's lives. It drives me bonkers ...' Lauren shouts. She drags her hand through her hair, flattening her bangs down with her palms, hands shaking with anger.

'Wow. Calm down ... overreacting much?' Cate says, completely shocked at Lauren's fury. 'The point I'm trying to make is too much social media isn't good for anyone's mental health. End of.' Cate is determined to get the last word in.

'I won't calm down!'

'You know yourself you're overreacting, try to rein it in,' Cate says. 'You must be due? Your hormones are all-a-crazy.'

Lauren rolls the window down.

'Jesus, stop! Both of you, just stop! This was a huge mistake! You're wrecking my head, even more than it is already,' Ava yells, dropping her head into her hands.

'I'm sorry, Ava. Whatever, Lauren. I really don't have to listen to this – nonsense.' Cate unrolls the magazine. 'This is about Ava, not us.' She buries her head in it again.

'Nonsense? You aren't *my* mummy, Cate.' Lauren imitates Cate's voice, grunting out a sarcastic laugh.

'What's that supposed to mean?' Cate drops the magazine beside her and sits forward in the back seat, gripping the bars from Ava's headrest. Lauren puts her thumb in her mouth and sucks hard, and Cate opens her mouth to say something as Ava hits the dashboard with her hand suddenly, making Lauren and Cate jump.

'Shut up, both of you! Fuck! How could Simon do this to me? I supported him all the time. I listened to him go on and on and on about his stupid band shit, and I put up with his weirdo friends eating me out of house and home – for what? The prick! While he lazed around at home apparently writing music. And then once in a blue moon when he was allegedly working he was really off shagging other women. Not only that, the moron was stupid enough to let her take sex photos of him! I mean, that says more about him than anything else. *That* was the level of respect he had for me, and now you two going at one another like old times. A pleasant reminder about why we all stopped hanging out together. I give up, I really just give up!' Ava's voice starts to crack.

'Sorry, Ava.' Lauren rubs her arm gently.

'Yeah, I'm so sorry, Ava.' Cate strokes her hair from the back seat. 'And don't worry, we exorcised you of that douche last night. Things can *only* get better. We will make a bigger effort with one another, right, Lauren?' Cate says softly and sits back just as the car alarm starts to shrill again.

'What the?' Cate whips her hands over her ears.

'Ouch! My head!' Ava sticks her fingers in her ears.

'Oh shit … not *again*,' Lauren shouts and indicates to pull over.

'What do you mean "not again"? And, um, Lauren, why is

your red engine light coming on?' Ava slaps Lauren's arm hard, gesturing towards the car's display unit.

'What. The. Actual? Oh no!'

The car stops dead in its tracks.

'Perfect,' Ava says. 'This is just perfect.'

9

Pump and Dump Emergency.

'GET OUT AND WALK?' CATE'S EYES ARE ON STALKS. 'In case you've forgotten, Stevie Nicks, I'm dressed like a hooker who just got a slap in the face from her pimp for not bringing home the bacon! Call the Automobile Association. I'm not moving. I have to pump my breast milk, for crying out loud! Can you please get my case from the boot? I'll change back here.' Cate wraps her trench coat tighter around her leaking chest.

'Try the engine again?' Ava says, aghast as the alarm emits deafening shrills.

Lauren turns the key. Nothing.

'The engine's dead. I told you it's been acting up, with the alarm going off all the time. Looks like it's run the battery down again.' She pulls the key from the ignition.

'You are fucking kidding me!' Cate shouts at Lauren.

'Language, please, Cate.' Lauren tuts in mock horror. 'I'll get your bags, girls.' She jumps out of the Range Rover followed by Ava, who looks up and down the deserted road for help. Lauren pops the boot open and stares in.

'I never normally use bad language, Lauren, but by God do you bring out the very worst in me, darling,' Cate shouts out the rolled-down window from the back seat over the car alarm.

'That's not quite true. I can vividly remember you being asked to leave Eddie Rocket's because you used foul language at our waiter. In fact...' Lauren rubs her temple. 'Hang on, it's coming to me' – she rubs her temples faster – '"Go fuck yourself, you lanky streak of piss" was what you said.'

'He felt my arse!' Cate protests loudly. 'And when I called him out on it, he said, oh so sarcastically, he hadn't enough *room* to pass me! He rubbed himself up against me, Lauren.'

'Still, you said "fuck",' Lauren shouts, then expends a breath. 'There is no good time to tell you this, Cate. Your tidy little blue case isn't in the boot.' Lauren moves her attention to Ava, who has wandered on up ahead, her red embroidered dress billowing behind her, just her suit jacket covering it.

'Hang on!' Lauren calls after her.

'What do you mean? You didn't grab my case? I've no clothes?' Cate yells out the window. 'How the hell will I pump?'

'Nope, and I don't know, maybe it's time you started looking after yourself, Cate! Now I have to go after Ava!' Lauren totters up the road after Ava, who she can hear talking to herself but can't quite make out what she is saying.

'Oh, I wish you were here, but what would I say to you now anyway, just as you found Suzanne?' Ava is rambling aloud to herself. 'I'm glad I didn't marry him, but those last ten years ... for what? It's a release to speak my truth, out loud ...'

'Yer one won't get out of the Range Rover,' Lauren says, as she catches up with her. 'We left her case, and apparently she thinks this is *Driving Miss Daisy*. We have to go back.' Lauren widens her eyes at Ava.

'What are we going to do? Can't we just google a number and call a tow truck?' Ava asks. 'Get the car fixed, then go on to Clare. I'll pay. I have our joint account bank card with me, and damn right I'm going to use it before Simon gets his hands on it!

I swear it wouldn't surprise me in the slightest if the weasel has cleaned that account out!'

'We could if there was any coverage on this road.' Lauren waves her phone at Ava.

'We have to walk to the next garage, or at least find somewhere where we can get phone coverage again.'

'This is really not fair.' Ava rolls her eyes as they trudge back to the car, the alarm still blaring. 'Whatever I did in a past life to deserve this, I am truly sorry for. I must have done something terrible. This is a real-life fucking nightmare. Excuse my language, but it is.'

'Oh, for God's sake, Cate, are you still sulking? Get out of the car!' Lauren yells over the din. 'Neither of us will change in the car, okay?'

'I need to pump, and I have to ring my wife and tell her where I am!' Cate, fuming now, extends her hands out the car window, exposing two damp patches on her coat.

'This isn't *Taken*, Cate. Liam Neeson isn't out looking for you!' Lauren looks left and right, dramatically, making fun of Cate.

'You really should have been an actress, Lauren. Maybe get a part on a reality TV show, you are *that* good! I'm telling you that we can't just go walking randomly. We have no idea where we are. It isn't safe!'

'Any brainwaves to offer, so? None of us have any coverage, so we're shit out of luck,' Lauren snaps.

'It's like she says, we don't have a choice, Cate,' Ava agrees, just as the car alarm stops and the welcome quiet of the countryside surrounds them.

'Oh, thank God, that was horrific.' Ava sighs. 'Is there a worse sound than a car alarm?'

'Three children crying at the same time,' Cate suggests.

'Nope, I've no bars at all still,' Lauren says, distracted, looking at her phone.

'I should never have left the kids, what the hell was I thinking?' Cate wails.

All of them stand silently, in their own worlds. The moment stretches out, until Ava speaks.

'What was *I* thinking? Never mind *you*! The way Stefan looked at me. I'm surprised she hadn't packed a lunch for him in her stupid little farmers' market brown paper bags for my wedding!' She realises what she's said, and looks at her friends. 'Why am I being such a bitch? Suzanne seems like a perfectly nice girl, and he likes her, and he's a great guy, and ...' Ava crouches down on the grass verge, tilting her head into her hands.

'What on earth are you talking about?' Cate looks at her, concerned.

'And now, well, now he probably thinks I'm ignoring him. He's tried to contact me ...'

'Is this the French lad she's on about?' Lauren asks, looking to Cate.

'What French lad?' Cate replies, looking back at Lauren.

'I don't want to talk about it, okay?' Ava tugs at a tuft of grass.

'Okay, well, when you do ...' Lauren wipes her upper lip again.

'Where are we anyway?' Cate gets out of the Range Rover, pulling her trench coat tightly around her.

'Not that far from civilisation, with a bit of luck.'

They sit in silence for a long five minutes before a car approaches and Lauren leaps to stick her thumb out.

'Open up your Inspector Gadget coat there, Cate, that will stop them in their tracks!' Cate whacks Lauren's hand back away, as she tries to tug at her coat.

'We are not stopping a random car! Not a chance! Smile and pretend we're going for a walk! If they're murderers and they smell fear, we're doomed,' Cate whispers through her gritted teeth. The car driver slows, looks at them, then speeds off.

Ava gets up and starts to move faster, walking ahead of them again along the narrow country road.

'Why didn't I just escape on my own? Oh God, what was I thinking? You're doing my head in. I need space … to be able to think straight.' She is ranting furiously to herself, as she strides away from the car.

'You okay, Avz? What are you saying?' Lauren calls after her, as she walks even faster.

'Nothing … there's got to be a pub up here or something. I mean, it's Ireland, you can't swing a cat without hitting one, right?' Ava calls, glad of the distance between them but still within earshot.

'God help her, what a disaster. I mean, not in her wildest dreams could she have imagined she'd be walking on a deserted country road on the first day of her honeymoon. Dressed as Frida Kahlo, no less.' Lauren shakes her head, looking at Cate next to her.

'It's just awful, I know, but it just shows you the best laid plans and all that. One time we had tickets for *Ben & Holly's Little Kingdom* in the Olympia. JP was so excited, couldn't sleep the night before, he was in and out of our bed fifty times. The morning we were due to go, he got his willy caught in his zipper. Had to go to Crumlin hospital, we missed the show,' Cate explains. Then, as she clocks Lauren's expression, she realises what she's said.

'I – I – I mean, obviously it's nothing like this, but my point *is* … best laid plans. Not the fact we missed The Wise Old Elf …'

'The Wise Old Elf?' Are you losing your mind? Ava, slow down!' Lauren calls out.

'He's like the head of all the elves …' Cate coughs into her hand and catches Lauren's eye. They both burst out laughing.

'Let her off,' Cate suggests, nodding her head along the road.

'Let's give her a bit of space.' They walk in silence along the country road behind Ava, who now is chuckling to herself, an insane conversation going on behind her.

'I'm sorry about the social media stuff. I didn't mean to upset you,' Cate says, putting her hand on Lauren's arm.

'Don't be, it's okay. I overreacted. I-I-I'm ... I'm, you see, I'm ...' Lauren starts, just as Ava does a U-turn and heads back towards them.

'Whassup?' Cate calls out.

'I really need to pee!' she says, as she stops and leans against a stone wall. She watches them pick up the pace. 'Why did I try to patch this friendship up?' she mutters, looking at her friends approaching. 'I know deep down you can't be arsed to stay with me for a few nights. Even after I was publicly humiliated. He's right, as always. I should have asked Stefan to be my maid of honour ... At least then it would be me and him together, stuck on this isolated road. What if he's really falling for Suzanne?'

'Who's Suzanne?' Cate asks, catching Ava's words.

'Hop over there. We'll keep sketch,' Lauren says, as they all look up and down the road.

'No one,' Ava says, not wanting to give anything away. 'I guess she's right.'

Cate leans against the wall and pulls off her shoes, rubbing at her feet. 'God, my feet are killing me.' She picks some gravel out. 'Go for a wee-wee now,' she tells Ava.

'Okay.' Ava squirms at being talked to like a child.

'That's what you get for taking off the heels and putting back on your sensible shoes this morning,' Lauren says, as they all look down to Cate's feet, clad in flat brogues.

'I can't exactly do the school run in stilettos,' she replies, watching as Ava throws her leg over the wall and clambers to the other side. Suddenly reminded of her family back at home, she snorts. 'I'm sure Lily must think I've completely lost my mind. I still haven't checked in, and it's after lunch now.'

'I'm not having a go at you, but does she not think you're taking care of your best friend during the worst time in her life? I'm sure she's not remotely concerned. Lily is pretty cool, from what I remember,' Lauren says impatiently.

'What is it to you anyway if I want to check in?' Cate snaps.

'Nothing, just feels a bit . . . weird.' Lauren shivers for dramatic effect.

'Weird? That I want to check on my sick kids?'

'They aren't sick, you said one of them had a bit of a cold,' Lauren challenges deliberately, taking her on again.

'Just because you have no one to check in with doesn't make me a weirdo,' Cate says.

'No, but your constant need to talk to your wife does.' Lauren scowls, all earlier apologies forgotten.

'Shut up, both of you! Just keep a look out!' Ava hisses from her squatting position behind the bush.

'Here's a car!' Lauren squints at the reflection behind her. 'Or is it a van? Hurry up! Pee faster!'

'I can't!' Ava hisses. 'You have me on edge. Now I can't go!' She grimaces and Lauren stands out in the middle of the road.

'Jesus, Lauren, you'll get run over!' Cate says, appalled.

'I need to use my phone for work. You need to phone home to survive.' Lauren points to the oncoming vehicle. 'We need a lift to the nearest town. End of.'

'How am I going to wipe?' Ava asks.

'Use a bloody leaf, if you have to!' Lauren says as the vehicle gets nearer. They can hear faint music now, accompanying the sound of the engine as it gets louder.

'Sounds like a travelling rave is approaching,' Ava pipes up, struggling to coordinate her dress and dainty wedding knickers as the music booms even louder.

'Is it a mobile disco?' Lauren asks, a flash of excitement in her eyes.

'No. But it is an ice-cream van!' Cate says, hand perched over her eyes now.

'Get off the road! I'm not stopping an ice-cream van playing that godforsaken rave music!' Cate moves away, but Lauren doesn't budge. 'Do you have a death wish?'

'We have no choice, Cate. And I've made a decision. I'm going to text Stefan!' Ava jumps out beside Lauren.

'This is insane!' Cate howls. 'I'm not doing this.' She climbs behind the wall to join Ava.

'Watch the pee!' Ava warns her.

'Too late!' Cate raises her sensible shoe; its laces are wet.

'And, Cate, might I remind you of the time we hitched from Salthill to Connemara a few years ago, after you hooked up with that girl at the local disco the night before? Shifted her to "The Lady In Red" and everyone in the hall was straining to get a good look at the pair of yiz! Remember how you made us help you track her down. Remember yer one Tara Durkin, Ava? The girl of your dreams, you called her, Cate, you thought she looked like Wonder Woman. We did that for you,' Lauren calls.

Ava remembers, nodding in agreement.

'When I was twenty-six years old, Lauren. It wasn't exactly a few years ago. I'm almost forty now and the mother of three young boys.'

'And a wife to Lily, don't forget that. You are also a wife to Lily!' Lauren holds up her finger, enjoying this. 'How can you fathom being away from your wife and kids for a whole twenty-four hours, Cate? How will they survive? *Who* is going to cut up their sausages?'

'Shag off, Lauren, I don't cut up their sausages . . .'

'Eh, the last time I was in your house you did, and you sugared Lily's tea, gave it a stir, then tasted it for her.' Lauren is on a roll.

Cate is getting more and more irritated. 'Do you know what, Lauren? I'm *so* glad we don't hang out any more! There's so much more to me than just my wife and kids. And you know what? It's you I feel sorry for. Sorry that you're so desperate to be noticed. Sorry that you're as single as a lone sniper and clearly oh so bitter about it. Don't hate on me for being happy, twisted sister!'

Cate looks over the wall and sees she's pushed her too far. Lauren's eyes well up.

'Oh, look, I'm sorry, Lauren. That was so out of order.' Cate tries to get over the wall to speak to Lauren, cringing at what she's just said. She makes it and hugs her friend.

Tears are streaming down Lauren's cheeks. 'I'm sorry too, Cate. I'm just winding you up, you should know that.' She gulps. 'But, hey, thanks for all those really lovely compliments. Who needs enemies with friends like . . .' Lauren's voice cracks.

'You started it, you always start it,' Cate quips.

'How can you say that when I . . .'

'It *is* an ice-cream van!' Cate cuts her off.

The rave-machine ice-cream van screeches to a halt, and the girls walk towards it, brushing away their tears.

'By the way, Avz,' Lauren says, stopping Ava briefly. 'A few minutes ago you said you had to text *Stefan* instead of Simon. A Freudian slip, yeah?'

'No, I meant Stefan. How did I not see what was staring me in the face? How am I so stupid? I really need to talk to him.'

Ava's smile is suddenly wild.

10

Don't Judge a Boy by His Ice Cream Van.

'I'M ACTUALLY AFRAID TO ASK IF THIS DAY can get any more bizarre?' Ava stands with her hands on her hips, her red and black dress billowing in the breeze.

'The universe works in mysterious ways,' Lauren says, walking down the middle of the road towards the van. 'You know, I've often thought that someone should invent ice-cream vans for adults but, like, one that serves wine, a wine-scream-van. Nice ring to it, no? Can you imagine the stampede of stressed-out mammies running out of their houses chasing the van when they hear that familiar music coming up the street?' Lauren laughs.

'Not all mammies are wine-aholics!' Cate reprimands her.

But then a ruggedly handsome guy jumps out of the driver's side. The three watch him as he fixes a large piece of thick rope that appears to be holding the van doors together.

'Nice day for a stroll, ladies. How are yiz? I'm Tommo! Out for a stroll or do yiz need a lift? Where are ye headed?' Tall, with floppy black hair and dark stubble, he extends his hand towards Lauren.

'Lauren?' Ava nudges her. Lauren doesn't move.

'Don't tell me, for the first time all day, she's lost for words?' Cate stares at Lauren, who seems to be completely hypnotised by the vision that is Tommo.

'Hiya, Tommo, I'm Ava. And these are my friends, Lauren and Cate. Thanks for stopping. That's our Range Rover broken down back there,' Ava tells him, gesturing towards the other two.

'Guessed as much. So yiz are looking for a lift, I take it? Where to? Deadly outfits, by the way!' Tommo pulls up his sagging black and white striped tracksuit bottoms. 'Nearly as smart as mine.'

'Eh, hi, eh, Tommo, well, we're not quite sure where we are at the moment. Like Ava said, Lauren's car broke down and we just need a lift into the nearest town. I'm desperate to ring home and there's no phone coverage. We're also escaping a cheating groom, our friend Ava here bailed on her wedding yesterday, but we're still going on her honeymoon ...' Cate is nervously babbling on, filling the awkward moment.

'Jesus, Cate, shut up!' Ava punches Cate on the arm. 'Over-sharing, much?'

'Ow! I was just explaining!' Cate rubs her arm, frowning at her friend.

'Sorry,' Ava whispers. 'What Cate is *trying* to say, Tommo, is that we need a lift to pretty much anywhere at this stage, somewhere we can phone a mechanic. Isn't that right, Lauren? *Lauren?*'

'It surrrre is,' Lauren replies, her voice a purr as she twists her hair around her index finger suggestively.

'Oh good God, make it stop.' Cate rolls her eyes.

'Well, I'm heading on to Clare, so I can drop yiz at the next hotel. Or a petrol station? Wi-Fi in these parts is still non-existent, mad in 2019 but there you go ... Welcome to rural Ireland.' Tommo shakes his head. 'Add that to the new drink-driving laws, where a remote farmer can't even drive to his local pub for a single pint after a hard day's graft, and you've an angry rural Ireland.' Smirking, he jogs backwards to the van. Pulling the frayed rope on the side of the van he swings the back doors open.

'Git, we've got company! Tidy yourself up! Come on, girls. Hop in!' He gestures for them to enter.

'We can't. It's too risky,' Cate hisses.

'He seems ... nice,' Ava whispers back, as Lauren struts past them towards Tommo

'Nice? Jeffrey Dahmer seemed nice. Even Hannibal Lector was charming. Look at how Clarice nearly fell for him, and she was an FBI trainee! Plus you still have the remains of a unibrow and he never commented on that. What does that say about him?' Cate continues, in a flurry of anxiety.

Ava rubs her head as she moves to the door and cautiously peers inside. Cate tight on her shoulder.

'I think we're safe enough, Cate,' Ava reassures her.

'For the record, I'm definitely not on board with this plan. They could be axe murderers or sex traffickers,' Cate hisses fearfully to Ava.

'I wouldn't worry, Cate, I think you are a little old for kidnapping and the other,' Lauren snips.

'That's not even funny, Lauren!' Cate scowls in disgust.

'And that would be?' Ava asks, pointing tentatively to a young man wearing pyjama bottoms and nothing else, lying face down in the back of the van. He appears to be asleep, but is still clutching a vape in one hand.

'That's Git. And Git is ... well, just being Git!' Tommo adds, winking at Ava, who is still rubbing her sore head madly.

'Have ya a headache?' Tommo asks her.

'No. Hangover. Is he stoned?' Ava asks, pointing towards Git.

'Ava! Remember your manners!' Lauren interrupts.

'No, no ... just off the ciggies three months, so like everyone in his position there is a vape constantly glued to his hand,' Tommo tells them. 'At least with the cigarettes ya only had one when the nicotine craving kicked in. This vape scene is crazy stuff altogether – a fella I know vapes in his sleep!'

'You two hop in there,' Lauren says, gently pushing Ava and Cate into the back of the van with the pyjama-clad Git. 'I'll sit up front with Tommo. Don't worry.'

'It reeks in here!' Cate protests through the closed doors.

'Spilt milk!' Tommo calls in. 'Nothing I do will get rid of that smell.' He gets in and sniffs the air. 'Sorry about that, ladies.' He sniffs again as Lauren clambers into the passenger seat beside him.

'You don't mind if I sit up front, do you, Tommo?' she asks, flirting, as she pulls on her seatbelt.

'Oh, Lauren, you are shameless!' Cate tuts.

'It would be my honour, Your Highness!' Tommo smiles at his new passenger and starts the engine.

'Love what you've done with the wheels,' Lauren comments, Cate snorting with laughter in the back.

'What's with driving an ice-cream van?' Cate butts in.

'Why not?' Tommo responds.

'Exactly! I admire that mentality!' Lauren positively beams at him.

'Actually, I'm going to Clare, too, Tommo,' Ava shouts impulsively up to Tommo from her bench-like seat against the metal wall of the van.

'Ava!' Cate hisses. 'I am *not* staying in an ice-cream van with these two weirdos for the next hour!'

'No problem, *senorita*! We're going to see the Clare versus Dublin hurling game. We can drop you off along the way. Wherever you're going, like. . .' Tommo turns to her, holding the wheel with one hand.

'Don't worry. You don't have to come. We can drop you at the next town,' Ava reassures Cate.

'So I can do what? Beg for a lift from another random stranger? Great suggestion,' Cate mutters, incredulous.

'So you can call Lily and she can strap the three boys in their car seats and come rescue you. She's only two and a half hours away. You aren't in outer Mongolia,' Ava replies, clutching on to the side of the seat as Tommo takes a sharp corner. Cate's phone beeps multiple times and she twists to tug it from her coat pocket.

'Phone coverage! Hallelujah!'

'Is it Stefan?' Ava asks, holding tight to her chest.

'I don't know him. How would I know his number? And how would he have mine?' Cate looks strangely at Ava.

'Oh, of course …'

'Here, call him, text him, tweet him, whatever, just hurry up, I need to call home!' Cate offers her phone.

'I would, but I don't I know his number and Lauren still won't give me my phone back!' Ava bangs her head gently against the back of the van. 'Although I could call the gallery, maybe?'

'You aren't calling anyone, we're taking time out. New horizons …' Lauren tells her from the front. 'Personal space is needed. Cate is right.'

'What?' Cate looks up from her phone. 'Do my ears deceive me? I'm *right*?' Cate puts one hand behind her ear.

'And I'll go all the way to Clare with you, Ava, if you want.' Lauren turns her head, beaming at Ava.

'You're too kind, Lauren, seriously, so selfless … always thinking of others.' Ava smiles sarcastically in appreciation.

'Ha! Of course she is.' Cate snorts.

'Ah, don't mention it. Sure, that's what friends are for.' Lauren inches her body closer to Tommo's as Cate shouts into her phone.

'Lily! Darling, it's me … Oh! Hi, boys! It's me, Mummy! Mummy's in an ice-cream van!'

11

She's a Maniac . . .

'THANK LILY FOR ME, WON'T YOU?' Ava whispers to Cate as she wraps up her phone call.

'You got the gist of that, then?' Cate exhales and suddenly relaxes back into the hard seat, hauling her feet up so she doesn't stand on Git.

'She wants you to stay with me?' Ava guesses.

'She does, insisted actually, and she has put me completely at ease. She said the boys are absolutely fine. She sounded cool as a breeze, has a spag bol on, and herself and the kids were all watching *Peppa Pig* while she was giving my defrosted breast milk to a very chilled-out Max. Not a bother on him, she said!' Cate's face eases of her frown lines. 'Now if I could just find a chemist to sell me a breast pump . . .'

'See, the show goes on, Cate. It always does,' Lauren calls from the front, winding down the window.

'Thanks for your concern, Lauren. You really are a martyr for the cause. All okay up there, Tommo? Still alive?' Cate shouts back sarcastically.

'Peachy keen, Jimmy Dean,' Lauren answers, channelling Rizzo from *Grease*.

'I'd never admit this to Lauren, but she was right . . . I didn't think Lily would be able to cope,' Cate whispers to Ava.

'Ever give her an actual chance?' Ava asks her, fidgeting with her mother's ring on her finger.

'Well, no, not really, now that you say it. Guess I'm used to being in charge at home. I want to do it all, Ava, is that so wrong? That was the deal. Lily is the breadwinner and works her fabulous ass off at the restaurant for really long hours. I'm the stay-at-home mum, but I suppose sometimes it does get a bit ... a bit ...'

'Monotonous?' Ava offers.

'Yeah, you could say that. It can be so isolating. It's tough having the kids for company *all* the time, ya know? I can't believe I just said that out loud ...' She shakes her head.

'Which is why you desperately need to make some time for yourself to get out and have conversations with adults! Those boys will be grown up before you can say *I-Never-Left-The-House-For-Eighteen-Years.*' Ava tilts her head, as Cate grabs her two swollen breasts and winces.

'I really have to pump soon and, I know, I just wish, sometimes ...' Cate leans far forward on the hard seat, but is rudely interrupted.

'What the actual ... ?' The bare-chested young man surfaces from the floor of the van. A ginger beard so full his face and features are barely visible appears before them.

'Who the ... ?' He rubs his eyes as he spots Cate from the floor.

'Hi ... G-Git, isn't it?' Ava asks the crawling man who is now staring intently at Cate.

'What the? Is this an apparition?' He rubs his eyes roughly again.

'Hiiiii ...' Ava tries again, with a small wave of her hand.

'Am I in Tír na nÓg? Historically dreaming?' He rubs his eyes vigorously, then gets to his stripy pyjama-clad knees, his eyes never leaving Cate.

'Are you ... okay?' Cate asks, more than a little concerned at his behaviour.

'Oh, more than okay. You're an absolute vision,' he replies slowly.

Cate clears her throat and inches back on her seat nervously, crossing her legs.

'Oh, well ... why, thank you ... Git,' Cate says, running a licked finger across her hairline.

'Wow ... what a stunner.' Git moves on his knees towards Cate, who can't help but look rather pleased with the compliment.

'What are you doing here? Are you a model?' Git kneels in front of her, his green eyes alight.

'Me?' Cate looks from her left to her right. 'Nooo, no way ... a model, me? Stop!'

'That body ...' Git mumbles, staring open-mouthed at her as Lauren swings her head around from the front seat.

'You might want to close your coat there, Cate. Your sexy lace undies are on show like Melanie Griffith in *Working Girl*,' she cackles.

'Oh, Cate, your coat is open! I'm so sorry, I didn't notice.' Ava leans across and tugs Cate's coat together to cover her.

'Oh, Jesus Christ!' Cate gasps as she uncrosses her legs and wraps the belt of her trench coat firmly to cover up her black underwear.

'No, it was beautiful ... You are a work of art,' Git tells her solemnly.

'I-I am a married mother. I do have clothes, but I didn't get to put them on because the rat was on me!' Cate beseeches Ava's help with her eyes.

'Yeah, Cate doesn't normally parade around in her sexy undies, Git. Long story short, we had to escape a rat-infested mobile home in a hurry. Just need to get to my new place in Clare and we can all change and stuff,' Ava explains, as Git pulls himself up onto the bench in the back to sit beside Cate.

'Well, I apologise profusely, Cate. I would never have looked if I had known that. I'm not that kind of man. Sure, I have daughters! You believe me, don't you? I'm one hundred per cent a non-pervo!' Git earnestly tries to reassure her.

'It's fine ... not your fault ... Git.' Cate smiles at him, blushing.

'Oh, thank God. You can't be too careful what ya say these days, and rightly so! I treat every woman I meet nowadays the same way I'd treat a man. Not that I fancy men, but ... I am aware you have to think before you speak. So, what do you do for a living?' he asks her, swerving away more talk of goddesses.

'I'm a mammy, full time,' Cate replies, matter-of-fact.

'Cool, yeah, but what do you do for yourself?' He stares into her eyes with such intensity. Cate smooths down her unruly red hair with both hands nervously.

'I – I well, I ... I get a takeaway cappuccino and a fruit scone every morning after I drop the kids to school while I read the noticeboard in SuperValu. Eh, I love reading when the baby is asleep. I watch *Dr Phil* ... sometimes ... every day ...' Cate's voice trails off.

'Yeah.' Git nods enthusiastically. 'Love a good fruit scone meself.' He rubs his beard. 'You *could* be a model by the way,' he adds, sincerely. 'And that's not sexist. I'd say that to a good-looking man, too. I've told Tommo that before, haven't I, Tommo?'

'Ya have, Git, in fairness. Fierce man for the compliments!' Tommo calls back.

'Stop the lights.' Cate licks her lips and laughs a flirty laugh she doubts she has ever heard come out of her mouth before.

'I mean it, not just the crazy powerful body. You're stunning. Like Helen of Troy.' He pulls at his beard again.

'I am not!' Cate protests, her voice several octaves too high.

'Jeez, Cate, I hope the windows don't shatter in the van,' Lauren remarks.

'Bite me, Lauren,' Cate shoots back.

'So, what do you do, Git?' Ava swoops in – to save Cate.

'I'm a dad, a Blackpool FC superfan and a wannabe gardener at the weekends,' Git tells them, as he slaps his hands together. 'Green fingers, that's what I have.' He wiggles his long fingers.

'How many kids do you have?' Cate asks him.

'I have three, a boy and twin girls. Will, and Leontia and Fiona,' Git replies.

'Leontia? What a gorgeous name!' Cate adds. 'So unusual. Bet she's gorgeous too!'

'Ah, she is, named after a Roman saint. They're all little smashers, all three of them. Myself and their ma split up a few years ago, but we've worked it all out between us, got a civil relationship going on now ... thankfully,' Git adds proudly, making the sign of the cross.

'Going to drop the girls off first, Git, and then head back up to the match, yeah?' Tommo calls in.

'Deadly, Tommo, bud.' Git gives him the two thumbs-up as he pads on his knees to the front of the van towards Tommo and Lauren. 'Sorry I nodded off, pal, haven't been getting much sleep lately, ya know yourself. Fecking box sets. I stick on one show and binge until it's four in the mornin'!'

'You dropped off as soon as we got past Newlands Cross, ten minutes after I picked ya up. A highly reliable co-pilot, what?' Tommo laughs.

'Ah, thanks, Tommo, needed that kip. Will's not sleeping great either, ya know. He took it the worst, me moving out. He's seven now, but still wetting the bed at night, so I'm up half the night changing sheets, washing him down in the bath and cuddling him back to sleep when I have them at my place.'

'Oh, Git, I so get it.' Cate's face crinkles in sympathy and Ava leans back against the cold metal of the ice-cream van.

'It'll all be grand. Just a phase.' Git's tone puts an end to the conversation.

After a pause, Ava turns to Cate. 'Imagine,' she says. 'It just hits me in waves. Simon still hasn't called my dad to talk to me, has he? Hasn't even called my dad's landline?'

'Bizarre.' Cate shakes her head. 'But, I think that says it all.'

'He's too selfish to face me. Isn't that insane? How can he not even write an email to apologise? Or check in to see if I'm all right? If my dad is all right?' Ava picks at the shreds of the remaining French polish on her fingernails.

'Maybe he's just not a good guy, after all,' Cate offers gently.

'He definitely isn't what you'd call a regular guy, that's the thing … he's not living on the same planet as we are. He's so completely lost in this façade that he's more important than everyone else, that he will not conform to societal values. Like he genuinely thinks he's above the regular tax-paying eejits like us. He sees himself as a working class hero. Oh, and he's absolutely certain himself and the band will headline Croke Park one day. So, right here, in this ice-cream van, I, Ava O'Hara, am stating out loud that I now realise how delusional I have been.'

'What do you mean?' Cate asks.

'Well, I think in a way he semi-brainwashed me into believing his theories, too. Ten years of listening to "When we make it big again" or "We're better than The Script", when it was never going to happen, was it, Cate?' Ava snorts.

Cate shakes her head slowly. 'I don't think so; reckon Seventh Hour had their fifteen minutes of fame. Let's be honest.'

'So, what was I going to do? Was I going to marry him and support him for the rest of his life?'

'Highly likely …' Cate's tone is soothing.

'I – everyone told me, but I didn't listen. My dad never liked him . . . Stefan didn't like him from the get-go, and I trust Stefan's opinion more than anything –'

'Stefan's opinion?' Cate is intrigued.

'Yeah . . .'

Cate holds Ava's gaze. 'Go on?' she encourages her.

'And . . . and the really scary thing is . . .' Ava holds her forehead. 'I think I really like Stefan, Cate. Like, in *that* way.'

'W-w-what?!' Cate says, as Lauren's head spins around again.

'Told ya! B.I.N.G.O. Bingo! Knew it!' Lauren sing-songs.

'Really?' Cate is wide-eyed. 'This must just be rebound stuff, you know, Ava. A way of protecting yourself or your heart, no?'

'It's not. Trust me. I mean, he's just amazing. In every way. So good to me. The thing is, I was never open to even considering anything because I was marrying Simon. And then Stefan saw some sketches I did of him in my portfolio – I can't even tell you about that yet, the mortification is still so real – so he knows I have a major thing for . . . or, well, I'm certainly in lust with him. And just as this realisation all comes together in my head, he falls for some random girl.' Ava claps her hands over her eyes with the horror of it all.

'Call him! You need to talk to him on the level, and be honest! What have you got to lose?' Cate urges, waving her phone in the air.

'My already battered pride maybe? That's what I'm most nervous about. What if I misread things? If I ruin everything?' Ava wonders. 'Anyway, I don't even know his number.'

'Easy. Call the gallery, like you said!'

'I don't know what to say.' Ava shakes her head.

'Just go for it. It'll come to you!' Cate urges.

'I can't.' Ava shakes her head. 'Anyway, the gallery is closed today.'

'Why do you think you might be falling for this fella?' Tommo joins in the conversation from the front of the van, turning down the music to listen.

'Why?' Ava leans her head back, but keeps her eyes shut tight. 'For starters, he came with me to pick my wedding dress, even though I sort of suspected he might sort of have a thing for me. He respects me that much ... He tells me all the time how talented I am ... He makes me look at the world in the best light, literally. He just wants me to be happy. And, Jesus, he is so unbelievably sexy. I look at him and I just ...' Ava opens her eyes now and physically shivers.

'Sound enough reasons for me!' Tommo says.

'Look, let's just get to Edenvale and get showered and changed, and make a plan from there? If someone can maybe lend me something to wear ...' Cate suggests. 'I'm over being dressed like a late-night kerb-crawler, and I'm also starving out of my mind. I mean, I'd eat a scabby man's leg through a gate. We haven't eaten since ...' Cate looks appalled. 'Since yesterday!'

'Welcome to my world, Cate!' Lauren says. 'I always detox for twenty-four hours before a big event. Torture! I thought for a long time it was my dryer that was making my clothes shrink – turns out, it was the fridge! My metabolism isn't what it once was, that's for damn sure.' She sighs dramatically.

'I've actually got a little bit of my appetite back now, food would be good! And thanks so much for coming with me, girls. Honestly, you'll never know how much I appreciate you two not abandoning me too,' Ava tells them, her eyes welling up.

'Sounds like you've got a heavy load on your shoulders, Ava. I'm sorry, but let me tell you: I've thought about running away more as an adult than I ever did as a kid!' Tommo tells her from the front.

'How true that is!' Cate agrees, laughing.

'It has been ... eye-opening, Tommo. Guess it's not every day you run away from your own wedding,' Ava muses.

'I can *only* imagine, a bride squad runaway, what? On that note, can I interest you ladies in a nice cold beverage?' Git extends his bare foot and pulls a black cooler bucket across the floor of the van.

'Yes, please, sir!' Lauren calls back. 'I'm in!'

'I better not, but thanks anyway,' Cate says.

'Go on then, I will too, I'm actually parched!' Ava watches as he clicks open the box to reveal a stacked pile of green cans of Heineken piled to the top, plumes of icy mist emerge.

'Oh, perfect! I could use some Vitamin H!' Ava says gleefully.

'Ah, go on, Cate, take a walk on the wild side for a change!' Lauren calls back.

'No ... I can't ... I – I don't want a drink at lunchtime, but hey, you all go ahead.'

'Fifty-five minutes to destination, lads! I'll pull in as soon as we get to a village. I'm starvin' myself and we'll keep an eye out for a chemist for you, Cate? Throw me up a bottle of water, will ya, Git?' Tommo asks.

'That would be great, Tommo,' Cate replies.

Ava pulls back the ring pull on her can and takes a swig as it fizzes over.

'Deal. Now, who's up for a bit of yeah, yeah funky yeah?' Tommo asks, as Lauren hands him a bottle of water and they all raise their hands rapidly in response.

'Yes! Yessss! That's my song!' Cate roars, startling Ava with her enthusiasm.

'Jesus, Cate! Keep yer wig on!' Ava laughs.

'Cate? The raver? Wonders will never cease.' Lauren's head spins round as she smirks at the commotion.

'Greatest song of all time, if you ask me. I'm with Cate there.'

140

Git nods vigorously and punches the air. 'Hit it, Tommo! Blast it, bud ... Are you ready?'

'Standby!' Tommo presses a few buttons on Spotify as the others sip the cold beers and 'Maniac 2000' booms in.

'*She's a maniac ... She's a maniac.*'

They all chant the lyrics at the tops of their voices as the vibrating ice-cream van tears along the country road.

12

Hello Whiskey, Goodbye Dignity.

'WHAT EXACTLY IS THIS PLACE?' Ava asks Tommo.

'The ... Ennis Bridge Hotel?' he says, wiping grime from the sign on the wall, as he hands Cate a brown paper bag.

'Eh, thanks.' Cate looks at him, eyes narrowed.

'Why is it so dark?' Lauren holds onto Tommo's arm, as they push open a door at the end of a long musty carpeted corridor.

Inside a disco is in full swing, the dance floor packed to capacity with elderly locals twirling on the floor. Stiffly permed curls and Brylcreem'd hair spin past them as they stand looking on in awe.

'So much talent!' Cate says. Then, at last looking into the bag, 'Oh, Tommo, you're a total lifesaver! I'll be right back!'

'So much ... old people,' Lauren remarks.

'Look!' Ava points at a banner. 'Over 70s Day Disco.'

'If my nightclub days turn into a day disco when I'm over seventy, well, let me just go walk off the Cliffs of Moher ... like, right now.' Lauren looks horrified at the sight before her.

'Aw, what is wrong with you, McCabe? I think it's so cute!' Ava gushes. 'Look how in time they all are! How happy! And look at love's young dream!' She points to an elderly couple waltzing around the room flawlessly to Neil Diamond. And they stand, transfixed by the dancers, as Cate returns.

'Where have you been?' Ava asks. 'You look like you've just won the lottery.'

'Pumping! Oh, the sheer joy of it.' Cate waves the damp paper bag at the girls. 'Tommo bought me a pump!'

'Okaaayyy . . . I mean it, if I *ever* utter the words, "Who's coming with me to the day disco?", just shoot me, like, immediately,' Lauren warns, deadly serious.

'That's so sad, what do you want to be when you're seventy? Cher?'

'Yes, Cate! Cher! That's exactly what I want to be. Whatever it takes. I want to be just like Cher!' Lauren nods, her head bobbing.

'Saddo . . .' Cate makes a face at her.

'Where's the bar in this hotel, Tommo? And for the love of God, don't say "This is it"!' Lauren lets go of his arm.

'No, I have your back, Lauren. There's another bar next door, if I remember correctly. Now, it isn't anything fancy like you lot are used to in Dublin, but . . .'

'I don't really like *fancy*, Tommo, it reminds me of work.' She links his arm again.

'Shameless.' Cate can't help but laugh as Tommo gestures to everyone to follow him and they exit the Day Disco and step into Fitzgerald's pub next door.

★ ★ ★

'Hang on a minute here, is this for real?' Lauren stops dead in her tracks, as she steps into the hallway. 'Fitzgerald's Bar has separate men's and women's bar areas?' She gestures to the individual 'Men' and 'Ladies' signs above the two frosted glass lounge doors as they enter. 'Did we just hop in a time machine and go back to the 1950s?'

'Don't worry, we'll go into the Ladies lounge area with you, girls. And yep, it's weird, but I presume they've had these rules for donkey's years ... Almost like heirlooms. Not to be taken too seriously, I'd imagine. I just want a good pint of Guinness, don't care where it's pulled,' Tommo adds, looking at Git for support.

'Yup, yeah, a few pints, a bit of craic, I tell ye something, my first weekend off from the kids in months and I've got a fierce thirst on me. I normally spend the weekend exhausted and standing pitch side.' Git nods firmly. 'I'm happy to go into either bar, sure I'm all about equality. And eh, not saying the wrong thing!'

'Nice to see you've changed out of your jammies, Git. Wouldn't recognise you in those jeans!' Ava slags Git.

'Steady on, sister suffragettes, where do you think you're going?' Lauren holds out her arm firmly to stop Ava and Cate in their tracks as they turn to head towards the Ladies bar entrance.

'Well, that sign says Men, so I'm guessing it's a really old-fashioned bar, probably where the auld fellas hang out, smelling of Guinness farts. The lounge is over here, so ...' Ava offers, trying to avoid a scene.

'If you think for one minute that I'm joining the bingo brigade in the Ladies lounge there, you've got another thing coming!' Lauren adjusts her outfit.

'She's right, I'm afraid, Ava, I have to stand with her on this one,' Cate chimes in, defiantly.

'*This* way, girls! You too, Tommo and Git.' Lauren instructs the group with a serious demeanour, swinging the door to the Men's bar open. The cheering inside stops and every man in the room turns to stare at them. Various hurling supporters sit huddled at tall tables, and older men sit at the bar drinking Guinness. A single dart flies by and hits the board.

'Oh my God,' Ava mutters under her breath to Cate.

'Jaysus, Noel, did they not read the sign?' A toothless elderly man pipes up, nudging his friend beside him.

'Okay, now I'm totally cringing and just want to get out of here. And I was right about the smell!' Ava mutters and sheepishly stands behind Lauren, who ignores her and waves down the male bartender.

'Ahoy! Hi, there, can I get two pints of Guinness, and what are you having, girls?' Lauren asks politely, turning her head over her shoulder to get the orders in.

'Not sure if you saw the sign there, but you may prefer the lounge next door?' the young barman suggests, uncomfortably avoiding direct eye contact with Lauren. A middle-aged American man, wearing a thick, cream Aran sweater with a grey tweed cap, stands up from a large table of men wearing Clare jerseys and swaggers across the bar dramatically.

'Yo! He said, not sure if you saw the sign there, young lady, but you are, in fact, in the men's section of the bar? Ladies is next door,' he bellows.

'Oh, I can read, thank you very much.' Lauren turns to face him. 'Putting letters together to form words, hard as it is, I have accomplished. Guess I just assumed we weren't in a ridiculous sexist time warp. Imagine that, a group of women who dare cross the men's sacred threshold?'

'Leave it, Lauren.' Ava puts her hand on her friend's arm.

'Oh, and she's feisty too, lads. A modern-day Maureen O' Hara if you's don't mind.' The American laughs and turns around to his friends, who all laugh back in support. 'Are ye in some sort of fancy dress?' he asks sarcastically, looking them all up and down.

'Um … we'll just go grab a table. Or we can go somewhere else, no worries, yeah?' Git says to Ava.

'No going back now – this is the Bull McCabe in action, Git. Lauren doesn't back down! Go hide at a table somewhere; I know you hate trouble. But I highly recommend you watch from a distance,' Cate whispers, winking at Git. He and Tommo disappear to the back of the bar.

'Lauren, let's just get out of here. I'm mortified dressed like this, and the yank is making a bloody show of us.' Ava looks to Cate, who is staring the obnoxious American down.

'Lauren! Come on, let's just go somewhere else, no place is worth this grief.' Ava tries one last time. 'I've enough drama in my life for now, thank you very much.' She rubs her temples, the stress of it making her feel faint.

'Now listen here, Mr Quiet Man. Why don't you just crawl back to your Guinness and leave me and my friends in peace, we just want to have a few quiet drinks. We've been dealing with a lot.' Lauren's voice is raised a little, as she turns to face the American, her hands on her hips.

'Well, let me explain it very simply to you, young lady. We have rules in this bar. Rules that have been abided by in here for decades. Us men like to have our few pints in peace. No nagging. No trouble. No women. Just us, the black stuff, some old-fashioned male company and banter. Isn't that right, boys?' The American's drawl sounds aggravated as he looks around the bar. The other punters drop their eyes to newspapers, beer mats – anything – while others avoid his gaze by looking up at the television screen.

'Oh, now I get it. We're in a gay bar?' Lauren quips back, smirking.

'A gay bar? Hell, no!' he protests, a little too firmly for Cate's liking, who straightens up.

'You're not even Irish!' Cate's voice bellows from behind Lauren.

'Excuse me?' The American looks shocked, turning to face Cate.

'You have the strangest Clare accent I've ever heard. And by

146

the way, sir, *no one* wears Aran jumpers in Ireland. NO ONE!' Cate tut-tuts at him.

'I'm as Irish as you are!' the American gasps. 'Been living in Clare for twenty years and counting.' He commands the room as he turns, the locals surrounding him all nodding to confirm this fact.

'Were you born in Ireland?' Cate steps up to ask him.

'Well, no, but my ancestors were, to be sure,' the American mutters.

'Oh, here we go again, with the "Oirish" shite!' Lauren rolls her eyes.

'Can you recite "The Lake Isle of Innisfree"?' Cate challenges him.

'Well ...'

'If you're Irish, like you claim, the answer should be an instant, "Yes, ma'am!"' Lauren shouts, triumphant.

'I will arise and go now ...' Ava starts him off.

'I know it ...' The American rubs his nose roughly.

'In your own time, so,' Cate says, folding her arms.

'I will arise and go now, and go to Innisfree, where a small cabin built there, of clay and waffles made ...' he proclaims loudly.

'Waffles?' Cate stops him mid-flow. 'Did you actually say waffles?' She laughs into the collar of her trench coat, as Lauren dissolves into fits of laughter.

Ava jumps in to diffuse the rising tension. 'It's wattles. W-A-T-T-L-E-S. We won, I think, so let's live and let live, yeah? Come on, girls.'

The American ignores her. He turns his attention to Cate, and looks up and down with disdain. 'Who are you? One of those gender fluids, I'm guessing?' he spits.

Cate moves her neck from side to side and shoves her hands in her coat pockets. 'Cate, that's who I am. Cate with a C – it's

trendier. And it's none of your business who else I am, you igno-
rant ass. My entire life I've put up with enough ridiculous rules
and insults. I've marched more times for my rights than you have
had bacon and cabbage.' Her voice rises as she hits her stride.
'So, listen here, you, there's only one thing to prove your true
Irishness ... Irish car bombs, you and me. Whoever can throw
back the most wins. And when I win, we'll stay, and that'll be the
end of this male chauvinist bullshit.'

'Cate!' Ava throws her head back in shock.

'Ava?' Cate moves to the bar and squeezes herself in between
two old men bending over the bar with crooked backs. 'I am not
to be messed with, okay? I've been instructed by my wife and
kids to do whatever I damn well want this weekend and that's
what I am doing. *Go, do what you used to do together, find your
smile*, that's what Lily told me!'

'My boss Mags told me the exact same thing!' Ava says, her
face still shocked.

'Right, this is on!' Cate turns now and waves to the young,
highly amused barman.

Ava finds Lauren in the crowd gathering and whispers in her
ear. 'Oh no, she's totally screwed now. We all are!'

'Deal!' the American adds confidently, slapping his hand down
on the bar. 'Lay them out there, Peter,' he instructs the barman,
who lines up glasses of Guinness and drops shots of Irish liqueur
and whiskey into the top of each glass. 'This will be a quick
slaughter!'

'You don't have to do this, Cate. You don't even drink any
more!' Ava hisses.

'You can do this, Cate!' Lauren deliberately contradicts.

'And let the games begin!' the barman announces with a smile.
'On your marks ... down them!'

Ava is cringing, a look of serious concern on her face. 'They're

Irish car bombs, Lauren! She doesn't drink any more! She'll end up in hospital getting her stomach pumped! Lily will go through me for a shortcut!'

'Shush, I've never been prouder! Let her have her moment. She needs to find her old self again. Unleash her suppressed wild side, even if it's just for one weekend. It will do her good,' Lauren hushes Ava, enthralled by Cate's unexpected act of defiance.

Meanwhile, Cate and the American grab their glasses at speed and lower them as fast as the barman can pull them.

'Oh my God, she's already slammed three!' Ava stares open-mouthed, watching Cate swiftly polish off the drinks laid out before her. 'She's on a mission!'

'And that's five. How are we doing there, Mr American?' Lauren asks sarcastically. 'You appear to be in a little trouble. You're trailing behind our girl!'

'Never!' he retorts indignantly, but then he bends over as if he's going to vomit. Next thing, he's shouting, 'You win!' as he slams down his glass and bounds towards the bathroom door.

'You'll be needing the bathroom on the right side there, sunshine. Look for the sign that says Ladies,' Lauren catcalls after him, as the bar erupts in laughter.

'He's not a bad lad,' the barman tells the girls. 'He's just seen too many bad Irish movies.' He wipes down the wet counter top, as he collects the empties.

'He needed a mighty big dose of reality!' Cate replies.

'I think we have a winner!' The barman raises Cate's arm in victory. The bar applauds, as Cate staggers back to the girls, smiling widely.

'So now, another mighty battle won, sisters. Who said I wasn't a party animal any more?' She sits, then falls backwards off the stool.

13

#Unfiltered

'W E *HAVE* TO GET CATE HOME. SHE'S PLASTERED.'
'Leave her, she just fell off a stool, so what? Let she who has never fallen off a stool drunk cast the first stone. And look, she's having *fun*. Letting her hair down for a change! We'll go in twenty minutes or so. I've googled Edenvale and we can be there in a taxi in ten. There's a local taxi number above the ancient payphone in the corner. You weren't joking when you said it was remote. We need supplies, though, no? Oh, and we'll most definitely need soakage for yer one for tomorrow morning.' Lauren nods to Cate, who's propped up at the bar, leaning in dangerously close to Git.

'Is she . . . is she flirting with Git, Lauren?' Ava says, concerned.

'Hardly,' Lauren replies, uninterested.

'She bloody is!' Ava tips her to look around.

'Well, good . . .' Lauren shrugs.

'She's happily married, but really drunk. That's not my defini-tion of *good*!' Ava focuses on Cate, who is now tenderly stroking Git's ginger beard while laughing and hiccupping hysterically.

'Oh . . . actually, maybe not good.' Lauren's eyes narrow.

'Oh, shit.' Ava pushes her stool back and stands up. 'Git is two seconds away from making a move on her! Let's go!'

Ava watches in horror as Git's and Cate's lips almost meet.

Just in time, Lauren pulls Cate by her trench coat backwards. Cate, unsurprisingly, nearly topples over.

'Let's try to sit you down again, shall we?' Lauren says carefully, as she leads Cate back to the table. 'Sorry, Git, I think we'll leave you guys here for the moment,' Lauren calls back to him over her shoulder.

'Cate!' Ava sits opposite her friend, holding her knees tight. 'What are you playing at? He's a . . . a man! Are you okay? Get her a pint of iced water, Lauren.'

'Thanks for the clarification there!' Git says sarcastically, as Lauren passes to get to the bar for the water. He's looking more than disappointed the moment was interrupted.

Ava and Cate sit looking at each other.

'That was a close call!' Lauren smirks, as she sits back down and Cate gulps the water.

'Oh my God, I nearly snogged yer man Git. What in the name of God am I doing?' Cate exclaims, her eyes glazed.

'Letting go? Living a little? Experimenting?' Lauren suggests.

'I don't want to let go! Why do you seem to think my life is so bloody boring, Lauren?' Cate hiccups loudly.

'I don't, at all. In fact . . .' Lauren says.

'Guys, don't start,' Ava groans.

'Can anyone finish a sentence around here? I –' Lauren tries again.

But Cate hiccups loudly, interrupting. 'Anyway, what would you know about letting go? You get to let yourself go every day. Your whole life is one big let go.' Cate wobbles unsteadily on the stool again and gulps down more water.

'Is that right, Cate?' Lauren stares at her, back to her old adversarial self.

'Please don't fall off the stool again,' Ava warns her.

'Yes, it is right . . . you . . . you look down on me because I don't get Botox . . . because I don't mind looking my age . . . because I have three kids and a wife and a full-time job as a mammy. You think that's sad, don't you, Lauren?' Cate makes a face, her drunken eyes trying to focus on Lauren as she sways on the stool.

'I think you're drunk, Cate.'

'Isn't that what you wanted? Me to be drunk? Well, here I am . . . drunk Cate!' Cate throws her hands up in the air and wobbles again. Ava reaches out to steady her.

'This isn't the time for this conversation, girls. Someone give me a phone? I'm going outside to call my dad. Keep your hand on her, Lauren, will you?' says Ava, standing up.

'Don't assume anything about me, Cate Connolly, I mean it.' Lauren leans across the table at Cate and grits her teeth. Ava sits back down slowly.

'Guys, come on, not again,' Ava pleads, as Cate leans forward now too, both inches from the other's face.

'I'd hate your life, Lauren. Living alone, no partner, no one to Netflix and chill with, working every hour of the day for someone else's business . . .' Cate holds the pint glass of water tightly between her hands.

'That's my life now too, Cate, okay? Drop it,' Ava says, perplexed.

'At least you were attempting to get married and have kids, but Lauren . . . way too selfish. Always was.' Cate hiccups and rolls her eyes to heaven melodramatically.

'I'm just going to ignore that comment, Cate. You don't know anything about the real me. Nothing, nada.' Lauren is trying hard to shut her down, not wanting to fight any more.

'Whateverrrr,' Cate slurs, sticking her tongue out.

'Mature.' Lauren nods at her. 'You're right to stop drinking. It really doesn't suit you.'

'Is that so?' Cate sits up straight now. 'I'd say you pour the second you walk in your lonely front door at night.'

'Cate! Enough!' Ava snaps.

'No, keep going, you're on a roll.' Lauren nods, as if encouraging a nervous interviewee.

'Let's revisit this again when we are all back home in Dublin, yeah?' Ava tries again. 'Let's just all go out for a bite to eat. We can talk . . .'

'No, let her spill, and since we're at it, go for a bite and talk? That's a joke, I don't see you, Ava, ever! You just fell away from me into your life with The Tuner. You moved out of our flat and right out of our friendship.' Lauren bites her lip, but the truth is spilling out too fast now.

'What? That's so not true. You know how much I tried to keep our friendship together!' Ava protests, astonished as Cate hiccups herself silly.

'Do I? I don't think so. No, you didn't . . . you invited me out with you and Simon all the time. Like a third wheel. I have no friendship with Simon. In fact, I knew he didn't particularly like me, but you still kept trying to shove us together. I just wanted to spend time with you. Like we used to,' Lauren says, more softly now.

Cate starts waving her hand to speak, swaying on her stool, desperate to have her say.

'Well, if we're being totally honest here, Ava,' she hiccups, 'the reason I didn't accept your bridesmaid offer is I knew I'd look like a big blob next to Lauren, who always looks amazing.' She looks to Lauren. 'Hate to say it, but you do. But . . . but instead of holding my head up and pulling on two pairs of Spanx and owning my new mammy belly for the third time, I was willing to sit at home and feel sorry for myself.' Her voice is starting to slur, now full of self-pity.

'You look amazing, Cate,' Ava tells her, automatically. 'Sexy as hell.'

'Blah, I don't *feel* amazing ever. Not any more,' Cate continues. 'And sexy? Bollocks. I couldn't tell you the last time Lily and I, well, you know . . .' Cate trails off.

'It was like that for me with Simon, Cate. It's being together for so long. It's normal. The "I want to rip your clothes off right now" chemistry fades a bit,' Ava tells her truthfully. 'Any married couple would tell you the same, if they're being honest!'

'So, when Git told me I was beautiful, you see how foolish I was behaving? I was giddy. Look at how pathetic I am! A bit of attention and I nearly snogged him. Who the hell am I?' Cate says.

'It's okay to flirt, Cate, maybe that's what's missing in your life. You feeling sexy,' Ava tries, hoping to reassure her.

'Yeah, I do need to make more of an effort. Just for me,' Cate admits. 'This underwear is magic stuff – it's true what they say – Lily would bust something if she saw me in this little number!'

'We all busted something at you wasted like that, Cate. And you know?' Ava pauses, getting her thoughts in order before she starts to confess them. 'If it makes you feel any better, I knew Simon was tagging along with me deep down, but I didn't want to waste those last ten years. I really wanted to marry him to prove to everyone – you two especially – that we were in love and we could be happy when, really, I knew we weren't. I was too stupid and stubborn to admit I'd made a huge mistake.'

'Us especially?' Lauren asks in amazement.

'Yes. I know this is the worst-case scenario for us to get together, my *abandoned* wedding day, but while we're having this little game of truth here, I've missed you both . . . enormously!' Ava's pale blue eyes start filling up with tears again.

'Me too.' Cate hiccups again. 'And by the way, Lauren, I do

154

read *Irish Gloss*. I look at your flawless picture on the inside cover while I stuff my face with Jaffa Cakes and hanker for all the crazy fun times.'

'Really? After all you've just said.' Lauren leans towards Cate now. 'I always felt you didn't like me as much as Ava, and I'm forty and I feel like a total and utter tit saying this, but I've always been jealous of you! You and Ava got on so well. Stupid, yes, especially coming from an alleged adult who should know better. But hey, it's just how I feel.'

'And there was I, feeling the exact same way . . .' Cate hiccups again. 'Jealous that you and Ava were closer.'

'And I felt I always had to be the peacemaker between us all. That you two actually had more in common.' Ava is laughing now. 'And it turns out, I was probably right!'

'That attention Git showed me just blew my mind. It's been so long since I've been out – any attention is weirdly intoxicating,' Cate adds. 'I didn't feel like just the boys' mammy, I felt like me, the old Cate. And even if it was male attention, I still liked it.'

'I get it. Six months ago, Stefan walked in the door of Art Gallery Space 1 and I just felt like a bomb went off in my head. I knew Simon was dragging his heels, I knew I was pushing him into the marriage, but I wasn't brave enough to walk away and take a chance. I can see he did me a massive favour now.' Ava exhales slowly.

'Maybe we all just needed each other but all of us were idiots about how we handled it?' Cate says, and they all nod. 'Listen to me, all wise now.'

'What the hell are we like, girls? Who *are* we right now? Sad bitches, is what we are!' Lauren throws her head back and laughs. Cate and Ava start laughing along with her.

'Let's do it . . . let's go on our honeymoon, girls!' Ava says, pulling her overnight bag from under the table.

'You're on!' Lauren says, getting her bag.

Cate cheers and raises her now empty water glass. 'Thanks, Lauren . . . But, Ava, I'm so hungry. Can we order some food?'

'Totally,' Ava says. 'A night of catching up and hating on Simon by the turf fire? Can we just agree to talk shit about Simon all night?'

'Sounds great! And easy!' Lauren agrees. 'I'm not so sure about ordering around here. We'll need to find a garage.'

'And, missy, you still haven't called Stefan.' Cate points at Ava.

'No, I haven't . . . don't think I'm going to . . . I think I just need to be with myself and you guys for now . . . if it's meant to be . . . well . . . it will,' Ava says.

Tommo appears at the table. 'You lot ready to rock now? To Edenvale?'

'You're still here?' Lauren says, surprised.

'Of course. I'm a man of my word. I told you we'd get you to your destination. You girls looked deep in convo, so we left yiz to it.' Tommo rattles the biggest bunch of keys in his hand.

'You've been drinking, though?' Cate looks at him through her own slightly glazy eyes.

'One delicious creamy pint of the black stuff and two Americanos, Cate. We've been here a while and I'm good to go.' Tommo holds out a small grey tube in his other hand.

'What the hell is that?' Lauren asks, virtually sprinting to stand close to him.

'Personal breathalyser. All good. Now listen, I was talking to a few auld lads with Git and apparently this Edenvale place of yours is pretty legendary, Ava, as was the bachelor who lived there. Freddy Curtis was his name, they said.'

'I'd heard a mention of a Freddy all right from the estate agent, but Simon was never keen to talk to the locals and hear more. I'm actually getting excited to finally see it. It's been months since we bought it. I can't believe this is my first time seeing the place! My new home!' Ava's eyes widen in her newfound excitement.

'Come on, pal!' Git pokes his head from behind Tommo, gently grinning at Cate. 'That was some place-putting you did with that weird American lad. Respect.' Git joins his hands together and bows his head.

'Oh, why, thank you!' Cate says, laughing now, and grabs his arm. 'I'm feeling those damn car bombs going off in my head big time and I'm sorry about, um, earlier. I'm a happily married woman . . .'

'Forget it, never happened! My fault, never make a move on a woman after an alcohol-fuelled duel. Friends?'

'Friends!' Cate grins at him and Git winks at her as they link arms. They walk outside Fitzgerald's and clamber back into the ice-cream van, the others traipsing behind them.

* * *

'That was some craic,' Ava says as the door of the ice-cream van closes behind them and Git and Tommo jump in front.

'We're never short of madness when we get together, that's for damn sure.' Cate smiles at the girls, sobering up nicely.

'No surrender!' Lauren chimes in.

'God, I feel so vilified!' Cate screams and stamps her feet.

'You were amazing!' Lauren high-fives her.

'Listen, back there, I . . .' Cate tries to apologies to Lauren again.

'History!'

The van edges out of the car park and they're bumping about in the back of the van, when suddenly Lauren shrieks from the front seat, 'Stop!'

'What? What's wrong?' Tommo yells.

'I just saw a garage, I see a garage! There, see! We need grub! Pull in, pull in!'

Tommo swerves into the garage, and they all get thrown around the back of the van. Lauren jumps out and heads towards the garage shop, as Git follows.

'Wait up, Stevie Nicks,' Git calls after her, as they wait for the automatic door to open and step inside. Lauren trails the two small aisles that sell everything from fire logs to sewing kits and Irish souvenirs.

'Make yourself useful. Hold out your arms there, Git. Like this!' She beckons him to follow her up and down the tiny aisles, grabbing packets of random pre-packed sandwiches, salads, crisps and chocolate, and drops them all into Git's open arms.

'Did ya ever hear of a shopping basket, Lauren? Amazing invention,' Git says, his arms feeling the strain.

'Do they have shopping baskets in garages?' Lauren wonders, playing along. 'I do all my shopping online, Git.'

'Eh, yeah . . .' Git nods his head to a pile by the automatic door. Lauren goes over and grabs a large one with a red plastic handle.

'Much better.'

Git throws the stuff in.

'Get another basket, too, Git, will you?' Lauren says, then does a double-take when she sees his face.

'What's wrong?' she asks him.

'The wife said the final straw in our marriage was that I wouldn't go shopping with her. It wasn't that I wouldn't go, but when I did I was useless. Anything I'd suggest she'd tell me no. Anything I put in the weekly trolley, she'd laugh at me and tell me to put it back on the shelf. Sounds ludicrous now, but it really affected me. Whenever I opened my own fridge it was like someone else's house. Nothing was mine. I'd no say in what we ate. The furniture we sat on in our gaff. My own clothes even! I know she was doing her best on a tight budget and getting the kids what they needed, but we fought about it all the time. Silly really . . .' Git is suddenly deep in thought, leaning against a fridge freezer.

'I'm sorry, marriage sounds bloody hard.'

'It shouldn't be though, that's the thing. It's why Tommo never jumped into it. Look, we're all grand now. I'm happier, we're all happier. No more fights. Kids should never have to hear their parents fight. I'm in a flat near the house now, so it's all good,' Git tells her, slapping a smile on his face.

'With a fridge full of food you actually like?' Lauren asks, smiling back.

'Isn't that mad, Lauren? I don't stock a fridge,' Git tells her. 'I eat out after work with a few of the lads most nights. Wednesday and Friday. Elaine, me ex, still cooks a family meal for us all. Normally a beef stew, which I hate but I shut up and eat it gratefully. I'd say my fridge consists of a plastic bottle of milk, a sliced pan and a bit of cheese. Oh, and a few cans of Dutch Gold,' he adds with a wink.

'There is always a catalyst, Git, and yours was a fridge,' Lauren says carefully to him as he nods.

'I've written enough articles for *Irish Gloss* about broken relationships to have learned a thing or two over the years. It's always the little things that end up being the explosive things. The little straws that finally break the poor old camel's back, ya know?'

'True.' Git smiles now, pulls on his beard and straightens himself up.

'Your marital issues weren't that simple, Git,' she says.

He nods, thinking for a moment. 'So, is Cate really happily married?' he asks coyly.

'As far as I know. Three young kids and still in love. Yeah, it's rough going in number eight Draggle Wood right now, but Lily adores Cate. Cate's very lucky,' Lauren softly tells Git.

'Cool . . .' Git's eyes slightly widen. 'I was definitely barking up the wrong tree there, so?' He laughs as Lauren smiles dramatically in agreement.

'And Tommo?' Lauren enquires, with all the subtlety of the ice-cream van's playlist.

'Ah, sure, Tommo's as happy as Larry on his own. He's a social worker, hard job, lives and breathes it. Some of the stories he could tell ya about families would literally have ya in tears. He works with a lot of families also in Direct Provision, it's a tough gig he has. Never moans though, he's a sound lad,' Git tells her, proud of his pal.

'Oh wow,' Lauren says. 'He does seem nice. Anyway . . . wine, where's the wine? And water? Lots of water!' she wonders aloud. Git nods to a section to his left, a display of wine stacked up on two crates, both red and white.

'Oh gawd, this is going to be like drinking turpentine, but hey, beggars can't be choosers!' She grabs three bottles of heavily discounted wine and three bottles of water, adding them to Git's heavy basket.

'Doing all right there, chicken?' she asks, not waiting for his response. 'Alrighty now, I'm going to guess there won't be any necessities at Ava's new place, so I know exactly what we'll need. Kindly follow me . . .' Lauren grabs toilet roll, a load of cleaning supplies, eggs, rashers, milk and tea bags and throws them in her basket. As they march up to the cash register to pay, Lauren stops. 'Throw something in the basket, Git,' she tells him, just before they reach the till.

'What do you mean?' he says.

'Let the shopping shit go, throw the stuff you want in the basket,' Lauren tells him as he scratches his ginger beard in thought.

'Like what?' he asks.

'Anything . . . whatever it is you fancy, drop it in the basket. Whatever it was you used to want.'

Git turns back and shuffles from foot to foot.

'I've a terrible sweet tooth.' He turns to look at Lauren.

'So . . . satisfy it.' She grins at him.

'These!' He raises them up before dropping a value size bag of Werther's Original Toffees into Lauren's basket. 'And these!' He drops a family pack of strawberry bonbons in too.

'That it?' she asks.

'Yeah, that's my dream shop. Thank you.' Git expends a long, slow breath and nods at Lauren in appreciation.

'You're an actual kid in a sweet shop now.' She gives him a big smile. 'Right, we're sorted, so!'

The guy scans all their stuff and Git packs six plastic bags before they bound back into the van.

'Onwards to Edenvale, Tommo! Take this single lady home!' Ava shouts, in greeting. 'Let's get this honeymoon started!'

14

'Let There Be Light'

'THIS CANNOT BE HAPPENING! It just can't be,' Ava repeats, perplexed. 'Tommo, are you sure you got the directions right? Maybe it just looks the same as my cottage? All old cottages look the same, right?' Ava's face is a picture of confusion, as she walks around outside the ice-cream van, staring at the small derelict cottage with its windows boarded up in front of her and its garden wildly overgrown.

'You said Edenvale, didn't you? This is the place, according to the GPS on my phone,' Tommo replies with certainty.

Cate and Lauren exchange shocked looks between them; the three of them stand in front of the van beside Ava, all staring open-mouthed at the dilapidated cottage.

'But, but this ... this is exactly as we bought it ... it was supposed to be my *new* house. I paid for the full renovations. The white pebble-dash walls and the picket fence. Where are all the renovations Simon's been telling me about? This place is a ruin. And, and what did he do with the money he's been spending?' Ava's voice is barely a whisper now.

'But you have a contract with the builders, right?' Lauren asks.

'Simon does.'

'But you have a copy?' Lauren persists.

'No. I've never even seen it. I asked him to leave it out for me, but he never did.' Ava swallows her emotion.

'This is your house, Ava. It was your money. End of,' Lauren reassures her. 'But never *ever* let anyone take charge of your hard-earned cash like that.'

Ava gulps. 'You know, this is even worse than that Chloe on the radio yesterday.'

Lauren exhales slowly, staring at the cottage. 'That absolute bast–'

'We can't sleep here!' Cate cuts her off in horror.

'Shush, Cate, not now,' Lauren hisses back. 'For God's sake!'

'I don't think anyone has lived here for a very long time. Some of those old boys in the bar I was chatting with were saying it was put up for sale last year. And then they heard it was sold to some rock star fella,' Git adds, trying to be helpful.

'Sold to a rock star! Oh, I've heard it all now.' Lauren snorts in disgust.

'Don't!' Now it's Cate's turn to shush her friend.

'Ava, let's just go have a look around,' Cate adds gently. 'Maybe it's better inside?'

'B-b-but, but I used all my inheritance money from my mother. I paid seventy thousand euro for this house, and another twenty thousand to fix it up so it would be ready for our honeymoon . . . I've worked in the gallery every weekend for months to pay for it.' Ava gulps again as the colour drains from her face.

'Absolutely nothing The Tuner has done even surprises me any more,' Lauren chimes in. 'He wasn't content screwing you over with other women, he just had to screw you over on the house, too. I swear, when I get my hands on him he's a dead man. We should sue his rock star ass!' Lauren spits.

'Again . . . not helping!' Cate shoots Lauren a filthy look.

'You'll need shears to cut away that ivy on the door, eh, so you can get in. Can we help?' Git suggests. 'I've stuff in the van.'

'We'll figure it out, everything is going to be just fine. Come on, girls. Boys, thank you, but you need to head off to the match or you'll miss it! Swing by in the morning, it definitely looks like we'll be needing some help here, if you know what I mean,' Cate adds, trying her best to take control of the situation.

'Bye, lads. Have fun tonight, behave yourselves!' Lauren adds, winking at them.

'Never!' Git replies.

'Watching the match is all the fun I want,' Tommo replies, his eyes locking on Lauren as he pulls up his sagging tracksuit bottoms.

'What size are you, Tommo?' Lauren says, distracted by the sight. 'I've a pile of really great men's designer stuff in the office . . . tracksuits, T-shirts, hoodies. I could . . . eh . . . courier you over some?' She moves back to lean against the van.

'Here, stick your number in and I'll text ya,' Tommo responds, handing her his phone.

'Right so, Tommo, think the girls want some space here, let's be going . . . twenty to the match whistle,' Git says. 'Mind yerself, Ava.'

'Oh, um, okay, we'll swing by tomorrow. Have fun tonight yourselves. I bet it just needs a good going-over, Ava . . . it's got a ton of potential. Things can only get better, right,' Tommo calls out to the girls as he takes his phone from Lauren and jumps into the van with Git.

'Thanks again, guys.' Cate waves, as Tommo revs the engine to life and the ice-cream van drives off into the evening.

'You've got to admit, that Tommo is *such* a nice fella.' Lauren sighs as she looks dreamily after the van.

'You are actually unbelievable,' Cate says. 'But yes, they both are. And here I am, always preaching to Lily and the kids that they should never judge a book by its cover, and I did that when we first met them. Shame on me.'

'I think I'm going to pass out!' Ava suddenly shouts. 'Am I the most stupid fucking woman in the world? I must be! I have to be!' She staggers, as the three of them stand in the long grass of the garden staring aghast at the derelict cottage. The faded red front door is completely covered with overgrown ivy.

'It's going to be okay.' Lauren grabs her.

'How many times have you told me it's going to be okay today? It's not okay. None of it is fucking okay!' Ava yells at Lauren, her eyes wild and desperate.

'Right, Ava, you stay here and calm down. Me and Lauren will figure this out.' Cate grabs Lauren's arm and pulls her towards the side of the house.

'Oh, hold on a minute there, let me just grab the magic bloody wand out of my bottomless handbag here!' Lauren whispers loudly to Cate as they pick their way through the overgrown grass. 'And how exactly are we going to fix this? This place takes a fixer-upper to a whole new level! Even Kevin McCloud would tell you to run a mile.'

'Maybe it'll be better inside?' Cate wonders aloud.

'Considering we have to find a way to hack our way to get to the front door, I'm fairly doubtful!' Lauren says, rolling her eyes at Cate.

'There! There's a clippers thingie!' Cate runs towards a rusty bucket and grabs an equally rusty set of shears.

'Oh, jolly good show, Cate! Sure, we'll have the place looking like the Chelsea Flower Show in no time, with your magical shears, darling,' Lauren slags her. 'God, I'd love to break The Tuner's neck. What has he done with all their money?'

'Let's not go there right now. If I saw him, this rusty, sharp implement would have a very unfortunate run-in with his privates.

I just need some help right now. Ava is practically catatonic. We have to do *something*. You keep an eye on her, and I'll try to sort this!' Cate determinedly starts attacking the overgrown ivy like a woman possessed. Twigs and tangled leaves fly everywhere. Lauren moves back carefully towards Ava to watch.

'Proper Hyacinth Bucket, isn't she, Avz?' Lauren whispers to Ava as they both watch Cate swiftly gain traction on clearing the cottage entrance.

'Who knew you were so green-fingered, Cate. Impressive!' Ava shouts at Cate, smiling reluctantly for the first time since they arrived, watching as Cate kicks the front door firmly and it slides open with ease. She raises the shears above her head in victory.

'Small victories, girls, that's what it's all about! If I can carry two scooters and two kids while pushing a bugaboo with Max full of shopping up a hill in the rain . . .' she calls as she bounds over towards Ava and Lauren.

'It's all overgrown so much in six months. We could actually get in the door when we were here last. I honestly don't think Simon has been here at all. Now that I think of it, he asked me to postpone the honeymoon . . . This was why! No doubt he had no intention of us coming here after the wedding. And, obviously, he was shagging that one Chloe from the radio when he was claiming he was supervising the builders down here. And to think I could have been ravaging Stefan. It . . . it makes my blood boil!' Ava physically shudders.

'Right, you take that side of Ava, I'll grab her on this side!' Cate gestures at Lauren.

'Excuse me?' Ava looks worried.

'What she said, say what now?' Lauren adds, looking confused.

'*We* are carrying Ava over the threshold to her new house, that's what!' Cate answers, nodding to Lauren.

They simultaneously grab Ava's arms and legs before she can

stop them and carry her, jubilant, through the rickety red door and over the threshold.

★ ★ ★

'Am I actually hallucinating?' Ava stops giggling the minute they enter the cottage. 'Are we in an ancient twilight zone?'

'Had you never seen inside?' Lauren asks her in amazement.

'Yes, but I didn't really take any of it. I just had this picture in my head of what it *could* look like, all pretty and painted and a big turf fire blazing. The estate agent just kept saying "Picture this" and giving me all these wonderful images to focus on. I had Simon in my other ear saying, "Buy it, buy it" and "Imagine what it can look like". So I did.' Ava shakes her head. 'I must have been mad.'

'Take my phone. Ring that prick right now and ask him where all your money has gone to?' Lauren rages. 'Or I will. Who the fuck does he think he is? He cannot get away with this!'

'She's right! By the looks of things, the only *fixing up* Simon did with your money was dates with other women! He makes me sick to my stomach,' Cate adds with bite. 'This place hasn't been updated in decades.' Then, seeing Ava's ashen face, tries hard to back-pedal. 'But it has a certain, um, rustic old-world charm. It just needs some TLC . . . I suppose . . .'.

'Tommo said it has potential, and he's right.' Lauren gives Cate the eye.

'Oh. My. God! What am I going to do?' Ava whimpers, sitting on the filthy floor with her head in her hands. Cate and Lauren walk around, inspecting the inside of the very old cottage. It's furnished with all the trappings of a traditional Irish household from times past. A hard-looking wooden chair sits in front of a big open-hearth fireplace. A large iron kettle sits on the block in the fireplace, and a traditional cottage kitchen dresser holds rows of mismatched crockery beside it.

'Wow, how *old* is this place? I feel like I just jumped into a time machine,' Lauren says, pacing around the tiny kitchen area, slightly mesmerised.

'Look at the calendar on the wall! It's from 2003!' Cate points to it.

'It's about as good as you get for seventy grand,' Ava tells her, her voice low with despair.

'I mean, it will look great . . . when . . .' Cate replies.

'We paint the walls with Simon's blood?' Ava suggests. 'We were told 2003 was probably the very last time anyone lived here, and the furniture is from decades before that.'

'But wow, look at these!' Lauren says, picking up an old-fashioned sterling silver condiments set still laid neatly on a rustic wooden table beside a dust-covered blue porcelain plate.

'Now, them I love,' Ava says, walking around the small room. 'Simon clearly spent all the renovation money, but this is still my house, right? I still have my job in the gallery, I think. I can stay at my dad's for as long as I want and save on rent. The commute is only an hour and a half to Dublin from Offaly?' She looks at the two girls for affirmation, as she walks round and round the table.

'Sue his ass for that money back! Judge Judy the hell out of that prick,' Lauren advises her.

'This would make a great holiday rental, Ava. Think of the summer income, if you market it correctly? And it's all structurally solid, like you said, so ya know a big push on how you wanted to keep it as authentic as you could. Sell it as the real Irish country experience. Tourists will lap this place up!' Cate says, full of enthusiasm, ignoring Lauren's negativity.

'Yeah, Simon can stay in that shitty flat, for all I care, and strum his stupid guitar until his fingers bleed and the landlord throws him out. I never want to lay eyes on him again. As long as I live.' Ava stops pacing and leans against the wall.

'Atta girl. Wash that man right out of your hair. Like, when you can actually have a wash . . .' Lauren tells her.

'Yeah, a shower would be nice, but you two must think I am as thick as two short planks!' She looks to them both.

'No,' Lauren says. 'You didn't ask for this. And you most certainly don't deserve it.'

'You trusted the man you were to marry, how is that stupid?' Cate adds.

'What was he going to say to me when we got here?' Ava shakes her head in disbelief.

'He'd have thought of something, I've no doubt about that. Bullshit artists always do,' Lauren says.

'You're right, he'd probably have told me that he put the money into recording the new Seventh Heaven album. He was crapping on about this studio time they were trying to afford a few weeks ago. I didn't entertain him. They were going to "storm the charts" with it, you know how Simon goes on.' Ava drops her head and clears dirt off the floor with her foot. 'I'd have probably accepted that. Made excuses for him, like I always did.'

Cate moves to be near her and rubs Ava's back gently, making soothing sounds as Ava leans into her friend for comfort.

'Oh gosh, look here, girls!' Lauren exclaims, picking up a brown tweed cap and pointing at a green wool cardigan draped on the back of a wooden fireside chair.

'The legendary Freddy Curtis even left his hat and good cardigan behind.' Ava squeezes Cate's hand, then moves along the dusty floor and approaches the big open-hearth fireplace.

'Oh bless, look at the turf and logs all neatly packed there. Like he went out for a stroll and just never came back. Now I want to know *everything* about the old man who lived here at Edenvale.'

Lauren is flicking intently through a thick book beside an old stove. 'Well, lookee here. You want to know about the old man who used to live here? I think I've just found the answers,' she says, thrusting a black leather-bound diary towards Ava, a discoloured *Irish Times* newspaper page folded inside it. Ava quietly scans the contents.

'Lauren! Cate! Sit down. I have to read this to you, it's amazing, I think I may have found a genius marketing tool for this place!' Ava gestures excitedly towards the girls.

'Just one second – first things first, if we're going to have a meeting.' Lauren walks towards her case and opens it, removing two bottles of wine, Tayto crisps, Curly Wurlys and a stack of paper cups.

'Tonight, we dine like queens!' She laughs, passing the chocolate around, as she pours wine into paper cups for each of them. 'To old times, the best of times!' She makes a toast, as Ava unfolds the newspaper article carefully across the table, smoothing it out with the palm of her hand.

'Look at this!' She points to a picture. 'That's what Fred Curtis looked like! This old newspaper article is an interview with him before he died. It's fascinating. Sit, sit, I absolutely have to read this to you, you know how much I love old things!' Ava enthuses, as Cate and Lauren hunch over the table to listen. Ava coughs to clear her throat.

'So, according to this news article, it looks like Freddy Curtis was born in Edenvale in 1902, was a publican's son and worked nearly all his life on a family farm in Ennis.' She reads to herself, her lips moving quickly. 'His poor mother died tragically at a local woollen mill in 1914 when he was only twelve and his father decided to move the family to the United States. But it was agreed that Freddy would stay behind here in Edenvale to look after an elderly aunt who was too old to emigrate. She had no one to care for her, so he stayed to look after her, and he never saw his father and brothers again. Imagine! That's so tragic!' Ava is almost teary eyed.

'That is so sad,' Cate says softly, her eyes getting a little watery too.

'And after his elderly aunt passed away, he inherited Edenvale and lived alone in this very cottage until he died. He didn't really want to change anything, guess he wanted to continue living in it like his family always did, in their memory . . .'

'That *is* your selling point!' Cate claps her hands. 'The history of this house! Frame every single piece of paper that references Freddy and this house. Tourists will be beating you up to rent this place. Especially the Irish Americans! It's seeped in authentic Irish history. Bravo, Ava!'

'You could be right there, Cate! Every evening, he sat on that hard chair by the fire over there and pored over books. Guess he was an avid reader, probably all there was to do back then, it's not like television was even invented.' Ava points over to the chair.

'God, I enjoy my me-time, but I can't fathom having nothing *but* me-time!' Lauren exclaims. 'I'd lose my mind!'

'Me too!' Ava agrees. 'But here's the thing, according to the reporter who did this interview with Freddy, he said he lived – I quote – "a rich if modest life and was a chatty and sociable man with all the locals. Went to the local pub in the town for a single glass of Jameson whiskey every night without fail, and then came home". Same routine, every single night of his life.' Ava shakes her head, her blonde hair falling across her face.

'Wow, wish I had that kind of discipline,' Lauren says, nudging Cate, who laughs.

'Wish I had the energy at night to have a drink instead of being asleep at nine o'clock in my clothes and runners, stone cold sober!' Cate quips.

'And check this out! Freddy also told this reporter a story about how he hid in a tree in the garden here, watching the Black and Tans burn a neighbour's house down. And when those brutes were gone, Freddy jumped out of the tree to go help his neighbours salvage what they could from the burning wreckage. What a little legend!' Ava is shaking her head in amazement at the story, getting more enthralled by the facts. 'I can't wait to devour his diary next. You don't think he'd mind, do you?' she asks them. 'I mean, diaries are supposed to be private.'

'He's dead now, Ava, I'm pretty sure he would love to know we were regaled by all his life stories. In his old house, no less.' Cate looks towards the window and sees it's getting dark. She stands up, trying to find a light, pressing everything that resembles a switch as she paces around the room.

'Ahem, as far as electricity goes, I think we might have a little problem!'

'What? Nooo!' Lauren looks horrified. 'We can't stay in this old house tonight in the pitch dark. I'll be petrified!' She shivers. 'Maybe I should ring Tommo?'

'No. This isn't an excuse for you to get down and dirty with Tommo. This is us-time, right? Anyway, I just couldn't find the switch. I didn't say we wouldn't have light, McCabe!' Cate adds, grinning, reaching into Lauren's case to pull out a plastic bag.

'What the hell is that you're pulling out of my bag?' Lauren asks.

'Ah, a little pressie I thought you'd like, was supposed to be a keepsake for you when you got home.' Cate opens the bag and removes the penis candle.

'Get lost!' Lauren laughs.

'We can light the fire there, as good old Freddy kindly left us plenty of logs. And we can add to it with the Simon the penis candle and his Pope friends. Tah-dah!' Cate places the familiar candles on the table and lights them. Warm candlelight floods the little room.

'Oh, thank God. Thank you, God.' Ava sighs deeply with relief. 'And Lauren, it's not a creepy old house any more. You're in *my* house now! Mine and Freddy's. He's left me a legacy, is what he's done. I'll just have to pick up where he left off. So, cheers to that!' Ava raises her paper cup.

'To Freddy!' Cate proffers. 'And to strong women!'

'To us,' Lauren replies. 'Now, let's get that fire cracking.'

Cate grabs the lighter and rolls up some old newspaper.

'Hey, that paper could be worth something!' Ava tells her. 'For my Freddy heritage cottage.'

'Yeah, heat! That makes it priceless in my book.' Cate strikes the lighter and the paper catches flame. 'Joking! It's a page of racing results. I checked.' She throws a fire log on top.

'I'm still roasting,' Lauren says, looking at Cate, backing away from the flames.

'Shall I prepare our fancy evening meal?' Cate removes the sandwiches and opens the crisps and they sit around the table.

'I'm starving!' Ava adds, as she rips open a smoked ham and lettuce sandwich, layers it with cheese and onion crisps and bites in hungrily. 'Oh, how great it is to feel hunger again!' She licks her salty fingers.

'Divine!' Lauren chews hers as she sips her wine. The fire takes hold and crackles warmly behind them. 'Not so bad now, is it? Cosy even!' Lauren says to Ava, who nods slowly as they all eat in companionable silence, listening to the crackling of the fire in the hearth.

'You're right, Lauren, I do need to get away from the kids more, don't I?' Cate ponders, as she chews her sandwich.

'Speaking of kids . . .' Lauren blurts out. 'Well, now seems like as good a time as any to tell you, I can't have any.'

'W-what?' Cate's head spins to look at Lauren.

'Whaaaaat?' Ava echoes.

'Nope.' Lauren inhales deeply. 'I'm deep into perimenopause . . .' She exhales. 'Fabulous, right? In case you didn't notice me constantly sweating! Basically that means I can never have children . . . so, I envy you, Cate. I envy you and your relationship with Lily and your three beautiful boys. I can never have that. Like I was trying to say earlier in Fitzgerald's, please don't blindly assume anything about me or my life.' Lauren sits up straight and gulps loudly, the bread now stuck in her throat as she reaches for her paper cup and takes a swig.

'Jesus, Lauren, I'm so sorry. Why didn't you tell me? I don't even know what perimenopause *is*? I've never heard of it, I don't think?' Ava reaches across the table and takes her hand.

'I hadn't heard much about it myself, Avz, and me, the editor of a women's magazine. Go figure! It's the not-talked-about precursor to the big meno.'

'So how did you know?' Ava says.

'Where do I even start? I didn't know for months. My periods were a bit sporadic, but then they always were. I was always skipping months in college, remember? But then other stuff started happening.'

'Like what?' Cate moves her chair next to Lauren's.

'Mainly night sweats. Sleeping was one long restless wet patch. Then it'd creep into my working day. I'd feel like I was permanently on fire. The only way to describe it to you guys is like someone is constantly pressing boost on my body heat. Eating brings it on. Drinking brings it on. Sometimes even water brings it on. Jesus, Tommo definitely brought it on!' Lauren tries her best to smile.

'That's awful,' Cate gasps. 'When did you get diagnosed?'

'And there I am bitching about bad PMS every month,' Ava mutters, utterly taken aback.

'I couldn't cope with the night sweats any more. I was permanently exhausted. Then I went to Paris on a shoot about five months ago. I was sharing a room with Julia, and I woke up in the middle of the night in – and I'm not exaggerating here – in a pool of sweat. Like, literally drenched. As in, had to change my pyjamas and wash myself down with a wet towel because I couldn't turn on the stupid shower, and I just crashed out on the tiled bathroom floor to try to cool down. Obviously I was getting completely freaked out, consulting Dr Google, we all do it. You know how it is. I convinced myself I was dying.' Lauren rolls her eyes.

'I hear you. Every time I have flu symptoms I'm convinced I'm dying when I consult Dr Google,' Ava agrees.

'Yup, guilty too!' Cate raises her hand. 'Dr Google is pretty much like consulting Dr Kevorkian, if you ask me.'

'When we got home, I knew I couldn't take it any more without seeing a doctor, so I investigated the Well Woman Centre's website and spotted they do a menopause test. Deep down I kind of knew. So I made an appointment and went for a full internal MOT, if you will.' Lauren cradles the paper cup in between her hands.

'You can actually do a menopause test? Amazing . . . well, not really amazing, but you know what I mean. What do they do exactly?' Cate sits forward, listening intently.

'It was painless, well, emotional agony: they took a detailed set of bloods, usual cholesterol levels, iron levels, but the most important one, my FSH – the hormone levels.'

'Can they tell you pretty soon after the test?' Ava asks gently.

'Well, not exactly. They can tell you if you are in menopause.

They can tell you if you aren't in menopause. But they can't confirm if you're on the way to having it. There's no test that can absolutely confirm you are in perimenopause; well, not one that I know of right now anyway,' Lauren explains, matter-of-factly, but with relief in her voice.

'So how do you know you have it for sure? I mean, you're way younger than most women are supposed to be going through it? Like, super young,' Cate says.

'I wish! That's another myth: there's no set age. Menopause is defined as twelve months without a period. I've gone eight months and then had a period . . . a super light one, but still . . . it wasn't on my radar. The doctor is pretty sure from all the tests and my ongoing symptoms that I'm indeed in the throes of it,' Lauren replies. 'Lucky me!'

'But you can still have a baby if you get the odd period, right?'

'No, I've also got premature ovarian failure. I've got it all, sisters!' Lauren's voice cracks. 'A loss of normal function at forty. My poor sorry ovaries don't produce normal amounts of oestrogen, or release eggs any more. Destination: infertility.'

'I'm so sorry,' Ava says.

'It's okay, feels good to get it out, to be honest. I've been living with a series of little earthquakes in my body. Some days I get all the symptoms, the hot flushes, headaches, crazy insomnia, memory loss, chronic fatigue. Some days I get none. It's pure luck really. Oh, and did you know, I may even grow a beard? That would be useful for finding a guy, wouldn't it? Me, a bearded lady!' She rubs her chin.

'Wait, what . . . you could grow . . . a beard?' Ava's eyes nearly pop out of her head. 'Like the bearded lady in *The Greatest Showman*? Attractive . . .'

'You'd still look hot with a beard, Lauren.' Cate tries hard to make Lauren smile, while absorbing everything she's hearing.

'Thanks, Cate! And by the way, I'm sorry I've been so bitchy to you, but I guess – well, you can guess for yourself now, right? If you add the dreaded irrational temper flashes to my laundry list there.'

'No sweat!' Cate replies.

'Is that a joke?'

Cate smiles. 'I think so?'

'It's a good one. But oh, how I wish there was no sweat instead of bloody buckets of it, constantly!' Lauren responds, smirking.

'So, you saw a fertility expert too, I'm guessing?' Ava asks.

'Yeah, after I got the perimenopause warning I went to see a fertility specialist . . . the nurse advised me.'

'And?' Ava's ears are almost pricking up.

'Well, long story short, he did another bunch of tests and told me it's not going to be possible for me to have kids naturally, which has been tough to process. Guess I always assumed I'd have kids . . . later on . . . when work quietened down and I found the right guy, you know?' Lauren bites her cheek.

'I didn't even know you *wanted* to have kids? I just stupidly assumed you had no interest,' Cate says. 'How thoughtless of me to just presume like that.'

'It's not. I wasn't the most maternal woman in the world, I hold my hands up. My job was my dream. When I made editor at thirty-four that was all I could see long term. And with all that, I was so busy . . . I –' She stops and regains her composure. 'I just thought the baby thing was next step. I never could have imagined it was behind me.'

'And there was me assuming you had the dream life I've always wanted. I was always so envious of your fabulous career and seemingly care-free life,' Cate admits. 'I'm sorry, Lauren, I've been a selfish bitch.'

'Oh, you haven't, Cate, don't say that. I haven't exactly been there for you either. I guess you just never really know what's going on with people in their personal lives, do you? I'm the one who's always been jealous of you, especially over the last year, when I've been dealing with this shit. You and Lily are living *my* dream! But it is what it is.' Lauren tries to sound upbeat again.

'It seems to me like the bigger problem lies with all of us not talking about what we're going through in an honest way,' Ava adds.

'Oh, Lauren. Truly – I don't know what to say. But I will admit this. Motherhood is really hard too. I mean, I wouldn't swap it for anything obviously, and Lily and I fought damn hard to have our kids and, honestly, cross my heart, hope to die, that's the truth. But it's still hard, *really* hard. You never have any time for yourself, ever. Most days I don't even get dressed, I put that trench coat on over my pyjamas and walk to the park like a zombie. I rarely talk to another adult all day. I have *Peppa Pig* on loop. I eat Coco Pops from the box. Life is so expensive and full on and busy, which is the really strange part, because it can actually be terribly lonely, too.' Cate picks up the wine bottle and fills their paper cups to the brim.

'Well, from now on you can get dressed and meet me for lunch on a Friday. How about that? We'll go to one of those centres that has a crèche and we can get a nice lunch?' Lauren suggests.

'Offer accepted.' Cate laughs. 'I will live for Fridays.'

'Hey, count me in on that and . . . this may sound like a really dumb question, Cate, but I've always wanted to know – about your boys. Tell me to mind my own business, but . . .'

'How do us lesbians have kids, you mean, Ava?' Cate laughs.

'Well, uhm, kind of, yeah . . .'

'Got to be honest, I'm fascinated, too, Cate. We've been friends for how long and I never had the balls to enquire in case I totally offended you!' Lauren jumps in.

'God, Lauren, I've no problem talking about it . . . I'm proud to talk about it, so ask away!' Cate replies, amused at their sudden interest and glad to provide a distraction. 'What do you want to know exactly?'

'Everything!' Ava chimes in.

'Okay, then, something that people miss all the time is that gay parenting is just parenting. Like the way our kids act, how they make us feel emotionally, or myself and Lily's deep-rooted desire to have them in the first place isn't determined by our sexual orientation, but, spoiler alert, obviously gay parents can't have kids by having sex with their same-sex partner.' Cate clasps her hand over her mouth jokingly.

'Oh, you don't say! But hey, for heterosexuals like me and Avz, there's no guarantees that we can create kids without needing help either, for all sorts of reasons!' Lauren chimes in, in agreement.

'Exactly!' Cate agrees. 'Where there's a will, there's usually a way.' She looks directly at Lauren.

'Anyway, Lily and me decided to take the sperm donor and intrauterine insemination route for our boys. We had to save bloody hard for years. I was lucky enough to be very fertile and Lily had a significantly lower egg count, so I carried our babies, but we needed the sperm obviously. Anyhow, we spent a year researching it all and talked to a lot of friends in the same boat and decided on this particular cyrobank in London that have a great reputation. For us, it was really important that the three kids had the same donor father, and that he was open to possibly meeting them after they turned eighteen, so they had that option if they wanted it. Listen, it isn't lost on us that we were very lucky that everything went our way. It's not easy.'

'That's amazing. Do you talk about it to the older boys?' Lauren asks.

'Yes, we do – they know they have a donor, not a dad. Our mission is to be honest and open from the get-go with the kids so there's no secrets. JP is eight now, but when he was about six, Lily and I began the conversation about how he was conceived, in a way that he could understand. There's tons of great books that were really helpful with explaining it. And when Jake turned six, we did the same with him. We'll do the same with Max when he's older too.'

'So, how do the boys explain it?' Ava asks, fascinated.

'Ask Jake and JP the next time you see them! They'll proudly tell you that they were made with lots of love by my eggs and the sperm of a special man who wanted to help their two mamas make a family! They'll also tell anyone very confidently that they have two mamas, not a dad. They're so young now, but their donor is an important detail in their history, but just one of lots of important details. We just wanted to be sure it was never a life-changing realisation for them when they got older. But everyone handles these things differently, and to each their own. Every parent's journey is different,' Cate adds again, purposefully.

'I can't even imagine how proud that makes you guys feel. Those boys are very lucky little dudes.' Lauren puts her arm around Cate, giving her a squeeze. 'And as Git reminded you, you're still sexy as hell!' Lauren whispers, winking, making the girls laugh.

Ava throws another log on the now blazing fire, then stands up and puts her back to it, warming her hands behind her.

'But what you guys were saying earlier is also true. I *have* lost myself in mummy world. I need to push myself out in the world again. I eat crap food all day, as I'm so busy running around. Lily is the same. And I am way less interested in anything romantic with Lily since I had Max and it has become a . . . well, a bit of an issue.' Cate shuts her eyes. 'I love our little guys dearly, all three of them equally, of course I do, but I'm constantly exhausted.

My life is passing me by, and all I want to do is crawl into my bed and sleep. It's ridiculous. I'm thirty-nine years old and I want to go to bed at eight o'clock every night. But' – Cate wags her finger in the air – 'I decided after that episode earlier today with Git, I clearly need some relationship therapy or something. Both Lily and I, that is.'

'Never a bad idea, Cate, people don't ask for help enough. It's so true,' Lauren adds.

'Trust me, Lauren, the daily reality of being a mum is mostly being wrecked, wishing you hadn't made plans, wanting to chill at home with your bra off, wondering how you can fall asleep and stay asleep, craving food you know you shouldn't eat, being forgetful, constantly worrying about things that haven't happened yet . . . Oh, and wondering how you got that massive bruise,' Cate adds, laughing.

'Maybe you just need some time away for yourselves and a load more of that really sexy underwear! What about a date night? A change of scenery now and then is good for the soul. I'll babysit!' Lauren tells her, her eyes serious.

'Maybe.' Cate nods and runs her hands through her wild red hair.

'I've been the editor of a woman's magazine for years. I can assure you this is a very common problem. In fact,' Lauren tilts her head to look at Cate, 'riddle me this, Connolly. I've been thinking about this side business for a while, an online business, starting with an Instagram page, and I've been looking for an agony aunt on relationship and marriage issues, a real-life married woman with kids is what I ideally want. I'll create a pseudo name for you obviously, but good pay if you were interested? I'd also like to touch on perimenopause, fertility issues in women under forty, and I can't believe the idea of you being a great fit didn't dawn on me until now.'

'Wait, are you offering me a job, Lauren?' Cate's mouth drops and she puts down the handful of mature cheddar cheese and onion crisps she was about to eat. She rubs her hands free of the crumbs.

'I think you'd be great at it!' Lauren takes a slug of wine.

'I'd love that . . . but, no . . . but the kids, I . . . I can't . . .' Cate protests, sadly.

'You can work from home, on your own schedule. I can't guarantee it will work out or even last more than a few posts, but we could give it a shot and see what happens?' Lauren tells her.

'Can I . . . I think about it?' Cate asks her. 'I can't get my thoughts straight right now I'm so gutted for you.'

'It's okay, honestly, it's so true a problem shared really *is* a problem halved. You can let me know by next week and I'll call off the agony aunt search! Julia is currently trawling every magazine agony aunt in the international mags right now, trying to poach them, and of course everyone operates under a fake name so it's impossible to track the real people down. Hmm, now I just need to think of a classic pseudo name for you!' Lauren smirks. 'And don't worry about me, Cate, I'm fine, honestly.'

Ava leaves the heat of the fire and sits back down at the table, picking up the conversation's earlier threads. 'But don't give up, Lauren. Like Cate was explaining, there's lots of other ways to have a family . . . like fostering and adoption?'

'I'll think about all my options, I promise, Ava . . . took me a while, but I'm starting to just accept it. Who knows what'll happen in the future. And hey, it's out of my hands physically – whatever will be, will be. Sure, there are those who will say I left it too late anyway. Maybe I did, but that's my decision and I have to make peace with it.'

'Would you tell a guy about your situation on the first date kind of thing, Lauren?' Cate wonders aloud.

'Funny you should ask. I told that RTÉ sports guy I went on that awful date with when I got hammered drunk. I don't know why I told him really,' Lauren admits.

'What did he say?' Ava asks.

'Wait for it . . . He said' – Lauren leans back and throws her arms out wide – '"*Oh, I assumed you were well past it anyway*".'

'That asshole!' Cate shouts, trying not to laugh.

'Nooo? Seriously though, maybe I should have a fertility test too?' Ava says to Lauren. 'I mean, we are practically the same age. I never even considered that I could be past having kids.'

'You still have your regular cycle every month, right?' Lauren asks. Ava nods. 'But then again, we are forty. Biologically our eggs aren't what they once were, so there's no harm to see where you stand.'

'Christ, how ironic that we spent all our college years desperate not to get pregnant, and now . . .' Ava trails off.

'I'm just so relieved to have finally told you both. It's been really weighing on me, as you can imagine.' Lauren sighs with relief.

'That's our girl, the Bull McCabe! We've got you. And call me emotional, but can we be really puke right now and hug it out? Come here!' Ava pulls the two girls in tight.

'By the way, I'm not having a glass of wine now, I'm having four, it's called a tasting and it's classy!' Lauren pipes up. 'Oh, and – friend disclaimer – due to the ongoing influence of hormones, I could either burst into tears or kill you both in the next hour!'

They throw their heads back and roar with laughter.

15

'You Oughta Know'

'JESUS, LAUREN! KEEP YOUR HANDS TO YOURSELF. You just hit me in the face – *again*!' Cate shrieks.

The three friends are lying top-to-tail in the small single bed in Freddy's sparsely decorated bedroom. A pile of blue-and-pink striped cotton sheets and ragged blankets are piled on top of them for warmth, as they lie virtually on top of each other.

Ava and Lauren readjust their bodies so they can see Cate's face.

'This is an old Irish bachelor's house,' Ava says, groggily. 'What did you expect, the Four Seasons? Of course it was only going to have a single bed. Sure, he was never married!' Her head lifts up from the other end of the bed; her hair's tied up in a scrunchie and generous blobs of Sudocrem adorn her chin.

'I know, but I think my back's permanently damaged from this stupid bed. Hard as nails. How in the name of God did poor old Freddy sleep in this all those years? I've got about twenty minutes of shut-eye and I can sleep in a cot!' Cate sounds exhausted, her hair a mass of tangles.

'Someone's toe is in my arse!' Lauren mumbles, still half asleep. 'And I am bloody hungover again. It's like my body is reminding me that I'm a total idiot. I just need tea and melted cheese on toast with a dab of Worchester sauce and I'll be right as rain ...'

'Hold on, I'll just ring the bell for Jeeves?' Ava sniggers, pulling on a rope beside the bed. A bronze bell does in fact tinkle loudly. The girls laugh despite themselves. A weak morning light is spreading across the room, and Ava gets herself comfy, looking around at her new future. 'Don't you just love all these relics everywhere?' Ava says, excited once again at her unexpected luck in finding this wreck in the country. She points at an ornate candlestick holder attached to the wall. 'I didn't even notice that last night. Stefan would absolutely adore this place. He's always sneaking off on his lunch break and wandering around the cute little antique shops on Amiens Street.'

'Let's just say it's more your thing, Avz. Give me a luxury king-size bed and a warm fluffy bathrobe any day of the week over this shit!' Lauren quips, removing five worn blankets off her to exit the bed. 'No offence, like.'

'None taken!' Ava smiles back, moving to fill the space Lauren's left in the single bed.

'Hear, hear! I'm with Lauren,' Cate chimes in. 'We better be careful here, Lauren, imagine we discover we have too much in common!'

'Oh, whatever, you two! You've no imagination. Let's just try to muck in and live a little!' Ava replies, rolling her eyes in mock frustration. 'I feel like a weight has been lifted off my shoulders this morning. I actually feel ... positive,' she adds, with a shrug of her slender shoulders.

'Well, that's good to hear. Me too.' Lauren turns back to them from the small square bedroom window she has been staring out of, taking in the beautiful view.

'And so do I,' Cate says. 'Without sounding like a total sap, I'm definitely feeling extra grateful for Lily and the boys.'

'This place will be absolutely stunning, Ava, just come here and look.' Lauren turns to her friend, beckoning her over.

Cate and Ava join Lauren by the small window and each take turns pressing their faces up against the grubby glass to look out at the rolling green hills and the riot of picturesque stone walls.

'It's so peaceful,' Ava almost whispers. 'I've been dealing with having to come home from a crazy work day to the band of tossers in my cramped modern apartment – I swear I've had a low humming headache for years and it's just lifted.' Ava rubs at the condensation on the glass pane.

'I'd have had a migraine, too, if I had been listening to their shite music for that long,' Lauren adds. They all laugh.

'Too right,' Ava says through her giggles. 'What a blessing not to have to pretend to respect their musical genius any more!'

'Lily would adore it here. She loves to get out of the city; we just haven't been able to. Money isn't exactly spare, if you know what I mean … it's crazy expensive to holiday with five of us,' Cate admits.

'Take the place whenever you guys want when it's fixed up a bit. And' – Ava looks around – 'imagine the boys here, Cate, they'd have so much freedom to run wild! All the fresh country air. But what I'd really like is if we – the three of us – could come here on this weekend, every year, just us, and chill? A kind of runaway bride anniversary?'

'I'm all over that plan!' Lauren says.

'And I'm in too. I needed this … I really did.' Cate smiles at them. 'Speaking of the house, we need to get it cleaned up. I've got to be on the road in a few hours. Lily has to work tonight and there's no way myself and Lauren are leaving you here on your own, Ava. The place is … well, unsanitary – and there's no electricity!' Cate turns on her mummy's-in-charge voice.

'I have to agree, I'm afraid.' Lauren pulls her phone out and breathes heavily. 'Julia has really let me down and I'm under fierce pressure now. I have to let her go when I get back. Her inability to work on her own initiative is downright scary. She has absolutely no idea how hard most people work to get a job in a magazine. Her dad is our biggest advertising client, so I didn't exactly have a choice, had to give her the job. And now I get to pay for that nepotism. It's my own fault!'

'Sorry, Lauren,' Ava says, feeling a bit guilty at causing her friend all this trouble.

'Oh, it'll be fine, don't worry, Ava. I've just told her a few home truths, actually, and she doesn't exactly take criticism well. I'll pay for it later, no doubt. Anyhow, let's get ready and take a shower,' Lauren suggests.

'Talking of home truths, I'm a bit giddy thinking about that agony aunt column stuff.' Cate bites her lip, and looks a bit sheepishly at Lauren.

'Good – because I meant it. You'll be great,' Lauren says.

Lauren heads towards the door, but turns back when Ava suddenly says, 'Eh, Lauren ... there's no electricity, therefore no hot water. What kind of shower did you have in mind?'

'Anyone for a whore's bath, so?' Cate jumps up to grab a giant box of baby wipes from her bag.

'Yes, me! Right now. Whore baths all round with these bad boys and then we'll get to work!' Lauren exclaims, laughing as she grabs the baby wipes and starts rubbing under her arms. Cate and Ava follow suit.

'Told you I'm full of solutions! Us mammies always are!' Cate adds. Smelling slightly fresher, Cate sets off out the door, shouting back optimistically, 'I'll look around for a brush and some cloths. Nothing a bit of soap and water won't take care of!' She disappears down the creaking stairs.

'I grabbed some cleaning stuff at that garage,' Lauren adds. 'The bags are by the kitchen table.'

'Our favourite scene in our favourite movie ever starts a bit like this,' Ava reminds Lauren, as they follow Cate down the stairs.

'Which one? We have a few, in fairness,' Cate says from the small kitchen, as she fills a pan with water. She moves to put it on the hearth, where the glimmer of last night's fire still flickers.

'*Calamity Jane*! When Calam invites Katie Brown to move into the cottage and it's a shithole, but, hey ho, all it needs is *a woman's touch*!' Ava dramatically puts her hands on her hips and juts out her chin.

'Such a class scene! We are literally living out our favourite movie scene right now!' Cate says, clapping her hands. '*We can fix it up …All it needs is a woman's touch*!' Cate spins around, her arms outstretched, playing along fully in her best Katie Brown accent.

'A woman's touch?' Lauren joins in. '*The magic of Aladdin …*!' she sings, slowly inviting the other two.

' *… She doesn't need a lamp*! That's me!' Cate trills, holding up the half-burned penis candle.

'*A woman's touch …the hocus pocus she does so well*! Oh my God, at last this song is actually about me. I knew the time would come eventually!' Cate dances around the kitchen like she's on a Broadway stage for *Dancing at Lughnasa*.

'Stop, Cate! I'm actually going to pee myself. Look at Lauren!' Ava's tears of laughter stream down her face and she crosses her legs as Lauren finds a red tea towel and ties it around her neck in a necktie.

'*With the magic of a broom …*' Lauren grabs an old sweeping brush and prances around behind Cate. '*… mesmerise a room …*' She star-jumps, making the other two explode in laughter.

Lauren clutches her chest, doubled over, as they sing at the top of their voices, and Ava grabs a cloth from under the sink. Cate removes all the cleaning products that Lauren bought and lays them out on the table.

'*With a rub rub here … polish up the winders …*' Ava sings at the top of her lungs, as she rubs the kitchen window so the view outside can be seen for the first time in what must have been years. She suddenly screams and falls back, dropping the cloth on the floor.

'What?' Lauren throws down the brush with a crash.

'What is it?' Cate stands up from the pot of water by the fire, then jumps up onto the chair. 'More rats?' she heaves, hugging her arms around her swollen breasts again.

'It's … it's …' Ava picks up the filthy cloth and moves away from the now crystal-clear glass and walks robotically to the door.

'It's what?' Cate asks her again from the chair.

'Simon!' she gasps, as Simon walks in through the rickety red cottage door.

★ ★ ★

'What are *you* doing here?' Simon asks Ava, his eyes on stalks as she stands cloth in her white-knuckled hand in total shock.

'Ava!' Lauren pushes her forward.

'What am *I* doing here? What the actual fuck, Simon!' Ava throws the filthy cloth and hits him smack in the face.

'Ow! Hey, not cool, man,' Simon says, rubbing his nose and pulling at his goatee beard as a rumble is heard outside and Lauren moves past Simon to the doorstep.

'You are having a laugh, Simon, right? Because you can't be fucking serious.' Lauren's face is pinched with disbelief.

'What is it?' Cate moves now just as four men, carrying drums, guitars, cymbals, a rolled-up carpet with a massive double bass all step inside the door.

'Ava, I'm sorry, baby …' Simon starts.

'Oh, crap! The Tuner's in for it now, dudes,' one of the band members says as he stops dead in his tracks spotting Ava and the girls.

'Mind melt, bro,' another one mutters under his breath.

'Sorry?' Ava spits the word at Simon. 'For what exactly? For having sex with other women behind my back? For treating me like an afterthought for the last ten years? For undermining my work as an artist? For lying to me? For humiliating me in the worst possible way? What part, Simon? What part are you truly sorry for, you stupid prick!'

Cate jumps down from the kitchen chair, and she and Lauren take up their defensive positions on either side of Ava.

'It wasn't like that, man ...' he starts.

'Eh, dude, where should we put all the gear?' another one of the band pipes up, puffing on a rollie inside the house.

'Eh, dude ... get the hell out! Now!' Lauren yells at him, stabbing her index finger towards the hall door.

'Ava, this is silliness, can we talk?' Simon asks, and beckons for the boys to back away, which they all do.

'You have five minutes, Simon.'

'Alone?' he asks earnestly.

Ava gives a small laugh. She picks up the sweeping brush at her feet and holds onto it for balance.

'These are my best friends, that you more or less tried to make me get rid of, anything you say to me I will say right back to them, just like you always feared I would, so it's up to you?' She clutches the brush handle like it's a staff.

'The thing is, it was a once-off. Coco – I mean, Chloe – was a once-off, well, ya know what I mean ... a one-time affair. You were all wedding talk all the time, and then I grabbed that cancellation to make you happy after I'd smoked a load of that hybrid grass ... but then it hit me that I didn't want to get married. To anyone. It wasn't personal, babe. But by then it was too late, it was all booked and your dad was getting involved and everything started moving so fast. I – I wanted to tell you how I was feeling but – I am sorry, Ava. That was a shit way to find out. Coc … C-Chloe was bang out of order, man.'

'Oh, I get it now. It's that girl Chloe's fault, she was just too irresistible, was she? She made you have an affair? And you, Simon, you were just this poor little lamb being led to the slaughter. So confused … so helpless … you couldn't help it, right? You were bullied into it, is that what you're trying to say?' Ava is incredulous, her face becoming a deeper shade of raging red by the minute.

'Well, she was … she was, eh, pushy,' Simon mumbles.

'And smokin' hot, to be fair. So were her friends …' The drummer of the band walks back in and catches on to the conversation, trying to come to Simon's aid.

'Budgie, man. Shut it. You're seriously not helping here.' Simon turns to shut him down quickly.

'Ohhh, I see, so she *pushed* you into an affair for a few months, helped you through a tough time … Did she help you spend all my money too?' Ava's sarcasm is totally lost on Simon. 'By the way, dickhead, she didn't know you were already in a relationship, let alone engaged!'

'I got in too deep, should have ended it, then I got scared …' Simon is sounding ridiculous. 'Men get scared too, you know,' he offers and then dips his eyes.

'Scared of some random girl, but not scared by the possibility you could be throwing your life with me away after ten years. Our plans to be married. Our new life here in Clare. Everything?' Ava hisses.

'Well, yes … I mean, no, not like that …' Simon stammers. 'I just needed to find myself, I guess.'

'And my money? When were you going to tell me there were no builders working on the house?' Ava shouts.

'Eh, I looked at it as more of an investment, man. These songs are gold – the album will win a Grammy. You'll get your money back, and then some.'

'I want every single penny of *my* money back that you've spent chasing your musical delusions, Simon. Or, and I promise you this,' Ava threatens, 'I'll come after you, and a court case will be the least of your problems.'

'Watch it!' Another bizarrely dressed band member steps inside the door. 'Crazy out of control Mr Whippy out there, dude, I'm staying indoors,' he declares, as Tommo and Git stride in, adding to the melee in the cottage.

'Everything okay here, girls?' Git asks, eyeballing the dishevelled band members.

'Couldn't be better, Git, thanks. We're just getting rid of some waste here,' Lauren shouts across to him, as she turns to face Simon. 'Did you just say "find yourself"? Here, let me help you. I can find your head for starters ... it's stuck very, very far up your arse.'

'I can't be selfish enough to keep you to myself, Ava. You can be free now, man,' Simon stutters, blanking Lauren. 'People can't be owned.'

'This just keeps getting better and better, Tuner,' Cate spits. 'No, really, keep going. I'm enjoying this bullshit. Maybe you could throw in a "everything is so perfect with us, let's break up now so we only have happy memories"?'

'Or perhaps a gem like "we've grown apart as people" or a "I think we should be free to see other people?"' Lauren spits sarcastically.

'Rich coming from you, Lauren, considering you can't keep a fella. The tide wouldn't go out with you!' Simon's face reddens dangerously, as he seizes his chance to bark back at her with venom.

'Watch your mouth, pal, this certainly isn't about Lauren's relationships,' Tommo says, taking a step towards Simon.

'Oh, who are you? Another one of Lauren's victims?' Simon is in a full rage, but he pales a little at the size of Tommo.

'This is the last time I'm going to say this, mate. Leave it out, or else.' Tommo's voice is steady, yet threatening.

'So, that's it? That's your explanation. For everything?' Ava sighs deeply, fighting to maintain her composure and get an answer from Simon.

'Yeah, I guess so,' he says, unsure.

'Bye-bye.' And she smiles at him and waves one hand slowly. 'I'll see you in court.'

'Oh, come on. It's not that simple, man. It was *our* money. I mean, we've got this house together now and, well, our apartment in town ...' Simon stammers.

'Oh yes, of course, darling! *Our* home, where *our* honeymoon and *our* new life was supposed to be. I was the one who actually worked long hours, weekends, all the hours I could muster to try to get that cash together. Not you.' Ava sighs.

'Hey, now, that's not fair! You know how hard I tried to look for gigs,' Simon points out.

'You know what? Even if you did try, here's a random thought, Simon: if you weren't getting enough gigs to actually live off, well, hey, maybe you needed to go get another job? A real job? Like me. Something that actually pays bills,' Ava spits, raising her voice, getting drawn in.

'That isn't me. You knew that when you met me,' he protests.

'Grow the hell up, Simon! That was ten years ago, and what if we had kids? What then, Simon?' Ava exhales heavily, totally exasperated. 'And why exactly didn't you spend my money on the renovations like you said you were? That's pure deceit and it's disgusting.'

'I was going to tell you. I wanted to ...I tried ...but me and the boys here ...we had this big dream of recording the album here in Clare ...just like The Waterboys did with *Fisherman's Blues*. And I needed the money to get the studio time, plus I knew there was no point in doing the house up before then as well ...we'd wreck the place so ...so I just decided not to tell you until we got down here. That's why I tried to delay the honeymoon a bit ...I hoped you'd understand.'

'Wow!' Ava looks at Cate and Lauren, who both shake their heads in complete disbelief. 'Get out. Get out of *MY* house, Simon.'

'But, but ...' he starts, as Ava moves closer to him and stares into his eyes. 'Wow ...what are you looking at?' Simon flinches and takes a step back.

'A silly question, but one I want to ask before you go: did you ever really love me?' Ava's voice finally wobbles and her eyes well up.

'Course I did, man.' Simon's nervous eyes can't meet hers and he stares down at his oxblood Doc Marten boots.

'What part? What exactly did you love about me?' she asks quietly, as Lauren takes her hand.

'What do you mean ...*exactly*?' He pulls at his goatee beard anxiously. 'Don't do this, Ava, please. I hate being put on the spot like this, man.'

'Go on, Simon. Tell me what you loved about me?' Ava demands, as her blonde hair falls loose from the knot on her head and tumbles down her back.

Simon stands very still, struggling to find the right words, to find any words.

'Uhm, I can't,' he whispers.

'Tell me,' she demands again.

'It's too hard,' he replies.

'Tell her!' Cate and Lauren say at the same time.

'This is pressure I don't need. Em...uh...' He rubs his temples then looks up as if he's just had an eureka moment. 'You always made amazing cheese and onion toasties!' he offers, his arms outstretched.

'Okay, get out! NOW!' Cate moves and grabs the rolled-up carpet and flings it into the garden, as Simon grabs the double bass and edges backwards, another band member coming to help him.

'I'll take these ...' Ava starts to lift the remaining equipment and kicks the cymbals onto the garden pathway; they clatter and crash loudly as they hit the ground.

'Hey, that is not cool, Ava,' the bass player shouts after her.

'No. And neither are you, Chad. None of you Seventh Heaven tossers are cool,' Ava adds, as she throws the last of the drum kit out. It clatters onto the pathway, as she flips them the middle finger.

'You heard Ava. Go. Move it. You're trespassing.' Git steps forward towards the band. They scramble to pick up their belongings from the ground and skulk away through the garden towards their transit van.

'Oh, and Ava,' Simon snips, now he's safely out of reach, 'the band don't really like you and, well, I certainly was never going to break up with them!'

'Just go, Simon. Get out of my sight. Get out of my life. For good. You'll be hearing from my solicitor.'

'Simon, yeah?' Tommo moves quickly and grabs Simon's elbow before he manages to escape.

'Yeah – what's it to you?' Simon glares at him angrily.

'What a blind idiot you were,' Tommo spits at him, his voice mocking, 'not to see she was in love with someone else all along.'

'Yeah right ... as if!' Simon snorts indignantly, as he stalks off.

16

Worn Once by Mistake.

'DRINK IT!' CATE PUSHES A MUG OF SWEET TEA across the table to Ava. The living room is now spotless and Mr Sheen-smelling. Lauren is standing in the kitchen on her phone.

'They really don't have to do that ...' Ava says, nodding to the window, where Git can be seen shovelling and Tommo raking leaves and cutting trees as music booms from the open doors of the ice-cream van.

'I guess they want to,' Cate replies, softly. Looking back at Ava, she asks, 'How long will you stay?'

'I don't know. I need to just sit and think, I guess. I'll work. Lauren brought me supplies and a sketch pad, so I can draw ... It will be good for me. God, I wonder if Stefan and Mags got Laurence Kilroy together for his exhibition. With all my shit going on, I forgot that his big exhibition is only two weeks away,' Ava thinks aloud as she takes a sip of her tea. 'Christ, Cate, is there tea in this sugar?' She winces.

'Good for the shock,' Cate says.

'Sugar's not good for anything, don't you read the news?' Lauren adds, wryly.

'It's the news that's bad for your health,' Cate says.

'I'm glad Simon came here, actually. Now I really never have to see him again.' The relief is clear in Ava's voice.

'He's some moron!' Cate agrees, pulling her hair into a bobbin.

Git knocks on the open window, startling Ava. Cate jumps out of her skin. 'Jesus, Git, you nearly gave me my second cardiac of the day!'

'Sorry, Cate! Hey, Ava, there's a bunch of tins of paint out here in the shed. What do you want me and Tommo to do with them?'

'Ah, just leave them there for now, Git, and thank you, you two are the real rock stars. I'll reward you richly in Dutch Gold when you're done!'

Git gives her a thumbs-up and disappears from sight.

'What is going on with her?' Ava nods to the kitchen, where Lauren is pacing up and down on her phone.

'Something to do with Julia is all I could make out,' Cate replies.

'She looks pretty perplexed,' Ava says, just as Lauren walks into the living room.

'What now?' Cate asks a red-faced Lauren.

'That bitch, Julia. She totally screwed me.' Lauren bites the top of her phone. 'Seriously, I'm going to need to go on the Valium.'

'Germs, Lauren!' Cate can't help herself.

'What do you mean?' Ava asks.

'I've been suspended while they launch an investigation.' Lauren tries to smile, but it turns straight to a harsh grimace.

'Suspended? You? How? You're the boss!' Cate asks.

Ava collapses back in the seat.

'Julia called up her rich daddy – you know, the magazine's biggest advertising client – and told him she had a recording of me, "her boss", saying that California Glow fake tan I'm promoting was absolutely shit. And then he called the magazine owner and grassed me out, while that stupid weapon Julia also uploaded it on Instagram. She also told my boss that I'm trying to start my online agony aunt business and I've been getting her to work on it for me during *Irish Gloss* hours.' Lauren shakes her head in total disbelief.

'But that tan is shite, isn't it? You told me it made you look like an Oompa Loompa?' Ava adds.

'But so is a lot of the crap I have to promote to make money on the side!' Lauren confesses.

'Wait, so they suspended you, so they can consult with the fake tan jury?' Cate is trying to calm Lauren down. 'What do they do, put a call into Willy Wonka and ask to speak to the little orange Oompa Loompas to ask their definitive opinion?'

Ava laughs, but Lauren doesn't.

'I'm such a fool. I knew Julia had an out-take from one of the videos we posted on Instagram a couple of weeks ago, but I never in a million years thought she'd keep it. And, worse still, use it against me! Apparently I said on the video, "How am I supposed to promote this absolute shit?"'

'So, what did she do exactly?' Ava asks.

'She uploaded it to the *Irish Gloss* Instagram account, hash-tagging bitchboss just because I had a go at her earlier over not doing her job properly.' Lauren squeezes her eyes tight.

'They won't sack you for that, will they?' Cate asks.

'I don't know. But Jesus, what am I doing it for anyway? I'm too old for all this bullshit.'

'You're forty, not ninety,' Ava exclaims.

'It's not that, Ava, it's all the screen time, I'm never off my phone. And this weekend for the first time in God knows how many years ... I haven't been checking my Instagram account at least every ten minutes to count likes, read comments and check up on everyone else's stuff.'

'Seriously?' Cates eyes are wide.

'Yep, sad but true.' Lauren exhales heavily.

'But, well, it's part of your job, isn't it?' Ava asks her kindly.

'No, it should be someone else's job. I mean, I have other stuff I could be getting on with, God knows. My life, for example! Instead I'm addicted to likes and follower numbers and comments and all that stuff. To be honest, it's just pathetic.' Lauren flops onto the hard kitchen chair next to Ava.

'Maybe they'll just make you calm down on the side gigs for a bit?' Cate suggests.

'Who knows. The problem is the owner, the publisher of *Irish Gloss*, isn't a huge fan since I – oh gawd, I can't even say it …'

'Uh-oh, what happened?' says Ava, her eyes widening. It feels nice to momentarily be drawn into someone else's horror story and escape her own.

'Uhm, so I was rushing around last week, trying to wrap things up before I left for your wedding and I needed to get the publisher's approval on some articles I was sending to press. I meant to type "Let me know when you get a sec?" and didn't check it before I pressed "send" … and it autocorrected to "Let me know when you get sex". Now, I copped it quickly, thank God, and tried to be funny and sent him another email that said, "Uhm, can I go home now?" to smooth it over, but he just blanked me. No response. It didn't help that a few weeks prior we'd done a piece – a huge spread on Viagra. We were sent samples in and I went looking for them, just to see what they look like, ya know? He'd taken them home! He's not exactly full of personality, and I'm sure he was appalled at how not seriously I was taking my job … Definitely doesn't help with this Julia double-crossing situation, though …'

Despite herself, Ava bursts out laughing. 'Damn autocorrect is here to destroy us all. Oh, Lauren, sorry for laughing, but that is classic! "Let me know when you get sex"!'

'Ah, sure here, I can match that, Lauren. I'm in one of those ridiculous, head-wrecking WhatsApp mums' groups for Jake's class at school. The devil's work. Anyway, instead of correcting some ranting mother on something with "I think you're wrong" it autocorrected to "I think you're whoring". I just about died! And no doubt a bunch of OTT mums are still discussing my vulgarity in yet another WhatsApp mums' group!'

'Brilliant! Those busybody mums at the school gates! Whoever decided on WhatsApp groups anyway? I hate them.'

Lauren looks at her two friends and can't help but join in their laughter.

'Seriously, though, Lauren. I think you should give it a day or so and let things settle at work. I'm sure they'll realise they're making a mountain out of a molehill at the magazine,' Ava says, in a reassuring tone. 'They'd be totally lost without you. You know that. Not to mention your big summer issue going to press shortly and all the work that's still to do on that?'

'She's right. And it's not like Julia can do your job, despite what she's up to,' Cate adds.

'I'm just so mad that I was so stupid. I hate that I was lying to people who probably went out and bought that tan.' Lauren puts her bottom lip over her top.

'Hang on,' Ava says, as she stands up. 'Tell you what. I just had an idea. Random, sure, but might be just what we need to let all our rage out. It'll be therapeutic, actually.' There is a mischievous glint in her pale blue eyes.

'Go out the back and kick lumps out of a tree for a bit, screaming like a banshee?' Lauren asks dryly.

'Oh, I've heard of those rage rooms, where you go in and smash up tellys and windows?' Cate looks around, mind spinning.

'You want me to trash my home? As if it isn't trashed enough, already?' Ava drops her hand on her hips and stares Cate down.

'Well, no . . . it just popped into my head.' Cate looks to Lauren, who just shakes her head.

'Wait a minute ... hang on ...' Ava moves away from the table and disappears up the winding cottage stairs, as Cate and Lauren look at one another apprehensively.

Ava reappears a few minutes later holding her creased and crumpled Vintage Brides wedding dress.

'Follow me, girls. Just trust me. This will be good!' She drapes her lace wedding dress over her arm and nods for Lauren and Cate to follow her. They traipse outside behind her.

'Hey, boys, you might want to stand back a bit,' Ava shouts over at Git and Tommo, who are chopping down the overgrown hedge. 'Git, where's those tins of paint you were talking about earlier?'

'Over there ...' Git points over to a couple of rusty paint tins stacked outside a small derelict shed.

'We're going to paint the house now?' Lauren asks, looking at her watch, seriously concerned. 'Oh, Avz, honestly, I can't ...'

'Wouldn't do the house, Ava,' Tommo tells her. 'That paint's been opened before, bit gloopy.'

'Are you all mental? Absolutely not!' Ava replies, walking over and grabbing the paint tins in her hands. 'First, we need to build ourselves a makeshift scarecrow or something.'

'A scarecrow?' Cate looks confused. 'What? That Worzel Gummidge shit?'

'Yes, don't worry there. We don't need anything fancy, Aunt Sally, we just need to build something to hang my wedding dress on,' Ava instructs light-heartedly. 'Lads, can you please grab some of those branches you've been clearing for me and drag them over here?'

'No bother, boss.' Git tips an imaginary cap to Ava, as they dutifully start dragging big branches towards the middle of the garden.

'You're the artist,' Tommo tells Ava.

'So Stefan says,' she mutters, as she starts to build a big stick-like figure.

'Tommo, grab some string or something out of the back of the van there, we need to tie Worzel up properly!' Once Git cops on, he starts taking the new construction project pretty seriously.

'Rope, sir!' Tommo throws a long rope towards Git, who proceeds to bind all the branches together in a giant matchstick man formation.

'Magnificent work, Git!' Ava claps her hands together excitedly. 'Who knew? Right now, for the *pièce de résistance* ...' She places the wedding dress over the scarecrow.

'Just a regular runaway, isn't she just lovely, gang?' Lauren adds, and they all laugh at the upright dress, blowing in the wind.

'A true stunner!' Git bows before the dress on its makeshift mannequin, as the others all nod in agreement.

'Now, for the fun part! Boys, help me open these old paint cans and then I want you all to grab one each,' Ava instructs her team.

'Say what now?' Cate asks. 'I'm confused. We're going to do what exactly to your dress? Destroy it with all this paint?'

'It will be art, Cate. And rage-release therapy for Lauren and me. And, well, whatever we want it to be really,' Ava replies, smiling.

'Give me a paint can quick, lads, I need to release a lot of rage!' Lauren shouts out to Tommo.

'Your paint, milady!' He bows neatly and hands her an open can of red paint.

'What colours have we got there?' Ava asks Git, who's bent over, busily cracking open the paint cans with a stick.

'Well, quite the rainbow, as it turns out. There's bottle green, yellow, black, and Lauren has the red,' Git responds.

'Perfect, green is my favourite colour, I'll take it. Cate, you take the yellow and Tommo and Git, you grab the black. I'm going to art direct this little creative experiment, so listen carefully . . . And be sure to follow my orders!' She giggles, gesturing wildly with her hands.

'She's mad but she's totally serious,' Cate whispers to Lauren.

'Okay, Lauren, you're up first. Stand six feet back from the dress and throw the paint at it. Whatever angle you like, it doesn't matter, just have fun,' Ava announces. 'Throw!'

'Are you sure? There's no going back when we start this, Avz.' Lauren looks worried.

'One hundred per cent! Get ready and on my orders . . . throw!' Ava shouts defiantly, as Tommo and Git stare on, eyes as wide as saucers.

'This is one for the books, wha' Tommo! Look at us, we're artists.' Git nudges Tommo, excited like a little kid.

'Jesus, that dress is a bit trashed, but I hope she doesn't regret this in the morning,' Tommo mutters, raising one eyebrow.

'Stand back, everyone! Ready, Lauren . . . three, two, one . . . go!' Ava calls. Lauren tilts the can of red paint forward and hurls it with all her might towards the floating wedding dress.

'This one is for you, Juuuuulllllia!' she screams. 'Screw you, you talentless double-crossing witch!' The paint flies in the air and splatters all over the bottom half of the delicate white dress.

'Epic job, well done!' Ava tells her, as she admires the intricate red patterns forming on the wedding dress.

'Next, we're going to add some yellow. Step on up, little Miss Sunshine!' She points to Cate and grabs her elbow, directing her exactly where to stand.

'And three, two, one . . . have at it!' Ava repeats, and Cate swings the paint can wildly, and yellow paint flies through the air in slow motion, landing with a loud squelch as it meets the dress.

'Wow, you girls are good at this modern art! Nice work, Cate!' Ava nods her approval at Cate.

'Right, boys, you're next. You know what to do!' she adds. Tommo and Git take each side of their paint can and swing wildly, laughing. Their black paint approaches the dress with speed, adding the next crazy layer of colour.

'And now for our grand finale,' Ava says, raising her green paint can, and aims it at the dress. 'Suck it, Simon. Permanently!' she shrieks, and the rest of the group applaud. Her green paint sprays the top of the now brightly splattered dress. 'Let's leave it outside for the paint to dry in the wind. Look at it – it's fabulous!'

They all nod in agreement, admiring their handiwork.

'Eat your heart out, Vera Wang!' Lauren exclaims.

'Yeah, take that Coco Chanel!' Cate adds, high-fiving Lauren.

'Jaysus, if someone had told me this morning that I'd be splashing paint at a wedding dress on a scarecrow, well . . .'Tommo winks at Lauren. 'And now look, we've created a masterpiece!'

'Haven't I always told you art is therapeutic?' Ava smirks, giving Lauren a knowing look.

'I think that was maybe the best rage release of my entire life. I feel so much better now. You're on to something there, Ava!' Lauren nods enthusiastically.

'I think we've created the most epic wedding dress of all time right there,' Cate adds, examining the dress closely. 'Look how brilliant those colour mix splatters are. Who knew?'

'Hey, girls, don't we all deserve a little reward now to celebrate our magnificent artistry!' Git is looking at the three friends with eyebrows raised.

'Yes! Five cans of Dutch Gold coming right up!' Lauren laughs at her false promise as she tidies away the paint cans with Tommo. Then they all stroll towards the cottage door giddily, pointing back at the rainbow dress, its colours drying in the gentle breeze.

'Ahem, don't you think it could do with some added layers for texture maybe, *mademoiselle* ... wild bird feathers or something? Maybe some natural foliage?'

Ava hears a familiar voice behind her and spins around.

'Stefan!' she shrieks.

17

Embrace the Glorious Mess.

'THIS IS BEYOND SURREAL,' AVA SAYS a week later, as she rubs at the condensation her breath has made on the glass in front of her.

'The last time you said those words to me, you then asked me to take a picture of your ass!' Stefan stands close, his leather jacket rubbing against her arm.

'Oh, I did, didn't I?' She looks up at him, grinning widely.

'I was happy with the request, not so much with the situation.' He laughs easily, rubbing his eyes.

'Yeah ... sorry about that, Stef.' Ava leans her head on his leather-clad shoulder and breathes him in.

'But you are happy?' he asks softly and places his hand across her forehead, her head still resting on his shoulder

'Happy doesn't come near how I feel. Which sounds completely ludicrous, considering I was humiliated live on air on the way to be married less than a fortnight ago – and then robbed.' She lifts her head. 'I didn't realise how much I wanted this. Physically needed it, even ... I can't believe it. I'm just over the moon. Honestly, I dreamed of this privately, but I never dared hope it would become a reality,' she tells him, openly.

'I always believed it would happen for you, and now ...' Stefan pulls his phone out of his back pocket, 'we have one hour before Ava O'Hara's "Finding Me" art exhibition opens.'

Ava looks through the long glass window of Art Gallery Space 1, staring at the walls lined with her art for the opening night of her very own solo exhibition. Ten of her paintings hang with small round red price stickers in the corner, prices that made her eyes water.

'Let's go in!' Stefan opens the gallery door and it gently tinkles behind them.

'Suzanne is coming, right?' Ava asks him. She walks in ahead, so she doesn't have to catch his eye.

'*Oui* . . . she said she would try her best,' he answers.

Ava takes a long deep breath in through her nose as her heels clack on the wooden floor. 'It's unbelievable, Stefan. But what if I don't sell a thing? Or worse, even, what if no one comes?' Ava's panicked eyes turn to stare at him, full of fear now. She feels sharp in her white dress suit jacket and tapered white trousers, her hair tied up in a high ponytail, with minimal make-up and a dark red lip, but her heart is trembling.

'They will come,' Stefan reassures her.

'It looks fabulous, Ava. You are one talented little curator!' Mags claps her hands and flings her oversized leopard print bag over her shoulder as she opens her arms in welcome.

'Mags, I can't thank you . . .' Ava starts.

'Don't thank me, thank him!' Mags nods her head towards Stefan. 'You know the funny thing?' Mags takes her arm and moves her away from Stefan slowly. They stand together under the painting she created of Lauren's flowers in the centre of the gallery wall.

'This is raw talent, Ava, real artistry. Though beautiful, these flowers are so sad.' Mags tilts her heads to absorb the picture in the centre of the gallery wall from all different angles. 'What blows my mind is that Stefan told me these were new blooms?' Mags looks quizzically, as she turns to look at Ava.

'Yeah.' Ava nods.

'That your maid of honour sent to you fresh that day and that you painted that night?' Mags enquires further.

'That's just how I saw them,' Ava admits.

'But they are all dead inside. The blooms are all bent and withered ... the brushstrokes limp and the colours dishevelled. Like the passing of time was incredibly slow and tough. It's absolutely brilliant,' Mags tells her. 'I mean, they are fresh flowers that look dead. Genius!' She adjusts her bag again.

'Guess I should have listened to my inner artist, and well ...' Ava looks to Stefan, who is moving to the back kitchenette, 'taken his advice.' She nods after his retreating back.

'And this,' Mags moves a step down to her left, 'this picture of the woman feeding her baby in St Stephen's Green. She looks so sad, too. Why?' Mags tips the bottom of the black-framed picture with her index finger.

'I felt she was alone,' Ava says.

'Feeding her child?' Mags asks, questioningly.

'Yeah, not all mothers feel fulfilled, Mags, you know – and that doesn't mean they don't adore their kids or that they don't worship the very ground they crawl or walk upon, but they still feel lonely. My best friend Cate always tried to tell me that, I just never really listened to her properly. Well, until our runaway, that is! It's okay to feel lonely as a mother,' Ava tells Mags, thoughtfully. 'We all need to talk more about that one!'

'When I had David ...' Mags stops short, and there is a short silence.

'Wait, you have a son?' Ava asks gently, more than shocked. 'I never knew that.'

'Well, now you do. He's grown-up, away at Manchester Met.

I got pregnant very young with him, raised him on my own. But you're right, it was a lonely time. Despite all the rewards of being a mum.'

'Why do you never talk about him?' Ava asks her. 'If you don't mind me asking.'

'I don't know ... I don't like the questions about who his dad was, how I coped alone. I'm private, Ava. I keep my private life private – that's okay, too, right?' Mags suddenly looks vulnerable in a way Ava has never seen before.

'Absolutely. That's totally understandable, Mags. I mean, it's like we are brainwashed into feeling that we shouldn't feel complete as women until we conform to the perceived norm ... which is happily married and then fulfilled with our babies – still in 2019! It's crazy. We all just need to find our own comfort zones and live our lives for ourselves. I nearly let my friendships go, and my friends are so important to me – they'll be with me forever – but I pushed that aside because I felt I needed to conform and keep you-know-who happy.'

Mags moves on to the next work, nodding slowly, her hand now gripping the shoulder strap on her bag.

'I bought this gallery and had to work my ass off to make it a success when David was very small. I rarely saw him as a baby – I had a live-in au pair instead.' She stops to look at Ava. 'I missed out on so much. I regret that now but, here's the bombshell, I didn't feel that way at the time. I was so much happier at work that at home,' she admits, her eyes sad.

'Don't look back, Mags, you aren't going that way!' Ava rests her hand on Mags's arm. 'Just for you – the wise words of my dad.'

'Thanks, Ava, and he's right, no doubt about it. You can only be who you can be in the present. And I did my best at the time. Actually, I'd never have introduced him before this conversation, but David's coming tonight, he's home for two weeks, so I'll introduce you to him later.' She nods slowly at Ava.

'I'd love that, Mags.' Ava smiles warmly at her boss, feeling a connection with her in a way she hadn't before.

'By the way, when that mad man Laurence Kilroy texted Stefan and cancelled his exhibition, Stefan came to me at my home in Dalkey with your portfolio under his arm. He told me we should exhibit your work. Homegrown talent, he called you, one of our own. I thought he was mad. He forced his way in, saying he needed to use the loo, which I now know was a pretty pathetic lie.

'But on his way out, as I was literally shoving him out the door, he showed me some of your work and, Ava, I marched him into the kitchen, we laid all the pieces on the table on the counter tops and on the floor and I was gobsmacked. Of course, I gave his plan my immediate approval, and we got to work on a new brochure.'

Mags straightens the picture of the red balloon in the sparse tree.

'Again this is heartbreaking, such isolation in your work, Ava.' Mags looks to Ava, as though seeing her properly for the first time.

'I know.' Ava bows her head, almost ashamed, and stares down at the gallery floor.

'Stefan always saw it,' Mags says, exhaling loudly.

'He is the best,' Ava admits awkwardly, as she shifts from foot to foot.

'He is. And I'm not one to keep quiet, so I saw the pictures you did of him, too, Ava.' Mags takes another step to her left, whistling loudly.

'Christ!' Ava drops her head in her hands.

'I actually wanted to display a few of them, but he wouldn't hear of it,' Mags says.

Ava feels the heat rise to her cheeks. She is mortified. 'He must think I'm a raving lunatic,' she says, cringing. She turns to Mags, her face burning bright pink.

'On the contrary, he loves them. He just didn't think you would be comfortable.'

'But *he* would have been?' Ava's eyes widen in complete horror.

'Oh, absolutely,' Mags tells her. 'I framed one just in case, but he said an absolute resolute "no" to displaying. Per your orders – those were his words!'

'I can't even bring that up with Stefan. The day he saw those drawings I nearly passed out. Mortified doesn't even start to cover it. Then Suzanne, his girlfriend, came in and I trashed my phone in a temper, then I became a runaway bride, thanks to the talk show revelations about my cheating, lying groom. And the rest is history. So . . .' Ava lifts her shoulders.

'Righto, well, I'm away now . . . I'm going to meet a man about a dog in the back of some van. Do not put anything here, please.' Mags motions to a free space in the corner of the gallery.

'I was wondering why you left that bare, it's one of the best exhibiting spaces in here.' Ava points over to the gleaming empty space, confused.

'It's my gallery, Ava. I can do what I like!' Mags snaps right back into boss mode and Ava flinches away. But Mags winks playfully at her, with a face so serious Ava snorts out a laugh. The day was proving exceptionally surreal.

'We have some press lined up for six o'clock, a few social photographers too, so be sure to smile a lot, and don't forget to name the gallery in any interviews.'

'Okay, of course. And, Mags, I've got to accompany my friend to a meeting as her witness now, but just one thing, before you go – my job as curator . . . Erm, it's still *my* job, right?' Ava asks nervously. 'I've been so busy curating my own exhibition, I haven't asked you.'

'I want you here, Ava, but I think you need to focus on your art. However, as I know too well, artists have to eat too! So let's talk about me commissioning you to do a Christmas exhibition, that way you can still work here, but perhaps we could make the storage room into a little art workshop for you?'

Ava almost hugs Mags with gratitude. She'd never dared dream of such a positive answer. 'Please. Thank you,' she manages to stutter. 'I appreciate –' She tries to regain her professional cool a little, seeing Stefan approach the gallery door from outside. 'I-I'd love that ... thank you,' she flusters.

'You should eat!' Stefan tells her, blustering into the gallery, coffee in hand.

Ava gathers herself to own the moment, as the gallery door tinkles open again and Lauren walks in, looking nervously at Mags, as Stefan makes his way towards the kitchenette.

'Oh, I can come back?' Lauren says.

'No, it's fine, I have a couple of hours before I have to get ready,' Ava reassures her.

'An hour,' Stefan calls out. 'And you have to eat!'

'Okay, an hour it is. I promise I will be back by four.' Ava grabs her sweater and, linking Lauren's arm, moves her back out the gallery door.

★ ★ ★

'I'm so screwed. I can feel it in my bones, Avz,' Lauren says now, as they stride through St Stephen's Green towards the *Irish Gloss* headquarters on Leeson Street.

'Don't be. I'm with you.' Ava squeezes her arm.

'I can't thank you enough for coming with me ... I just want this waiting bullshit drama to be over, I haven't slept in a week.' Lauren jabs at the button on the pedestrian crossing repeatedly.

'Listen, just be yourself, McCabe. Be honest. And if they can't respect honesty and having the balls to own up, well ...' Ava offers her best gentle support and puts her hand on Lauren's to stop her frantic jabbing.

'From your lips to God's ears! Okay, we're nearly here.' Lauren sighs, as she fixes her packed shoulder bag. Together, they approach a bright red door and nervously enter the vast office building.

'Are you sure I can come in with you?' Ava hisses.

'They *told* me to bring someone! A witness, remember? Oh, hi, Jenny ... sorry ... I'm here to see Dir ... Carl Diggler.' Lauren gasps. 'Holy shit, Ava, I nearly called him Dirk Diggler for real,' she whispers.

'Just take a seat over there, Laur ... Miss McCabe. I'll let him know you're here.' The immaculately dressed receptionist looks at them both a little coyly as she flashes her pearly white teeth, gesturing towards the chic waiting area.

'That was definitely not the time to be accidentally comparing the magazine's owner to a porn star,' Lauren whispers, as she pulls a chair over.

'Can I get either of you some coffee, or a Ballygowan? Mr Diggler and Miss Payne will be ready for you in a few minutes,' Jenny, the receptionist, asks politely as Lauren sits down.

'No, we're fine, Jenny, thank you.' As the receptionist retreats, Lauren mutters under her breath, 'Any chance of a stiff G & T instead?' Ava giggles quietly.

Lauren takes out her phone and studies the screen for a moment. 'Oh shit! "THE NOTORIOUS PAYNE" from human resources is going to be in the meeting. I have to tell Cate this. She's heard the stories about that weapon!' She begins to type furiously.

Cate's response pops up on her phone a split second later: 'WTF???'

'You've got this. Inhale, exhale. Just breathe.' Ava pats her friend's bare knee. 'Stay away from any extra drama.'

'Lauren?' A glamorous young assistant in a white shirtdress and designer flip-flops interrupts Lauren's text conversation with Cate, and Lauren stuffs her phone into her bag.

'Hey, Aveen! How was the retreat?' Lauren smiles genuinely at her, then her smile fades as the assistant looks to the ground.

'If you'd like to follow me. And you are?' She looks to Ava, ignoring Lauren's question.

'Ava O'Hara, I'll be accompanying Miss McCabe today.' Ava extends her hand.

'This way, please.' She leads Lauren and Ava towards a large glass-fronted conference room and they enter. A man in a dapper pinstriped suit is pacing up and down.

'Good morning. Take a seat, please, Lauren,' says a woman, sitting at the large conference room table. Ava notices that she's wearing a badly fitting navy suit; her jet-black hair is scraped into a severe bun, which makes her pinched face look even more pale and stern. 'And you are?' she snaps at Ava.

'Ava O'Hara. Lauren's best friend,' Ava says confidently as she sits.

'Hello, Ava. I am Tori Payne, the human resources manager. I'm here on behalf of the magazine. I'm glad to see you brought your representative.' She then nods at the man in the suit. 'And this is Carl Diggler.

'Thank you both for joining us,' Tori Payne adds, in an overly official tone. 'Let's get straight down to business, shall we? As you are aware, we have had a week to review this situation. To be honest, we were completely shocked by what transpired last week when your personal commentary about an important client's products were widely shared on social media.'

'B-but may I please explain?' Lauren tries to interrupt. Ava places a firm hand on her leg under the table.

'I will give you the opportunity when I am finished, Miss McCabe. If you'll allow me?' Miss Payne responds coldly. 'Mr Diggler and I, and our lawyers, have spent the last week thoroughly investigating this situation, while trying to manage the wide backlash we have received here at the magazine. We have lost four highly valuable advertising clients as a result of your irresponsible behaviour as the editor of *Irish Gloss* magazine. And, quite frankly, it is completely unacceptable. At no stage were we made aware by you officially that you were operating a side business on Instagram promoting products and being paid for it. It is a gross conflict of interest that has now escalated into an extremely grave situation with our advertising clients. I mean, the magazine's reputation is completely compromised . . .'

'And we received word today that the lawyers for California Glow are threatening a lawsuit for slander and business losses, yet another highly concerning development. If Julia hadn't brought it to our attention, well . . .' Mr Diggler builds on the accusations.

Ava squeezes Lauren's leg, trying to keep her friend calm, but it doesn't work. Next moment, Lauren explodes, the words gushing from her mouth before she can stop them.

'Julia Neiman, let's be honest, couldn't organise a piss-up in a brewery. I've suffered her for quite long enough. And this . . . this situation clearly demonstrates the type of person she is. It's also exactly what happens when you hire people based on pure nepotism.'

'I would remind you that Julia is the daughter of our biggest advertising client, Lauren. It's business,' Mr Diggler adds. 'Pure and simple.'

'It's people like me and others here who are forced to deal

with the consequences of your decisions, Mr Diggler. People who genuinely bust their behinds at work that end up paying the price for people like Julia,' Lauren bursts out. 'People who don't have a rich, connected daddy in their back pocket to cover for them. And when their ongoing lack of ability is reported professionally to HR, the people in charge turn a blind eye in return for profit. I've already reported her total ineptitude to you, Miss Payne. It's impossible – she's impossible!'

'I talked to Julia, and she assured me she had the magazine's best interests at heart.'

'And what would you know about best interests exactly? With all due respect, the California Glow customers should be suing the company for turning them orange!' Lauren spits.

'I would respectfully ask that you keep your opinions on a valued client's products to yourself, Miss McCabe.' Mr Diggler's loud voice booms out.

'This matter isn't just about you being caught on video sharing your personal opinions. It's a wider matter. When our lawyers conducted their investigation, they unveiled some extremely concerning facts, Lauren,' Mr Diggler says sternly, raising his voice. 'For example, you bought tens of thousands of followers for the *Irish Gloss* Instagram account on your corporate credit card.' His already flushed face is becoming even redder with anger.

'That was a business decision that paid off and it massively increased magazine sales, and ...' Lauren jumps in, trying to justify her actions.

'And, on close review of some of the Instagram posts, it also was brought to our attention that you were claiming to be places you were not on behalf of the magazine – the island of Capri last May, for example. When we checked your calendar, you were on a print check in Wexford. And we found another false post in August, where you claimed to be hashtag "living the life" in Barcelona, when you were, in fact, at a new business pitch at the St Stephen's Green Shopping Centre.'

Ava looks at her friend, trying to hide a slight smirk at the list of accusations being levelled at her friend.

Diggler carries on, really hitting his stride, ranting about the magazine's public humiliation by an anonymous blogger – 'BS Exposer', Diggler confirms, in his choked voice, who is going on a rampage exposing fake Instagram influencers.

Diggler is now on a fiery roll. 'The hashtag "Irish Gloss Their Loss" is trending, and we're seeing the impact of all this on our bottom line in a very concerning way!' he says, coming to the end of his tirade.

'How about I write something on behalf of the magazine?' Lauren suggests, as if she might be able to defend herself. 'I'll sort it all out, like I always do.'

'You owe her that at least,' Ava chimes in.

'We think you have done quite enough damage, Lauren,' Mr Diggler says abruptly. 'You have left us with no choice but to terminate your position as editor of *Irish Gloss*. We wish you well with your future endeavours.' He gets up and walks towards Lauren, to offer her a professional handshake, then starts to exit the conference room.

'You total douchebag,' Ava whispers to herself under her breath.

'You're firing me?' Lauren calls after him. 'Hang on a minute! I've dedicated nine years of my life to this magazine. I've built everything from the ground up to where it's at today. I'm sorry – yes, maybe I've made some questionable decisions – but I was fighting to retain our position as Ireland's number one publication. I did what I felt I had to do. Nothing I did was done with malice or bad intentions, I only cared about being on top. It was all about winning – haven't you always said that at company meetings, Mr Diggler?' Lauren is breathless and aghast. 'So I got a bit carried away, got a little reckless in my pursuit of success, but –'

'Miss McCabe,' Miss Payne cuts Lauren off. 'To be very clear, we have made the decision to officially terminate your position here. I'll escort you to your office now, so you can gather your belongings. If you can review the termination paperwork in this package, you'll see that we have put together a most generous exit package for you. If you agree to the terms, you shall receive payment to your account in two weeks. Please call me if you have any questions. I'll just need you to return your corporate credit card and your security passes. Thank you in advance for your cooperation.' Miss Payne hands a large white envelope across the table.

'I don't know what else I can say,' Lauren mutters, visibly shaken. 'Other than I'm sorry.'

'There is nothing else left to say. Just review the documents and let me know if you have any questions. I'll need everything signed and returned asap.' Miss Payne is determined now to end the conversation, directing Lauren and Ava towards the conference room door.

'That Instagram critic – I'm curious, what was her Insta handle again?' Lauren breaks her shocked silence as she walks towards the glass door, Ava by her side.

'I believe he or she goes under "BS Exposer", Lauren. I'd recommend not engaging with this poisonous person. Certainly not in any way connected to the magazine, now you're *no longer* an employee . . .' Miss Payne emphasises this, without emotion.

'You certainly don't need to worry about that. I've given quite enough of my life to this place. Precious time I can never get back. Oh, and I'd rather not parade to my office with you as my, eh, security guard. So I'd appreciate it if you could just box up my stuff and send it to my home address. I'll review everything in this package and will return any required signed documents to you if I accept the terms, Miss Payne. Goodbye. For good,' Lauren says with her usual authority, as she takes Ava by the hand and together they march, heads high, out of the *Irish Gloss* headquarters.

★ ★ ★

> Lauren was fired. Going for a quick pint before I have to run, can you make it? Take over for me?

Ava is typing into her phone as they stomp down Baggot Street towards O'Donoghue's pub, Lauren muttering obscenities under her breath at her side.

> What the actual fuck? This is unreal! Am on my way.

Cate's reply pings into Ava's phone. Another message quickly follows.

> Order me a soda water and lime. And whatever you're both having yourselves ... on me! I'll be there in fifteen.

★ ★ ★

Fifteen minutes later the three girls are sitting in a booth at the back of the old Irish pub.

219

'I can't believe they did this to you, Lauren, I really can't. You *were* that magazine.' Cate shakes her head, blowing on her cream-topped steaming Bailey's coffee. No soda and lime in sight.

'They were so obnoxious, Cate. The way they spoke to her!' Ava spits, sipping an iced water.

'Who's going to take over now? Demon child Julia? Best of luck to her in attempting to spin decent copy from the burning fires of hell. Karma will bite her in the arse ... *eventually,*' Cate adds, crunching her face up in disgust.

'One can only hope. She makes me sick. What a jealous, incompetent back-stabbing piece of work she is ...' Ava nods.

'It's shocking and dramatic, yes. But it's my own fault,' Lauren responds. 'Why did I dedicate the best years of my life to someone else's business? How could I be so blind? I got totally carried away with what success looks like and, I guess, some notion about my big career validating my entire life. And I made stupid decisions in the stupid head spin of the dog-eat-dog magazine business. But now – now I've got to take responsibility and pay for it. I'm done with all the bullshit. It's taken over my entire life for too long, and for what? Everyone is replaceable, no matter how great you think you are or how much blood, sweat and tears you pour into a job. Any job!' Lauren responds glumly. 'People always forget that they'd be replaced in a week if they were run over by a bus.'

'How sad that is,' Cate concurs.

'And you should have seen the look of pure joy on the Noto-rious Payne's face, Cate. She has hated me since I reported Julia to her the first time – "causing unnecessary waves", she called it. God only knows what the background politics are with that whole situation. She's a weapon, that one, head buried so far up Dirk Diggler's arse ... I'm so angry at myself!' Lauren rolls her eyes.

'Imagine burying your head up five-foot Dirk Diggler with the Napoleon syndrome's arse...ew! I don't know how you controlled your mouth around him earlier, you've always despised him. My mouth would have taken over as my head imploded.' Cate laughs, trying to cheer Lauren up. 'Just think about it, Lauren. You're done with all of those nimrods. For good. Freedom, my friend, is a beautiful thing.'

'I know, but don't you just hate all the secret management politics.' Ava sighs. 'The downfall of all the genuine hard workers in the world? I swear, you have to have eyes in the back of your head to keep a handle on all that crap. Honestly, I don't know how anyone actually gets any work done, with all the rampant nepotism and back-stabbing. It's everywhere. I can only imagine what level of fuckery you were dealing with at *Irish Gloss*.'

'I'm actually completely mentally exhausted after nine years of watching my back for flying knives. At least I got a decent exit package to pay for my wounds – well, some of them anyway!' Lauren taps her back jokingly. 'Huge stab wound right there, right now.'

'Just take some time off to figure out what you want to do next. You're so much bigger than that, Lauren. We know it. You know it. Anyone with half a brain knows it. You're the Bull McCabe, for God's sake. I want to see those bull horns return!' Cate smiles, raising her glass.

'She's so right, Lauren, eff'em all. You'll be back with a vengeance. Bigger and better than ever,' Ava firmly agrees.

'Thanks for knowing exactly what to say, girls.' Lauren half smiles. 'You know how much I appreciate you both. But first I need to figure out who this "BS Exposer" undercover Instagrammer is. Seriously, my head is wrecked with curiosity. Who is this person? Why is she doing this? Think I'm going to DM her and see what happens.'

'Do you really want to go there? Why bother?' Cate asks. 'This person is anonymous, they'll never agree to reveal themselves.'

'Because I need to try,' Lauren insists. 'For my own sake. I want to find out who this person is and why they do what they do. There's something on my mind that requires secrecy, and I think she can help me.'

'If you're sure?' Ava adds, unconvinced.

'Nope, I'm not sure of pretty much anything in my life right now. But hey, there's only one way to find out.' Lauren has a glint in her eye, as she grabs her phone and sends a quick message. 'I'm going to get all Nancy Drew and track him or her down!'

'What did you write?' Ava asks.

'Just "Hello, BS Exposer, it's Lauren P. McCabe, ex-editor of *Irish Gloss*. Can I pick your brain?"'

'Right. Well, I have to run,' Ava says, with a quick glance at her watch. She drains her water and stands up. 'Cate can take it from here, and I'll see you both at six sharp? Chin up, Lauren. Trust me, you've got this!'

Ava kisses them both and dashes out of the bar.

★ ★ ★

'You should eat,' Stefan repeats the second Ava steps back through the door of Art Gallery Space 1.

'Oh, I couldn't! My stomach is like a washing machine!' Ava tells him. 'All the adrenaline from Lauren's meeting and this – *my* exhibition!'

'Come on, just something small even?' he suggests.

'Go! Have a nice little glass of wine and some food, settle the nerves,' Mags orders them, as she struts around the gallery.

'I think it's a good idea,' Stefan says.

'Okay, but knowing me I'll spill tomato sauce all down the

front of this fabulous white suit. I got it from Lauren herself – it's pure designer!' Ava says excitedly, proudly turning around in it.

'Eat plain pasta,' Mags says, as her phone beeps and she reads a text message swiftly. 'I'm gone, lock the door behind you.' Mags whizzes past them.

'Did she offer you your job back?' Stefan unwraps a stick of gum and folds it into his mouth, his eyes questioning as he creases up the paper wrapper and plays with it between his fingers.

'You won't believe this, she offered me an artist-in-residence position … I think!' Ava bites her lip, then squeals and jumps in the air. 'I've only just worked that out, but that's what it was.'

'*Très bien*! Let's go,' Stefan says, chewing hastily. Then putting his cup down on her desk, he leads her out of the gallery, pulling on his flat cap as he goes.

★ ★ ★

'You know when Mags asked me to try and find him – Kilroy, I mean – to give him one last chance, I was always convinced that this was your time, Ava,' Stefan tells her as he leads her from the gallery up Grafton Street on a classic balmy July evening.

'She told me all you did for me,' Ava says, music filling the open air as buskers sing their best Irish melodies on every corner. The street is crowded with after-work commuters heading home, and busy shoppers and tourists fill the cobblestone streets. 'Thank you, Stef,' she adds, as he weaves them expertly through the crowds.

'*De rien*,' he replies.

'Are we going to Rosilita's?' she asks him now, as he takes the familiar route, more than a little deflated in case Suzanne is working.

'*Oui*,' he says, and she can't help but clock an admiring glance from a group of passing students.

'Suzanne working this evening?' she finally remarks, as casually as she can, as they step around a mime artist who has attracted a large crowd that's blocking the entire street.

'Perhaps.' He shrugs.

'Oh,' she says.

'Actually, you just reminded me, when we order I need to pop out to get something. I won't be five minutes – gives you the time to go over your speech, *oui*?' he says, and she nods. They push open the glass door of their regular wine bar. Ava makes a beeline for their usual seats, the high stools.

'*Non, mon amie*, this way ...' Stefan leads her to the restaurant part of the bar, down three granite steps to the ornate ground level.

'Good evening.' A smartly dressed waiter in a white shirt and black tie is standing at a podium to greet them, a small black book open in front of him.

'But we never sit down in the restaurant!' Ava says.

'A reservation for two, for Stefan Beaubien?' He ignores Ava and speaks to the waiter, who ticks his name off in the little black book.

'You made a reservation? I thought we were just grabbing a snack?' she asks, slightly bewildered, holding her stomach again.

'Follow me. This way.' The waiter lifts two menus and slots them under his arm as he leads them to a corner table, dimly lit by glowing candles with a red and white linen chequered cloth covering the table.

'Stefan?' Ava stares at him quizzically.

'You like?' He pulls out her chair for her.

'Of course, but ...' Ava looks around her at the other diners.

'It's a special occasion, *non*?' he asks.

'I suppose ...' She sits carefully in her sharp white suit and opens the black and gold padded menu.

'Oh, it's a different menu, too ...' She reads down the list of dishes. 'And ... oh, actually they do the spicy meatballs tapas we love ... I like ... we liked ...' She stammers and looks up at him, but he's engrossed in the menu. 'Right, that will do me so, with a big side order of a glass of freezing cold white. It's okay for me to have a glass of wine before the event, don't you think? To settle my nerves?' Ava fixes her hair, tightening the slim silver bobbin.

'In France, we don't have so much this crazy abuse of wine,' Stefan says. 'We use it for taste, relaxation, digestion ... not to get pissed, and almost always with some crusty bread. You are perfectly entitled to take a glass of wine and not feel bad about it, *amie*!' He stands up from the table and removes his leather jacket. He is wearing a light blue dress shirt over his jeans and she sighs at how he looks the very picture of sexy and sophisticated. He hands his jacket across the table to Ava. 'Put this on?'

'What?' she says, completely unclear now as to what he's at.

'I know you will spill sauce on that white suit.' Ava laughs in understanding, and reaches up and takes the jacket from him and pulls it on. She is immediately floored by the lovely weight of it and how it smells of Stefan's cologne.

'Can I get you a drink?' Suzanne is suddenly standing at the table looking down, tightening the ties on her black apron skirt, unsmiling.

'Oh. Hi ... Suzanne! Sorry, I – I – I am messy ... He was just giving me his jacket to protect my ...' Ava lays her hand across her chest and trails off as Stefan pushes his chair back, rises and kisses Suzanne on both cheeks.

'*Ça va?*' he asks her.

'Yeah, grand, thanks ...' she replies, scribbling her small red pen on her white pad to ensure it's working.

'A bottle of the Pinot Grigio, please, Suzanne.' He points to the specific bottle on the extensive wine list.

'How are you keeping?' Ava asks her, looking up.

'Good, thanks,' she answers. 'Won't be a sec.' She moves away quickly.

'Won't be a *sex*, huh?' Ava says to Stefan, sniggering to herself.

'Pardon?' Stefan sits again, and places his white napkin across his lap.

'Oh, nothing, just Lauren sent this text to her boss and the word "sec" autocorrected to "sex" . . . You had to be there, it's the way Lauren tells it.' Ava drops her head.

Suzanne returns to pour the wine just as the waiter comes to take their order, and Ava is relieved there is no time for more awkward chit-chat.

'The meatballs tapas, please,' Ava says, pointing to the dish on her menu.

'Actually, can we get the main meatballs to share?' Stefan looks at her questioningly and she agrees.

'Yep, perfect – probably works out cheaper,' Ava responds for Suzanne's benefit, who has started to walk away from the table again. 'Eh . . .' Ava looks after her and then back to Stefan.

'Cheers!' He lifts his glass, so she reaches hers and they clink.

'What a week it's been. I mean, it seems like bloody years ago you showed up at Edenvale like that and told me about the opportunity for the exhibition.' She lifts her glass to her nose and smells the bouquet, then gently swirls the glass anti-clockwise.

'It does. It was a hard place to find for a Frenchman. Some of those Clare accents . . . I had no idea what people were saying to me when I stopped to ask directions. But oh, wow, Ava, that home . . . *magnifique!*' He joins his finger and thumb together in appreciation.

'It is, isn't it?' She crinkles her nose as she smiles at him. 'Eh, sorry, but I have to ask, it's the elephant in the room – is Suzanne okay, she seems . . . in a really shit mood?'

'Perhaps she is having a really shit day?' he tells her. '*D'accord* . . . Okay, so this speech of yours?'

'I hate public speaking, but I've written a few bits down, but it will be very short and sweet.' Ava rummages in her red clutch bag and pulls out a crumpled-up piece of paper.

'Read it, in your head,' Stefan advises her, as he sits back into his chair. 'Be familiar with the words, but be yourself.'

Ava looks over the few words she scribbled down the previous night at dinner with her dad and, when the meatballs arrive, she continues to read over her speech and they both eat in comfortable silence.

'I have to grab something, keep going over your speech, and do it for me when I come back, *oui*?' He pushes back his chair, wipes his mouth with the napkin and drops it on his plate.

'Hurry up, I hate sitting alone in a restaurant,' she tells him, looking around her.

'Well, don't, you shouldn't,' he replies. She watches him take the three granite steps in one and then exchange a few words with Suzanne.

'*You lucky bitch*!' Ava mumbles under her breath, thinking of Suzanne. 'Pardon my French.' She drinks the last of her wine and goes back to concentrate on her speech.

'Can I top you up?'

Ava jumps; Suzanne is standing over her.

'Oh, sorry! I was miles away,' Ava flusters. 'Go on then, just a tiny bit. I hope to see you later?' Ava holds up her glass, her finger indicating the low level she wants poured.

'Yeah, I'll try to pop by. Stefan just told me about it, that's so great for you.' Ignoring her request, she fills Ava's glass to the brim and replaces the bottle noisily in the iced wine bucket.

'Oh, okay, um . . . I – I thought you were, I thought you knew . . . I mean, I thought you were already coming?' Ava says, suddenly very aware she is sitting at a candlelit table with Suzanne's boyfriend and also wearing that boyfriend's leather jacket.

'No . . . Stefan . . . let's just say his attention was never really fully on me.' Suzanne wipes her hands on her apron and turns abruptly away from the table

Ava gulps at the wine.

When Stefan reappears, Ava is curious. 'Are you two fighting or something?'

'*Non.*' He sits back down a little breathless.

'Why is she acting so weird with me?' Ava asks him.

'I don't know. Really. *Je ne sais pas.*'

'Excuse me,' she says, 'did you run all the way or something?'

'A little jog. I think we need to get back soon, I don't want you to be late.' Stefan rolls up the sleeves on his dress shirt. Ava thinks she'll never tire of the sight of his arms under the tight linen.

Ava bends across the table to him. 'Okay, you want to hear this speech or what?' She clears her throat just as he reaches into his back pocket and pulls something out. He slides a red velvet box across the table to Ava.

'What's this?' She looks up from her piece of crumpled paper.

'A gift.' He shrugs and leans back.

'What?' Her eyes look from the box to his face and back to the box.

'Open it,' he tells her, smiling now.

'For me?' she gasps.

'Well, it's not for Suzanne, that's for sure.' He only half laughs, looking over his shoulder.

'What is it?' She swallows hard. 'Stefan, what's going on?'

'Is just a gift, there is no label on it; it is just a gift from me to you. Something I thought you would like. That is all. Simple.' He lifts his glass and toasts the air.

Ava slowly lifts the red velvet box and prises the lid open.

'Oh. Oh. No way? O-oh, you didn't?' Her face falls and her mouth drops wide open. 'I don't believe it,' she gasps.

'Is the right one, *non*?' He looks carefully at her.

'It is.' She removes the ring from the Harlequin jewellers' box that she had originally been saving for. 'The rose flower diamond I wanted . . . but w-why?' she whispers to him.

'Why? Because I wanted you to have it, because you loved it, Ava. Like I said, it is just a gift. No strings,' Stefan assures her.

'But I can't have you waste your money on me like this . . .' She lifts it out carefully, turning the neat metal circle over in her fingers.

'It was not expensive . . . You always worry about me and money, Ava. I'm not The Tuner; I have savings. I am a big boy, you know. I worked hard in France for years before I travelled to experience the world. I am forty-five years of age and I am not stupid. I think you fear every man is stupid with money?' Stefan says.

'Thank you. It's the most beautiful ring.'

'Along with your mother's,' he adds.

'Along with my mother's, which is safely back in my dad's house in my jewellery box, where it belongs,' she tells him.

'Does it fit?' he asks now. 'Try.'

And she slides it on the second finger of her right hand.

'Perfectly,' she tells him. 'But . . . I really can't accept this, it's too kind, Stefan. I know how much this cost and I know it's not the end of the world expensive, but still, and I don't care if you've saved your tooth fairy, communion, confirmation, paper round money and teacher's salary all your life. It's way too thoughtful,' she tells him, a lump lodging in her throat.

'It fits. Wonderful. Now, let's go.' He stands and opens his wallet, and puts some money on the table.

'You are not paying for the food and wine as well! No bloody way!' She jumps up and folds the money back into his top shirt pocket, opens her bag and puts a stack of cash down herself, along with a very generous tip.

'I feel we won't be using this as our regular any more,' he says, looking over his shoulder to Suzanne, who turns her back on them and walks away.

'Why? What happened?' she asks him, still in a complete daze.

'Let's just say it wasn't meant to be. She is a very lovely girl, but she was looking for more than I could offer ...' He trails off without a proper explanation, as he leads her out into the sunny evening. She squints at the dipping sun, then stops under the orange canopy of the wine bar to take off his jacket.

'No, come on, what really happened with Suzanne? Spill!' She hands him the heavy jacket as he pulls a face. She has him cornered. 'You really liked her. You said she was *really special*, you even brought her to my wedding, Stefan!' She pushes him, not quite sure.

'*Oui.*' He slides his hands into his jacket pockets, looking uncomfortable.

'Why did you do that?' she whispers.

'Why?' He stalls.

'Why?' Ava won't let it go.

Stefan leans against the pole of the orange canopy; he rests his head back against it and closes his eyes. Ava stands opposite him.

'I'm still waiting?' she tells him.

'I wanted to get over you,' he tells her, as a passer-by with a dog walks around them and Ava gets caught up in the lead. She untangles herself and moves closer to him.

'Get over *me*?' Her breath comes rapidly. 'What?'

'*Oui.*' He opens his eyes and pushes himself away from the pole, then shoves his hands deep into his pockets. He looks vulnerable, unsure, and Ava suddenly feels an electric bolt of feeling between them.

'I'd prefer if you wanted to get *under* me ...' She gulps, dizzy from wine and a Dublin summer evening, and then laughs in breathless wheezes.

'I should have told you before, in words not in innuendos, and when I saw the pictures you drew of me, then I knew, but when I returned soon after lunch that afternoon and you had left ... Mags said you would probably never be back. I tried to call you but you'd also disconnected your phone, you'd decided to still go ahead and marry that awful Tuner, so I had to respect your decision. I had to stand back ... and let you be.'

Ava takes a step towards him. 'I'm beyond embarrassed of those pictures.' She looks up at him.

'*Pourquoi*? They are fantastic.' He smiles at her. 'Handsome, *oui*?'

'I drew you not far off naked, Stef ... that's all kinds of creepy love.' She shuts her eyes tight and when she opens them he is just inches away from her face. And her lips.

'Suzanne knew I was devastated ... I told her I was in love with you that night you left Rosilita's and she said she'd make me forget about you,' he tells her truthfully at last.

'In love with me?' Her words are barely audible.

'*Oui*.' She can feel his breath on her face, smell the lingering traces of La Nuit de l'Homme by Yves Saint Laurent.

'*Oui*?' she says again.

'You know I am *fou* about you, Ava O'Hara,' he tells her.

'I wasn't altogether sure, but ...' Her heart is beating so hard in her chest she holds it and leans into him.

'*Merde*! Shit! The time! Let's go,' he suddenly shouts, and she nearly falls over, her body bent forward, her lips ready to meet his, her eyes half closed in anticipation.

'W-what?' she heaves, almost toppling as he holds her upright.

'You have important work to do! It's exhibition time!' Stefan drapes his heavy arm around her shoulders and walks her quickly back to the gallery, while Ava smiles so hard her cheeks hurt and her feet barely touch the pavement.

18

Nothing Compares to Vous.

'Oh, stefan,' ava says, as they step inside the packed gallery. 'The place is buzzing.'

'At last! Here she is!' Mags shouts over the chit-chat, as everyone breaks into a round of applause.

'Hiya, Ava, this is bleedin' deadly!' Git clasps his hands, dressed in three-quarter length khaki shorts with a white shirt and spotty bow tie.

'You're a dark horse, Ava!' Tommo, in jeans and a suit jacket, says, as he looks around in admiration.

'You came!' Ava wraps her arms around the pair of them.

'Course we did ... wouldn't miss it for all the All Ireland hurling finals in the world! Plus, we had to go and pick up the centrepiece. Didn't you know?' Git looks at her, confused.

'Centrepiece? What centrepiece is that?' she asks, as the crowd breaks and she spots something in the corner of the gallery she thought she'd left behind. The space Mags told her to leave open. Her paint-splattered wedding dress.

'What was it yer man Oscar Wilde said again? "One should be a work of art or wear a work of art,"' Git deadpans, giving Ava a playful nudge. 'Just look at our masterpiece now in all her glory!'

Ava remains gobsmacked.

'That man about the dog I had to go see ...' Mags winks, and moves in beside Ava, smiling. 'Stefan saw it at your house in Clare and told me about it. I thought it was a spectacular thing to create, so I sent for it.'

'How?' Ava asks. 'I mean, what on earth for?'

'For the gallery! Stefan arranged it with your buddies there, the Git and the Tommo, is it? Anyway, I don't know, nor do I care, but I just love this piece! That is pure art, Ava.' Mags turns to look at it again. 'And I want to buy it from you for here, for the window. We'll talk cost when you are back to work after a few days off, yeah?'

Git leans across and offers Mags a bag of Werther's Originals.

'No, thank you,' Mags looks at him with interest, 'though how delightfully arbitrary.' She then sashays away as Git pops a toffee in his mouth.

'Ava?' he offers now as she walks to her wedding dress. She touches the paint-splattered lace just as Stefan did that morning in The Vintage Bride. How life changes in the most unexpected ways, she thinks, as someone taps her on the shoulder.

'Hi, sorry to interrupt?'

'I'll leave you to it,' Git says as he disappears into the crowd, sucking on his sweet.

'Thanks, Git,' Ava says as she turns to see a young woman.

'I don't know if you might remember me, but I was in a couple of weeks ago? Had my niece in the buggy.' Ava recognises the woman immediately, just as her dad comes in with Gina, his next-door neighbour. He positively beams at her. Ava waves back, frantically excited.

'Oh, yes, hi. Look, I'm really sorry, Laurence Kilroy's exhibition has been postponed ...'

'No, I came back for that.' The woman points to Ava's picture of the woman with the piercing blue eyes feeding her baby in St Stephen's Green. 'It was on the floor by your desk that evening.

It's perfect,' she tells Ava. 'Please tell me it doesn't cost a small fortune?' she adds with a wince.

'Oh, really? Oh, um . . .' Ava catches sight of the sticker below the painting, and cringes when she sees the price: eight hundred and ninety-five euro!

'Yes, I'll take it!' the young woman says.

'Thank you! It was for your sister, wasn't it?' Ava remembers.

'Yes, she's doing better, she had bad post-natal, you see. I stepped in to mind Emmie, my niece. This painting just struck me, you know, that mothering can be challenging, too,' she says to Ava, and the two women take each other's hands in understanding.

Mags steps in to follow up the sale, her hand on the small of the young woman's back, leading her gently to the counter. 'It's a stunning piece, will increase in value, I have no doubt. We'll have it wrapped for you.'

'Well, this is something else, O'Hara, what?' Lauren cheers giddily, as she and Cate approach.

'Hi! Are you okay, Lauren? I feel like a bit of a shit neglecting you with all this *Irish Gloss* nightmare going on!'

'Well, don't! I'm bursting with pride here!'

'But tell her, Lauren!' Cate urges.

'Tell me what?' Ava asks.

'It isn't the time,' Lauren says, looking around her, as if searching for a different answer.

'Tell me!' Ava tilts her head at her, her eyes imploring. 'Now!'

'*Later*!' Lauren nods to the people spilling in around them, sipping champagne and flicking through the exhibition brochure.

'If it affects you, I want to know right now.' Ava puts her hands on her hips.

'Okay, really fast. So, the mysterious BS blogger. She got straight back to me, she was in a café nearby, and she came to see us in O'Donoghue's when you left,' Lauren explains, talking at a million miles an hour.

'She honestly did!' Cate jumps up and down.

'Get away!' Ava's eyes widen.

'Yup, one Michelle O'Reilly, she was. An attractive older woman. Not at *all* what we were expecting.' Lauren looks to Cate, who nods in agreement.

'So cool!' Cate adds. 'My new idol!'

'What did you say to her?' Ava asks. 'Did she apologise? Like grovel?' Ava shakes her head as the gallery around her buzzes with people talking art and – incredibly! – buying *her* art.

'In fairness she apologised about what happened with my job, it wasn't her intention to see me thrown under the bus like that. I guess she was just incensed at *Irish Gloss* in general for not accepting any responsibility when she uncovered things. It was nothing personal. And, well, my comments blew up on social and, well, the rest is history.'

'Firing squad history?' Ava raises her eyebrow.

'No, I told her I was completely at fault for what happened at the magazine,' Lauren admits. 'It was my editorial ship and, honestly, I steered it all over the place, and made really stupid mistakes. No one on the planet is madder at themselves right now than me for being so bloody stupid.'

'You're not stupid!' Cate takes her arm in hers.

'Anyway, I congratulated her on creating such a strong online presence for herself, but what I really wanted to get to the bottom of was why she felt compelled to take this influencer issue on. I told her I'm working on a new venture and I think what she has to say will be really insightful and, obviously, super helpful.' Lauren's eyes light up now.

'Champagne?' a passing waiter offers, but only Lauren takes a glass.

'So, it turns out she's actually an English and social studies teacher at Sancta Maria College in Rathfarnham,' Lauren explains, as she takes a long sip of champagne.

'A secondary school teacher? Wow, quite the contrast to an anonymous Instagrammer persona!' Ava is completely surprised. 'See how fake it all is?'

'Right! So, yeah, she's been teaching young girls for years. What started all this was that she's seen some really worrying changes in her fifteen-year-old pupils. Their lives are pretty much run on social media, never off their phones. But, for Michelle, the really worrying thing was just how impressionable these teens are. As a social studies teacher, she feels like it's her responsibility to start asking questions. Anyway, Ava, we can finish this later, you really need to mingle.' Lauren looks over her shoulder, almost guiltily. 'It's your big night!'

'I need the distraction right now, please! Let them mingle among themselves a while longer. Let them have a glass or two more of free bubbles, loosen their purse strings. Go on ...'

Lauren doesn't need asking twice. 'My take was that she genuinely believes that a lot of it is pure fraud. At a dangerous cost. And she can't get over how anyone and everyone seems to be calling themselves an "influencer" these days. Myself included,' Lauren accepts.

'Yeah, she was saying kids are looking at all these glamorous young girls and guys portraying these fantasy lives, self-titling themselves as influencers,' Cate adds. 'You know how it is with them all posting filtered selfies non-stop with their equally touched-up mates, all portraying these seemingly amazing lives. Jetting off here. Drinking this diet tea product there. Hawking fake eyelashes to beat the band ...'

'Ho hum, the plot thickens, McCabe,' Ava says.

'Tell her!' Cate urges.

'Well, with all our runaway bride revelations, then hearing about Git and his ex-wife, and my own lengthy experiences in relationships gone wrong – it's given me some food for thought. I've got enough of a profile that I can genuinely help people, for a change. So, drum roll, Avz, I've decided on a brand-new direction for my future. I want to help people escape dysfunctional relationships, personal and professional, and Cate is coming to work with me. Well, out of her kitchen to be specific – you can't swing a cat in my overpriced apartment on the docks. Still plenty to figure out, but we're pretty damn excited!'

And, at that, Lauren and Cate high-five.

'We want you to design the company logo. We can all work together – like, literally, bride squad revisited.' Cate squeals in excitement.

'Pure genius! I'm in.' Ava beams at them both, then they all swivel at the sound of two young boys chattering and laughing.

'Hello, all!' Lily greets them, holding the hands of her and Cate's two older sons, as Lauren hurriedly digs in her bag for comics and chocolate bars.

'Bribes okay?' She looks up to Lily and Cate.

'Absolutely!' they respond in unison, as the boys scarper away to the back room and Lily takes two flutes of champagne from a passing waiter's tray and hands one to Cate.

'Cheers, Lil,' Cate says to her wife.

'Cheers, love.' Lily toasts her with a gentle kiss on the lips.

'Ava, I really need you now.' Stefan squeezes through Lauren and Tommo to take her arm gently. 'They are waiting for you to say a few words.'

'Oh, sweet Lord above, every time I see that man!' Lauren can't help herself and even Tommo laughs. 'Stefan, *salut*!'

'Ah, Lauren, *bonjour*!' He kisses her warmly on both cheeks, as Lauren catches Ava's gaze and dramatically rolls her eyes so only the whites can be seen.

'And you remember Cate, of course?' Lauren composes herself as fast as she can, and Cate kisses him on both cheeks too.

'Ah, *oui*, the best of best friends,' he tells them, tickling baby Max under his dribbling chin. 'Let's go, we shall have a celebratory drink after, *oui*?' Stefan says over his shoulder, and they all nod and raise their glasses in acceptance.

Ava makes her way through the heaving crowd and to the top of the gallery. She takes a deep breath and removes the microphone from the stand.

'Hello ... and ...' It squeaks, so she moves the microphone back from her mouth and composes herself, glad that she's memorised the words of her speech.

'Hello, everyone, and thank you for all being here. I promise this will be short and sweet ... like my wedding day ... No. Too soon?' She smiles at Lauren and Cate, who have pushed their way to the front of the crowd and are laughing hysterically. Stefan stands to her left.

'But seriously, I'm so privileged to show my work here tonight, it's about the reality of life and nature and unexpected circumstances – well, my personal take on it all. I've been painting for a long time but never had the confidence to see it through to a night like this, so thank you, Mags, the owner of this gallery, for giving me the opportunity to do so.' She raises her glass to Mags, who raises hers back with a warm smile, her handsome son David at her side. 'I have so many people to thank. I've had an ... an interesting few weeks.' Ava looks to Stefan, who smiles encouragingly at her. 'The truth is, in life everyone is capable of hurting you, you've just got to find the ones worth suffering for, and I'm feeling stronger and more independent now than I've ever been my entire life.' Ava looks around the gallery, people watching her intently, drinks in hands.

'I need my art, my dad and my friends, and I need to figure

out exactly what I want from my life. That's okay though, it's all a work in progress. I actually like this new blank canvas that is my future. I thought I had to follow the female formula I was brought up with, you know, marriage, babies, without really questioning if that formula worked for me. But the one thing I have learned, the one thing that I know for sure, is that true friends are the most important thing of all. And the only way to have great friends is to be one.'

'Whoop!' Lauren heckles happily, as Tommo hands her another flute of champagne.

'True dat!' Cate shouts, as she wraps her arm around Lauren's shoulders.

'So, without further ado, thanks again for coming, please take a look at the art, and I'm happy to answer any questions you may have. Most importantly, enjoy the evening!' Ava replaces the microphone in the stand and moves away, as the crowd clap loudly and then disperse to look at the art and mingle again.

'Another woman of many talents,' Tommo says to Lauren and Cate.

'That's our Ava,' Cate says, then knowingly drops her arm from Lauren's shoulder and steps out.

'I was going to text you,' Tommo says, 'but then I knew I'd see you tonight and I'm more a face-to-face kinda guy. So, I was hoping you might like to come see Mark McCabe do a DJ set with me next weekend. That way, I can spin ya round the floor to "Maniac 2000"?'

'Now that sounds like some fun mischief, Tommo.' Lauren raises her glass. 'Cheers to that plan!'

'Deadly.' He drapes his arm over her shoulder as a beaming Ava pushes through the crowd to stand in front of them.

'I can't get over how my dress looks,' she tells them. 'All my life I've tried to create my masterpiece, my inner angst, and now that dress is always going to be something I'm known for. Imagine that?'

'I'm a firm believer in everything happens for a reason,' Tommo says.

'Like that, is it?' Ava nods to Tommo's arm around Lauren.

'Another great result from our bride squad.' Lauren laughs.

Stefan's head appears over the crowd behind them as he nods towards the kitchenette. Ava waves at him and excuses herself as she follows him in.

'I hate public speaking.' She shakes her head as she leans against the sink. 'Was I okay? My mouth was so dry.'

'It was more than okay. You were brilliant and honest. Well done!' He smiles at her.

'I was honest and, guess what? Looks like Lauren and Tommo are a bit of an item! I'm so happy for her, things have been really shit for Lauren.'

Stefan looks at her, more than puzzled.

'*Pourquoi*? I thought you said Lauren had it all. What was it you said, that Lauren just wins at life.'

'I was wrong. Whaddya know, Stefan, it was me who was the rubbish friend. Turns out I was wrong about a whole lot of things.'

'You have good friends, forever friends, you're lucky.' He takes a glass from the counter and runs the tap.

'I am lucky,' she agrees. 'But what's that?' She points to a picture wrapped in brown paper that's on the floor by the sink.

'I bought a little something,' he tells her, handing her a glass of water.

'What did you buy?' Ava is intrigued as she gulps the glass down.

'A work of art. Take a look!' He winks now as she puts the glass in the sink.

She bends down and tears a tiny corner then gasps.

'Oh no, you didn't!' She shuts her eyes tight.

'I've always wanted a good nude of myself in my prime, even if it is just from your imagination,' he says in total seriousness.

'Well, now you've got one.' Ava moves in and leans her head on his chest to hide her embarrassment. He wraps his arms tightly around her waist. They stand motionless in the quiet kitchenette for a few minutes, listening to each other's breath. Ava inhales the scent of his cologne.

'You better get back to your after-party. I shouldn't keep you,' he says quietly.

'But I don't want to leave this moment,' she admits.

Stefan's hands move gently up her back and rest on her neck as Ava lifts her head from his chest to look up at him.

'From the very first day you walked through that door ...' she starts.

'Same.' He nods.

'I guess we have art to thank for ... *us*.' Ava pulls him close.

'Remember, the principle of true art is not to portray but to evoke ...' he reminds her.

'And do I?'

'Every day.' Stefan leans down and finally, tenderly, they kiss.

Acknowledgements

For Des Carey and Kevin Cassidy – the happiest husbands in the world (*blows kiss*) – we know *we're* the lucky ones. Thanks for all the love and support, and (ahem) for putting up with us. And to our children John Paul Carey and Grace and Maggie Cassidy. You are our sunshine, and we're so proud of you all and the epic mischief-makers you have become.

To our amazing parents Ray and Jennifer Knott, and Robert (aka Robbie Box) and Noeleen Grace. We're officially sorry for all those elaborate stories we conjured up as teenagers to get out of being grounded. It led us here, no?! We adore you. And to our fabulous sisters Tanya Knott, Ruth Knott, Sarah Knott, Samantha Doyle, and the equally fab non-female, Keith Grace. To say 'you're the greatest' is a total understatement. And yes, you're all total rides.

Lots of love to these real-life rock stars, too. A million thanks ... for everything!

Our incredible team at Black and White Publishing, especially our editorial goddesses Emma Hargrave and Alice Latchford.

Ray Carter. Johnny O'Loughlin. Jaime Carter. Jake Carter. Max Carter. Will O'Loughlin. Jenny O'Loughlin. Charlie O'Loughlin. Fiona and Cathal McAuliffe. James McAuliffe. Sarah O'Reilly. Sharon McNiffe. Jane Higgins. Caitriona Barrett.

Tara Durkin O'Brien. Joanne Wrenn. Deirdre Norris. Jennie McCarthy-Sanborn. Nuala Breslin. Sarah Fingleton. Debbie Molloy. Roisin Breslin. Sheila Cullinane. Ruth Major. Sinead Hayes. Robert Massey. Jason O'Mara. Una Fox. Ciaran Walsh. The late great Gar Brown. Conor Dalton. Aongus and Gavin Ralston. Nikki and Craig Atkinson. The Modem SF gang. Vincent and Bonnie Cullinan. Susan and Richie Saville. Catriona Carey. Cian Mulhall. Brian and Eileen Carey. Niall, Muvashni and Rohan Carey. Bobby Hawkshaw. Nuala Kane. Clodagh and Billy Davis. Brenda Cooper and family. Paul and Eileen Hickey. Brian, Conor and John Davis. Margaret and Donal Hickey and family. Aisling Griffin. Gina and Ger Quinlan. Howard Shapiro. Debra Drucker. Fiona Mahon. Kate Fox. Jennifer Kane. The mighty O'Keeffe clan. Our class of teen rebels at Sancta Maria College (and FYI Sister Pauline and Sister Basil . . . we're *not* in jail!). Marina Rafter. Elaine Crowley. Caroline Cassidy. Sarah Flood. Leontia, Bryan, Ollie, Arthur and Ted Brophy. Ruth Kavanagh. Aveen Fitzgerald. Susan Loughnane. Roisin Kearney. Amy Conroy. Elaine Hearty. Peader and Damian McGuone. Gail Brady. Amy Joyce Hastings. Barbara Scully. Fiona Looney. Claire Moran. Shane Guest. Annemarie Naughton. Sinead Dalton. Kelly Edmonds. Suzanne Kane. Graham Cantwell. Sonya Macari. Victoria Smurfit. Linda Maher. Maia Dunphy. Melanie Finn. Janine Curran. Eimear Ennis Graham. Maeve Callan. Marie, Dave, Paul and Nicola. Claire Woodcock. Niall, Mia & Zoe. Cillian, Olivia, Conor, Jay, Ava, Rian and Evan. Angela, Jimmy and family. Auntie Kathleen and the Blackpool posse. Ciara, Sean, Ben and Katie Ashmore.

All the cast of Park Pictures: Kevin, John, Erik Paul, Dawn and Catherine.

All *The Elaine Show* panellists over the years and the super crew. A not so *Quiet* shout out to the fabulous, Ciara Geraghty, who truly understands what a belly laugh 'dressing up' can still be!

All our pals in Rathfarnham, and the legends who joined us frequently on the moving dance floor at Club Sarah. The Glenbrookers. The Willowbankers. The Knocklyoners.

The fantastic team at the Sarah Jennifer Knott Foundation, and all our supporters.

Our fellow writers whose support is always astonishing: Carmel Harrington, Claudia Carroll, Liz Nugent, Marian Keyes, Claire Allen, Hazel Gaynor, Nick Kelly and the dearly missed Emma Hannigan.

And to you, our readers, without whom we'd just be talking to ourselves.

In celebration of the beautiful lives of Sarah and Jennifer Knott, and our grannies, Bridget (Birdie) Hickey and Margaret Kilroy. '*They lived. They loved. They left.*'

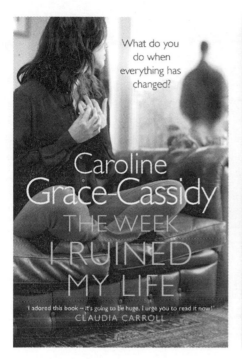 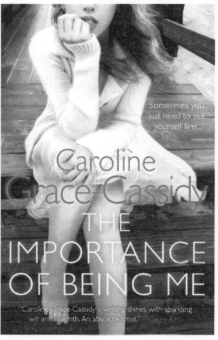

'I adored this book – it's going to be huge. I urge you to read it now!'
— **Claudia Carroll**

'Caroline Grace-Cassidy's writing shines with sparkling wit and warmth. An absolute treat.'
— **Cathy Kelly**